THE
WATERUBAS
BOOK 1

To James —
Enjoy!!
All the very best
[signature] xx

Text copyright © 2024 by Jocelyn Stevenson.
Original Wateruba Design copyright © 2024 by Brian Froud.

ISBN-13: 978-1-964108-00-1

Mystery School Press
P.O. Box 63767
Philadelphia, PA 19147
mysteryschoolpress.com

Cover art and black and white illustrations by Natacha Du Pont De Bie
Book design by Lorraine Inglis

Printed in the United States of America.

THE
WATERUBAS
BOOK 1

Jocelyn Stevenson

To Ismay, Reuben and Sorley

It wasn't exactly water

MIRIAM was in her pyjamas... *Nothing strange about that* ...in a blizzard. *Wait – what?!?* She was surrounded by snow – whirling, swirling snow. *How how how did I get here? Ouch!* The snow stung Miriam's eyes and got up her nose. *That hurts!* The howl of the wind pressed against her ears like an incredibly loud hat. *Brrrrr! I'm freezing! Why am I here?* Then something large fell out of the sky and landed at her feet. *Is that a person? Is that Mom?* Whatever it was didn't move. *Mom??* Miriam leaned over to get a closer look, and hit her head on a large piece of ice.

Ow!! Miriam pushed away the laptop she'd left in her bed. *Not ice. Laptop. Not a blizzard – another Mom dream...* She rubbed her face. *No snow, no wind. Is it time to get up?* She looked at the clock. *Almost, but not quite...* She turned over and put the pillow over her head. *I miss Mom. I want to see her in real life. She's got to come home soon.* Then waking life took over, and her whole body tensed. *Oh no! Science Camp today!*

"MIR-I-AM! YOU'RE GOING TO BE LATE FOR CAMP!!" Grammy's voice came up through the air vent that brought smells and sounds from the kitchen straight to her room. Along with Grammy's voice came the smell of Grammy's coffee.

"I'm coming!" Miriam called back towards the vent. She scrambled out of bed to grab some clothes. As she pulled on her favorite hoodie, she saw the picture of her mom she kept beside her bed. It was taken just before her accident in Greenland. She was standing in the snow with Uncle Eddy, who was her research partner on this trip. Eddy

5

looked serious, but her mother was smiling like mad. "You'd be so proud of me going to Science Camp," Miriam whispered to the photo.

"Two minutes!" Grammy's voice came up through the vent.

Help!! Miriam put a leg into her jeans, then hopped towards the bathroom as she shoved in the other leg. *Multi-tasking!* Glopping toothpaste onto her toothbrush, she jiggled it around her mouth, *Mmmm, minty!* then turned the handle on the faucet to rinse...

But all that came out was a GROOAAAAAAAAN. Like a tuba being squeezed through a rusty pipe. Miriam looked up into the faucet. "Awww! Do NOT old house me now!" she burbled through a mouthful of sticky toothpaste. "Water! Please!" She spun the faucet handle and heard the sound again. Then a big drop bulged out of the faucet.

Phew.

But there was something very strange about this drop of water. It wasn't exactly water. It had a shape – like something MADE of water. And it was glowing – a yellow-y color. *What is that??* As Miriam watched, it dropped out of the faucet, plopped into the sink and sloshed around. She leaned in closer – then froze, barely breathing. Something was taking shape right there in front of her. Something... alive. *Wha-what's happening?* Then, from the water, a head with two big ears appeared, with a tentacle sticking out on top.

Two little eyes blinked up at her. "Freida?" it said.

Miriam's whole body started to tingle. "N-not Freida, Miriam," she said.

"Miriam!" A whirl of water belatedly exited the faucet, submerging it. "See you when I see you!" and it spiralled down the drain.

Staring into the sink, Miriam gulped down the toothpaste. Her hands shook so much it was hard to turn off the water and put her toothbrush back in the glass. She almost couldn't breathe. "Did I just see … a Wateruba??" she whispered.

Miriam ran into the hall where the walls were covered in children's drawings – drawings by Miriam and her brothers Albert, Jeff and Erik and drawings by her mom when she was little. *Grammy keeps everything. Where is it where is it where is it?* Until… she lifted up one of Erik's many drawings of tractors and… *Yes!* There it was. A drawing of a strange watery creature with big ears that looked remarkably like the strange watery creature with big ears Miriam had just seen. And next to it, in her six-year-old mom's big, curly handwriting: Wateruba. *No! Not possible…* Miriam tore the drawing off the wall and raced down the stairs to the kitchen.

Wateruba

And there was Brad

GRAMMY was at the sink, humming to herself, when Miriam burst in. "Grammy!" Grammy jumped a mile, splashing dishwater onto the floor. "Your name is Freida, right?" said Miriam, sidestepping the puddle Grammy had just made.

"Yessss," said Grammy. *She obviously doesn't have a clue why I'm asking.*

Miriam held up the drawing. "And this is a Wateruba. Something that is not real. Something that is just a story. True or false?"

"True," said Grammy. "Your mom drew that after I told her my favorite story of seeing one in the sink upstairs when I was thirteen. It asked me my name and told me it was called Krakey. It was magical… but I have a very magical imagination. It's one of the best things about me," she smiled. "You know that, right?" Miriam nodded. *She makes up stories all the time. But I think this story might be true! But how could it be??* "Do you also know if you have everything you need for camp?" Grammy handed Miriam a piece of paper. *Way to change the subject.* "Eleanor and her grandson, Brad, will be here any minute to pick you up. He's staying with her for the summer so he could go to camp for another year. He loves it. *Good for Brad. Why are you telling me all this…?* Maybe you and Brad can be friends." *I get it now.*

"Is that why you want me to go to camp, Grammy? To make friends?"

Grammy sighed. "With your dad and your brothers in France for the summer, I just don't want you to be lonely."

I love Dad and Albert and Jeff and Erik, but the only person I'm lonely for is Mom… Miriam looked down at the list. She gasped. "I'm supposed to bring in 'something related to my favorite science topic'!"

She started to pace. "What, what, what, what??"

"Maybe you should've thought about this yesterday…?" Grammy said quietly.

Not helpful! "My favorite science topic?"

"Glaciers," answered Grammy.

"Correct. But I can't bring a glacier, can I? They're too big. And they're melting." *I don't want to be sarcastic, but I can't help it. Science Camp is not my idea, and it's beginning to annoy me.*

"Maybe you can bring one next year when they're smaller. *Really, Grammy…?* Sorry," she said. "So bring an ice pick or a snow globe or your mom's camera…"

Annoying! "Don't have one, don't want one, and mom will kill me the second she gets home if I take her camera."

Grammy looked sad and tired. "Sweetheart… it's been eighteen months…"

"Please, Grammy. Now is not the time for the you-have-to-accept-your-mother's-death lecture," said Miriam. *I'm sick of everyone giving up on Mom. There are so many more reasons to believe she's alive than…*

"I've got an idea!" said Grammy, pulling a jar of rice and bags of lentils from one of the many cupboards that lined the room, until… "Ta dah!" …she whirled round with a big rock, housed in a glass display case. "Take this!"

"Your grandpa's asteroid?" said Miriam. *Wait… Is that thing… glowing – or is it my imagination?*

"Why not? It's not doing anyone any good just sitting in the back of that cupboard. I'm sure Grandpa George would want you to have it. He gave it to me when I was 11, and now I'm giving it to you when you're 11! Seems right somehow. Careful, it's heavy." Just as she handed the case to Miriam, the doorbell rang. Bunster, Grammy's dog, started barking. "That must be Eleanor and Brad! Do you want me to get it?"

No thank you. You'll ask them in, and I need to finish packing up for camp without strangers watching. "That's OK, " said Miriam. "I'll go say hi and tell them I'll be out in a minute." She approached the front door, still carrying the glass case with the asteroid inside. "Bunster! Basket!" she said to the barking dog. She balanced the asteroid on one arm and opened the door with her other hand.

And there was Brad. He was wearing baggy shorts and a T-shirt with the periodic table on it. *He looks dorky and friendly, in a nerdy sort of way.* He had white stuff streaked on his face – *sunblock?* – and band-aids all over his arms and legs. *Accident prone?* "Hi! I'm Brad!"

"Hi…" said Miriam.

But before she could tell him she'd be out in a minute, Brad was already in full flow, "Are you as excited for camp as I am? I went last year and I loved it! I bet you'll love it, too. *I can't say yes, so I won't say anything.* What are you bringing to science show-and-tell? I've got this!" He lifted his T-shirt to reveal a rash on his stomach. *What am I looking at??* "Remind you of anything?" asked Brad. *Um…* He whipped out a picture of the Milky Way and held it up next to the rash.

"The Milky Way…?"

"YES!" said Brad triumphantly. "My topic is astronomy."

"Mine, too," said Miriam, hefting the asteroid in its display case.

Brad leaned in to look at it, eyes wide. "Whoa! Check out that 'roid!"

'Roid?? "Yeah well, I'll just grab my stuff and be right out."

"No problemo!" said Brad, heading back towards the car. "It takes me a minute to get the seatbelt on without pinching my fingers anyway." He wiggled two fingers wrapped in band-aids. "See you in the car!"

Miriam closed the door. *Brad and I will definitely not be friends. He's far too… nice…*

Miriam ran back into the kitchen and tried to stuff the asteroid into her bag. But the glass case made it unstuffable. *Go in go in go in go in!* "What can I do to help?" asked Grammy knowing there was nothing she could do to help. Just then, a tuneful honking came in from outside. Grammy chuckled. "Eleanor loves her crazy car horns…"

Annoying! "I'm coming! Just cool it!" said Miriam, trying to stretch her unstretchable backpack. Meanwhile, Grammy filled a clear glass water bottle and set it down next to Miriam's bag. "I'll check 'water bottle' off the list." The horn blared again.

"AAAAAARGH!" howled Miriam. Beyond frustrated, she shoved the display case as hard as she could. "GO IN!!!" That's when it slipped from her hands. No!! She watched as the glass case with the rock inside headed towards the floor, almost in slow motion, then hit it and smashed into pieces.

"Oh no! Grammy, I'm so sorry!" *Glass everywhere! What have I done?* Miriam quickly reached down to grab the asteroid. The second she touched it, BOOM! FLASH! ZZZZT! Miriam's entire body vibrated for a moment and her hair stood on end. *Is that rock giving me a shock??* Then the shaking stopped and bit by bit, her skin seemed to... dissolve. *What's happening? Where is my skin going? Help!!* Her muscles softened... her bones liquefied... *I can't feel my feet! Where have my legs gone? I can't stand up! Everything feels all mushy! Am I melting?* And then, with a sploosh... Miriam cascaded into the puddle on the floor. She had turned into water.

Puddler

"*WHAT is happening???*" screamed the voice inside Miriam's head. *Do I even HAVE a head? This is so weird! How did this happen?? I feel like I'm made of... water!* She waved what she thought might be her arms. The motion spun her around so she was facing downwards. *That's the floor! Am I in that puddle of dishwater?? How?? What's going on??* Then she heard a voice from above. "Miriam??!" She twisted to look up and, through a layer of water, saw Grammy.

Miriam screamed as loudly as she could – "GRAMMMMMYYYY!" Strangely, the sound was clear, not bubbly.

Hearing Miriam's voice, Grammy turned and stepped right in the dishwater puddle. As the pressure wave hit her, Miriam twirled head-over-heels, flowing to the edge of the puddle, right under Bunster who loomed over her. "BUNSTER!" Bunster sniffed at the water. *Oh no! Don't drink me don't drink me! Bunster, please don't drink me!* Bunster sneezed, blowing Miriam backwards. "EEEUGH!"

"Miriam! Where are you?" called Grammy.

"I'm right here," cried Miriam. "GRAMMY!"

Just then, a voice came from somewhere close by. "Hel...lo!" A watery creature appeared next to Miriam in the puddle. *What is that??* It was kind of like the watery creature she'd seen in the sink earlier, only this one had a completely different shape. Not compact and stout, but longer, with more legs. It had a thin snout and what looked like a watery mane. And it glowed red. It waved.

"Are you another Wateruba?" asked Miriam.

12

"Mmmm!" nodded the Wateruba, rippling as it moved. *Are those legs and arms? Or just ripples?*

Miriam looked at her watery body with her own shapeless arms and legs. "Wait! Am **I** a Wateruba?"

"No…" said the Wateruba. "You… Puddler."

Puddler? I'm a Puddler??? What's a Puddler?

Just then, the water in the puddle – the water that was not only water but also Miriam and a Wateruba – reached the base of the counter under the sink. There was a roar as the water rushed in a mini-waterfall down to the subfloor. The Wateruba and Miriam were both part of the sudden current. The Wateruba was exhilarated, waving its appendages. "Woooo- hoooo!" Miriam wasn't. *Oh no no no! I don't want to go down there!* She struggled against the flow as the Wateruba was sucked down into the dark. "See …you…!" it said, and disappeared.

Miriam fought the riptide. She was overwhelmed with fear. "NO!" she screamed and… schwoop, she turned back into a girl with solid muscles and hard bones and nice, firm skin.

As Miriam stood in the kitchen panting, Grammy stared at her, open-mouthed. "Miriam? Are you OK? What just happened?" she whispered.

Miriam spoke slowly. *Please let what I'm about to say make some kind of sense.* "The asteroid zapped me, and I think… I turned into water! I was in a puddle on the floor. There!" She pointed. "And, Grammy, Waterubas are real!" She picked up the drawing. "I saw this one in the sink this morning." She turned the drawing over, took a pencil out of her bag and tried to draw the other one. "And just now, I saw this one! They spoke to me! They're real, Grammy – they're real!!"

Grammy gasped, then her eyes widened, and she whooped. "Woo-hooo! It wasn't a dream! I didn't make it up!" She danced around the kitchen. "I'm not insane! Waterubas are real!! I knew it I knew it I knew it!!" She grabbed Miriam by the shoulders, suddenly serious. "What do you suppose it means?!?" Another tuneful honk from outside snapped them back to reality. "Miriam, what do you want to do? I'm not sure camp is a good idea."

Yes it is! It's the best idea ever. I can't believe it but it's all I want to do. I need normal! "So what do we tell Brad and his grandmother? That I'm bagging camp at the last minute because I saw some aliens and then touched a space rock and turned into water...?"

Grammy thought about this for a second. "I take your point. I'll clean up – you go to camp. But maybe you should take something else for show and tell."

"No kidding," said Miriam. "I'm not touching that asteroid ever again."

Grammy looked around the kitchen. "Something science-y, something science-y – I know!" She grabbed a magazine with a young Egyptian boy on the cover. "Take this." She stuffed it into Miriam's bag. "It's published by the Water Authority, and I wrote the cover story – about this boy who can find water in the desert, and nobody knows how. Now go! Have a good day – a good, solid day!" Miriam nodded, grabbed her water bottle and hurried out the door.

Samir

THAT Egyptian boy was Samir.

13 years old. A thoughtful person with dark hair and deep, serious eyes. At that moment, this dark haired, sensitive 13 year old was standing outside his house in rural Egypt next to a rain barrel that was nearly empty. His mother stood in the doorway waiting for Samir's younger sister, Asmaa, to return from fetching water. Samir could tell that his mother was worried, no matter how hard she tried to hide it. But he also knew that he could help.

Behind him, on a windowsill, sat a piece of asteroid. Whereas Miriam's piece was basically a rock, Samir's was a large, flat shard. But both Miriam's rock and Samir's shard had the same soft glow. No one but Samir had any idea what that shard had done to him as he'd held it in his hand after digging it out of the wall when he was eight. Just then, Asmaa returned from the neighboring village. When Samir looked into the jerry can she was carrying... "No water from the pump?" Asmaa shook her head.

Their mother called from the house. "We have a day's drinking water left, maybe two. What then?"

Samir's youngest sister, Layla, put her arms around his waist. "Don't worry! Samir will save us. He always does."

Samir smiled and gently pushed her away, embarrassed. No one could know what he was able to do. "I'll check out the pump," he said and headed off, turning as he ran to make sure no one was following.

Science camp

ONCE out the door, Miriam headed towards Brad's grandmother's car, shoving the water bottle Grammy had filled for her into her backpack. "Wheeeee!" said a voice. *What?!*

Miriam picked up the bottle and peered in. As she stared, a shape emerged out of the water – big belly, little elephant ears, a wafty tentacle, yellow glow. The same Wateruba she'd seen in the bathroom sink! *I can't believe it! It must've come out of the faucet in the kitchen when Grammy filled the bottle. I've got a Wateruba, here in my bag!* "Hi there!" it said. "Hi," Miriam whispered. *If I can hear it, can everyone else?* She looked up. Brad and his grandmother were talking to each other. *Phew. No one heard it.* Miriam pushed the water bottle into her bag, burying it under her spare T-shirt and socks. She hopped into the back seat next to Brad. *I am absolutely not ready to tell anyone about any of this.*

"Hello, Miriam," said Eleanor, Brad's grandmother. "Are you as excited for camp as Brad…?"

"Letsgoletsgoletsgoletsgo!" Brad interrupted, throwing his arms in the air.

"Not quite," said Miriam, smiling. *Whoa, Brad! Down boy!* "LetsgoNanletsgoletsgoNanNanNan!" continued Brad.

"Then let's go!" said Eleanor, putting the car in gear and pulling out with a final blast on the joke horn.

"I'm so glad you're coming to camp!" said Brad. "Making a new friend is the best, don't you think? *I'm not sure I know how anymore.* And you know what else is cool?"

"Meeee!" said the Wateruba from inside the bag. "Wheee!" said

Miriam, trying to cover. "Mayflies!" said Brad.

"What?" said Miriam. *Oh good. He didn't hear the Wateruba.*

"Mayflies!" repeated Brad. "There's a pond near the camp that's famous for them. Everyone says mayflies only live for a day, but when they're larva, they live for up to TWO YEARS at the bottom of a pond. So cool."

Brad kept talking, but Miriam couldn't think about anything except what was in her water bottle. *Sorry, Brad!* She peeked into her bag and lifted the T-shirt. The Wateruba was joyfully morphing in and out of the slosh in the bottle. One second it seemed to be clear water – but then, look! There was its belly, its funny little feet, its ears, its tentacle. It was a Wateruba! *It's magical, and it's real!* Then it vanished into the water.

Just as Brad was pulling up one leg of his shorts to show Miriam his collection of mosquito bites, they pulled up at Camp. Miriam hopped out of the car. "Thanks for the ride!" she called to Brad's grandmother and headed in, leaving Brad struggling to get out of his seat belt. "I'll catch up with you, new friend!" he shouted after her.

Where can I go? Where can I go? All Miriam wanted was a few minutes alone with the Wateruba. *I have a Wateruba – in my bag! So many questions!* She looked into her backpack and saw it inside her water bottle. It waved. "What are you, exactly?" Miriam whispered, "Do you have a name? What's a Puddler? And why is all this happening?"

"Wateruba. Krakey. Person who can turn into water. Asteroid," said Krakey. "Next?"

"Uh-hey?"

Miriam looked up to see that she was surrounded by campers. "Hhhey!" she muttered, quickly zipping her bag closed. *So embarrassing!*

"Do you talk to your backpack a lot?" said a girl. *She's so pretty. And so confident!* "No judgement."

Before Miriam could answer, Brad scurried in, breathless. "Hoooo! Hey, everybody! This is my new friend, Miriam! She's super awesome;

she lives with her grandma who's a science writer; she has a dog; we're space twins; and here's my show and tell!" He pulled up his shirt.

The confident girl took a close look. "Is that the Milky Way?"

Brad nodded, pleased. "Good one, Jin!"

Are these guys Brad's friends?! "I never thought you'd top last year's poison ivy Picasso," Jin continued, "but I guess turning twelve means you've upped your game." She then turned to Miriam and said warmly, "Welcome to Science Camp, Miriam."

FWEEEEEP!! Two camp counsellors approached the group. Steve was the one blowing the whistle. FWEEEEE-EE-EEEP!! *Annoying!* "Look alive, campers! Straight line! Sound off! Anu? Roll call!" Anu, the other counsellor, (no whistle), rolled her eyes. *Ha. Interesting.*

As Anu called out everyone's names, Miriam whispered to Brad that she really needed to get somewhere private. Brad whispered back that he'd made her a map to show where the bathrooms were, and handed it to her. *Thanks, Brad!* FWEEEEP! Everyone flinched. *Really? Again with the whistle?*

"Talking during roll call?" sputtered Steve, frowning at Miriam and Brad, the whistle still in his mouth. "Not a great start, campers." *Nope. Don't like him.*

"Dude, chill," Anu interrupted. "It's only nine a.m., Day One." She removed the whistle from Steve's mouth, then turned to Miriam. "Miriam, right?" Miriam nodded.

"Miriam," said Steve putting two fingers up to his eyes, then pointing them at Miriam. Anu calmly pushed Steve's fingers away. "Cool," she said to Miriam. *But I do like her.* Anu then turned to the other campers. "All right. First assignment! Find a bunch of nature stuff to make art with and bring it all to the Arts & Crafts cabin."

As the kids scattered, Steve hollered after them. "Stay within the very clearly marked boundaries of the camp. And stay away from Mayfly Millpond! Why? Because it can suck you in! That means you, Brad!"

Samir will save us

ABOUT 6,130 miles or 9,865 kilometers away and 7 hours ahead, Samir ran, out of breath, into the village near his home. One of the villagers was vigorously working the handle on the water pump, but nothing came out. Samir ducked into the shade, where the barest trickle of water dripped from a junction in the pipe that fed the pump. He looked around to make sure he was alone, then stood very still. He inhaled. As he slowly exhaled, Samir relaxed and whispered to himself. "Let go… sink… dissolve… flow…" He felt his hair liquefy. And then his whole head turned into water, followed by his neck, shoulders, chest, arms… until his entire body was liquid and spilled down to join his watery feet. In other words, he puddled.

Watery Samir joined the water trickling onto the ground and kicked his watery legs as hard as he could to flow up the pipe.

Mayfly millpond

MEANWHILE, at Science Camp, Miriam was hiding behind a tree, not far from Mayfly Millpond. *Alone at last!* Well, not entirely alone. "Hi, Miriam," said Krakey as she opened her bag.

"Hey, Krakey," said Miriam. "Tell me everything." And then she added, "Please." *I wonder if Waterubas care about manners...*

"I'll try!" it said cheerfully. "81 Waterubas including me came to this planet four billion years ago on an asteroid called the Asteruba. The rock you have in your house is a piece of the Asteruba – and not just any piece – it's a big piece of the core. That's why we keep coming back. The Asteruba is like a magnet to the Ruba in us." As Krakey said the word "Ruba," it glowed more brightly, a beautiful yellow.

"So your Ruba is your glow?" said Miriam.

"It's our glow, and it's the glow that keeps us in the know and helps us go, go, go!" said Krakey. "Ruba Ruba Ruba!" It whooshed around the water bottle, glowing. "Every Wateruba's Ruba is a different color. Mine is bumblebee yellow."

"It's so beautiful," said Miriam. *Really beautiful.* "So when I touched our piece of the Asteruba, I became a Puddler?"

"Yes!" Krakey stopped whooshing and looked at Miriam. "A Puddler is a human who can turn into water. I've never actually met one before, so I don't think there are many of you." Krakey smooshed its little belly flat up against the glass to get as close to Miriam as possible. "This is very exciting!! Why? Because humans desperately need Waterubas, and Puddlers are the key to everything!"

"Wait, what?" said Miriam. "But didn't you just say that **I** was a

Puddler?" *Being the key to everything sounds like a big job to me.*

"There's a reason we're meeting now. The world is changing. I've been around over 4 billion years, so I know! But you're the first Puddler I've met. That's significant."

What?? Krakey whirled and twirled around, almost completely disappearing into the water, then stopped. It took shape again. "Krakey, what's significant? How am I the key to everything?? What's everything??" Krakey raised a watery arm to point at the magazine that Grammy had put into the bag. "Maybe that boy's a Puddler too."

"A Puddler?" Miriam pulled out the magazine and looked at the picture of the unsmiling boy on the cover. "This boy…? Really?" When Krakey didn't answer, she put the magazine back in the bag and took out the water bottle. She pressed her face up against it to look right into Krakey's two little eyes. "How am I the key to everything? *I need more information!* Why do we desperately need you?" *None of this makes sense!*

"Can I see you puddle?" asked Krakey instead of answering her questions. "Please please please? I didn't have a good view when it happened."

Miriam shook her head. "Absolutely not. Besides, I don't have the asteroid with me, so I can't. I'm never touching that thing again." *Whether I'm the key to everything or not!*

"But you don't need to. One zap from the Asteruba is all it takes," explained Krakey. "A blast of Ruba and your molecules are transfigured. So just relax and think like water, and you'll puddle. It's your superpower! Try it!" Then Krakey's glow became even more radiant and it made the sound that Miriam had heard in the bathroom when the faucet didn't work.

"Huh?" *That sound is so relaxing.* Miriam found herself taking a deep breath, and noticed that her feet felt sloshy. She looked down. *Wait a minute… My feet are… water! How can this be happening?? I'm turning into water! Now!* "NO!" she screamed. Then she heard Brad's voice.

"There you are!" *Quick! Hide, Krakey!* By the time Brad joined her behind the tree, she was picking up rocks near the path. Her feet were normal feet again. *Phew!*

"You found me! I'm looking for the perfect rock! *Be casual!* I had to leave the, uh, 'roid at home."

Brad was genuinely disappointed. "You did?! Why?" *Good. He bought it.*

"It was too big for my bag," said Miriam. "So now I need another rock – an earthy rock, not one from outer space."

Brad joined in the search. "So we're looking for an igneous rock, then. There are two types – intrusive and extrusive."

OK, but all I want to do is talk to Krakey! Miriam sighed. *I can hear Mom saying, "Feeling frustrated because things aren't the way you want them to be isn't going to help." Focus on finding a rock!* She looked around to see what was there. *I want one that doesn't look anything like the Asteruba.* "This one's nice," she said. She picked up another. "Oooh, I like the feel of this one. But this one has good earthy colors …" She carefully put each rock into her bag. "Want to help?"

"Already on it!" As Brad concentrated on collecting rocks, Miriam edged away, positioning herself so she could talk into her bag while keeping an eye on him. "Krakey!" she whispered. "What did you mean when you said Puddlers are the key to everything?"

Just then, Brad held up a rock he'd found. "Miriam! It's not as cool as an asteroid or mayflies, but this granite is pretty dope!"

"Sure is!" said Miriam. *I need to get Brad off my back.* "Are there more?"

"I'll keep looking!" said Brad. *You do that.* As he turned his back, Miriam ducked behind a tree and pulled the water bottle out of her bag. "Please tell me why Puddlers are the key to everything. What's everything?"

"Well, to begin with…" began Krakey. But it stopped talking when Brad came around the tree.

"Did you find anything back here?" he asked. "The closer we get to the pond, the better the rocks are!"

"NO!" yelled Miriam. *Ooops. That sounded angry. I don't know him well enough to yell at him.* Then she realized that Krakey was in full view in the water bottle. She quickly put it behind her back.

"That's okay," said Brad. "I've got enough rocks for show and tell AND for our art project. Can I have some of your water? Rocks are hard work! Geddit? Because they're hard?" He reached behind her and took the bottle from her hand. He saw Krakey. "Whoa! You've got yuck in there!"

"I know," said Miriam. *Oh no oh no oh no oh no!* She took back the bottle. "Yuck! I can't let you drink yuck!"

"And I can't let YOU drink yuck!" said Brad, grabbing the bottle and twisting off the cap. "Do you want dysentery? Trust me. You don't want dysentery. Or cryptosporidiosis. Or cyclosporiasis. Or e coli." *What is he talking about?* Miriam tried to yank the bottle away, Brad yanked back. And that was when the water – along with Krakey – went flying into the pond.

Miriam ran to the water's edge as Krakey landed, waved, said "See you when I see you!" and splished out of sight.

"No!!!!" cried Miriam. She stared out helplessly over the pond, watching the Wateruba that she'd only just found disappear forever.

We'll get what we need

IF we'd been in Egypt at exactly the moment Miriam lost Krakey, and we'd been staring at a certain pipe snaking its way through the desert, we would have seen that this particular pipe was broken. It looked as if the water had been diverted into another pipe. What was going on? Then some water pooled where the pipe was split. Before it dripped into the ground to be absorbed, it rose into the air and took the shape of a person. The watery shape solidified – it was Samir.

Samir was panting. He'd had to swim against the trickle of water going down the pipe to get all the way up it. If there was one thing he'd learned from his adventures as a Puddler – because just as Krakey thought, Samir was, in fact, a Puddler – it was that going against the flow of water took a lot of energy. He steadied his breathing, stomped his feet to make sure they were completely solid, and looked around. The water that should have been available to his village was now going somewhere else. But where? Samir saw a number of crates, piles of bricks and other building materials. Then he heard voices, and ducked behind a crate, keeping low to the ground. Peeking up over the top, he saw a group of construction workers and a man who seemed like the boss striding towards them. Curious, Samir darted behind a crate closer to the group.

"Has all the water been diverted from the village pump to the resort grounds?" Resort?? This was the first time Samir had heard anything about a resort. "We're going to need it all for the swimming pools, water slides and fountains."

"We'll get what we need," said one of the workers confidently.

Another looked out over the barren landscape. "Won't the locals be a problem when their wells go dry?"

The boss laughed. "By the time they figure it out, it'll be too late!" Samir grabbed some tools. He was about to prove them wrong.

Be like water

BACK at Science Camp, things were tense. *I can't believe Brad just threw Krakey into the Millpond!* "Why did you do that??" Miriam yelled. *I don't care that I don't know him that well. I'm really mad at him!!*

Brad blinked at her. "To save you from drinking a big blob of unidentified yuck. It could've been a deadly mixture of algae and cyanobacteria. It could've been MOOSE POO!"

I can't listen to this! Miriam dropped her pack, kicked off her shoes and waded into the water. "Krakey! Where are you? KRAKEY!"

"You need to get out of there. The muck could suck you in!"

"KRAAAAAA-KEY!!" called Miriam.

"Does 'Krakey' mean 'leave me alone' in some weird language?"

Miriam turned to Brad. "I have to do this on my own, so go away. Now." She waded deeper into the pond. "KRAAAAAAAKEEEEY!" When she turned around, Brad was gone. *Good.* "KRAAAAAAAAKEEEYYYY!" Miriam waited a few moments, listening. Nothing. *Where is it?! How am I ever going to find it??* She felt sadder than she'd felt in a long time, and that was saying something. *I can't believe Krakey's gone! And it's all Brad's fault.* She waded back to the shore and slumped to the ground. She buried her head in her hands, close to tears. "Mom," she whispered, "I actually had a Wateruba, a real Wateruba, and I lost it!"

She remembered the night before her mother had gone on that last trip to Greenland. Her nine year old self had been in bed trying to sleep while her mom had stroked her hair. *I could never get to sleep on the nights before Mom went away.* "I won't be gone long, my love – six weeks, eight max." *Six weeks! That seemed like forever! But now it's been a year and a half... I miss her so much... Will the missing ever stop?* And then her mother had said what she always said: "I wouldn't go at all if I didn't know it's the only way for me to be the best possible human being I can be, and to help us all live on this planet." *That's when I started to cry. I couldn't help it. I was proud and sad all at the same time.* Her mom had leaned in close. "Shhh... no tears...." Then she'd gasped. "Wait! I think I saw a... No. It couldn't be!" Her mom had brushed a tear from her cheek and held it up. "Miri, look! A Wateruba!" *If there had been a Wateruba, it could've been Krakey! But back then, we didn't think they were real. She was just trying to cheer me up.* In the memory, her mom had gathered her into her arms. "Come on, honey. Relax. Breathe with me. Be like water, and just let things be as they are... Breathe in... breathe out..."

As Miriam sat on the ground next to Mayfly Millpond remembering this moment, *I wish I wish I could be with my mom again right now!* she took the same calming breaths. In... out... in... out... Thinking of her mother, her heart expanded with each in-breath, her body relaxed and ... her feet started to feel oozy and watery. *What??* When she looked down, she saw her toes turning to water. *Look at that! Don't be scared, don't be scared! I want to know what happens next!*

Both feet and ankles were now water. *If I'm water, maybe I'll find Krakey! Maybe it's the only way!* She closed her eyes, and kept breathing. In... out... in... out... The watery feeling moved up to her legs, then to her belly, chest and arms, neck, head. *Now what? I will not freak out!*

What happens next?? Am I water yet? Almost... Her hair was the last thing to puddle. *It's not wet like in the bath; my hair isn't hair anymore – it's water!* With one final out breath, Miriam flowed into the pond.

You'd think this would be like swimming underwater, only it's not. When you are water, you don't need to swim – you just drift... drift... drift. And I can breathe! How cool is that? Miriam drifted in the pond, weaving through underwater plants. It was like being in a rippling forest. *This is a whole other world!*

Who knew all this was here? Look, a newt! She watched a newt swim around a submerged tree branch. She was concentrating so hard, she was almost cut in two by a great diving beetle heading back up to the surface for air. *Whooooaaa!!* Startled, she tensed. Her feet began to feel solid... *No! Not yet!* Trying to relax again, she closed her eyes. *Be... like water... Need to find Krakey... Feet still oozy – can't feel my bones – good.* Miriam continued to go with the flow. "Krakey!" Again, she noticed that her voice didn't sound watery, as you'd expect, but clear, like whale song. "Krakey!" Soon she noticed that wherever she pointed her head, she moved in that direction. "Krakey!!" She pointed her head to the left, and glided left; to the right, she wafted right. "Krakey!!" And then she heard a sound... like a distant tuba. "Krakey!?" Once more, the tuba sound. *Did that come out of me?* No, it seemed to be somewhere below her. "Krakey?" she called. Closing her eyes, she pointed her head down and sank deeper into the pond.

When Miriam opened her eyes again, she saw that she was heading into the gaping mouth of a frog. *Uh-oh.* But there was nothing she could do to stop herself, so she went with it. *Good thing I like frogs!* Everything went dark for a moment, and then she came out into the water again. *I was just inside a frog?!? Wait 'til I tell Grammy!* Then she heard a familiar voice. "Hi, Miriam!" *Krakey!! I found you!* Krakey bobbed in the mud among some mayfly nymphs.

Miriam was so relieved she almost cried. *Can water cry?!*

While Miriam was wondering if water could cry, Brad was stomping through the woods with his big backpack of rocks. Branches whacked him; nettles stung him. But he was too furious to even notice. He was also worried. As he stomped, the worry gradually became stronger than the fury, until he stopped, shouted out in frustration, "AAAAARGH!!", then turned around and headed back to the pond. But when he got to where he'd last seen her, there was her bag, but no Miriam. "Miriam? MIRIAM??" No answer. Absolutely positive that she was stuck in the muck at the bottom of the pond, Brad's worry completely washed away the last of his fury. He had to save her.

Meanwhile, Miriam was anything but stuck. She was having the time of her life, joyfully floating around Krakey, who exuberantly floated around her – as if they were dancing. "I still can't believe I found you," she said.

"Of course you did," said Krakey. "We're connected."

"We are?" said Miriam. *How?*

Krakey then passed right through her. *Whoa! That was weird!* "We're all water," it said. "It's in us and around us – it IS us! All water everywhere is connected." Krakey made the deep resonant tone Miriam had come to associate with Waterubas. She felt her watery self pulsate with the sound.

"What's that music you make?"

"The Wateruba Tuba," said Krakey.

Just then, the water roiled, tossing them in different directions. "Help!" *I mustn't unpuddle before I finish talking to Krakey!* Not unpuddling just yet was her plan – until she saw two pudgy legs approaching, one of them red with nettle stings. As the legs stirred up silt and mud, Miriam heard a voice coming from above.

"Miriam! Where are you?!?"

"Oh no! It's Brad!" *He sounds scared!* Miriam saw that Brad's legs were approaching a ledge where the water got deeper. Much deeper. "No, Brad, stop!" she called. But too late. Brad stepped off the ledge and onto nothing. His terrified face sank past her as he was dragged down by his backpack full of rocks. *He is scared! Really scared! And way too heavy!* Brad thrashed and kicked, sending Krakey spinning away.

"I have to help Brad!" Miriam yelled and waved.

"See you when I see you!" called Krakey as it spiraled away in the current.

Brad struggled in vain to get to the surface. *He's going to drown!* With that thought, fear instantly took hold. And as it did, Miriam felt her bones, her muscles, then all of her skin. She was a solid girl again. *Yes!* She dove down, pulled Brad's pack off his back, and yanked him up. He bobbed to the surface, gasping. Half-swimming, half-running, Miriam dragged him to dry land.

Coughing and spluttering, Brad rolled over onto his back and saw Miriam looking down at him. "Brad? Are you OK?"

"Miriam? You… you saved me!" He gratefully burped up a slimy blob of pond water.

"Yeah. Call it a moment of weakness," said Miriam, not quite ready to show Brad how relieved she was. He smiled at her, and she smiled back. Brad struggled to sit up. Then a voice – "What is going on here?!" Steve. And he was not happy. *Just what we need. Not.*

"Did I or did I not say NOT to go near Mayfly Millpond!"

Miriam and Brad couldn't disagree. "You did," said Brad, shivering.

Steve pointed at Brad. "You're twelve," and then at Miriam, "and you're eleven, right?" They nodded. *What is your point??* "Then you're old enough to know that when you break rules, there are consequences. Consequences like getting expelled from the camp."

"What?!?" said Miriam. *That's not fair! It was my fault, not Brad's!*

"This is what happens, Miriam," Steve lectured. "I've got to set an example. I mean, I get it. Mayflies are wicked-awesome, but they are no reason to wade into a pond that is off-limits. UNDERSTOOD?!"

Miriam stared at Steve. *The more I know you, the less I like you.* She looked at Brad, who was clearly crushed. *He loves this camp. He does not deserve this.* Miriam took a deep breath, then turned to face Steve. "It wasn't Brad's fault," she said. "I dragged him out here because I had to see the incredible mayfly norwads." "Naiads," Brad whispered. "Whatever," said Miriam. "I got stuck in the muck, just like you warned us, but Brad helped me out. He's a hero… and a good friend."

Brad was so happy to hear this, he forgot how angry he'd been and that he'd almost drowned – all because of Miriam. He grinned from ear to ear. Steve frowned. He looked at Miriam. Then at Brad. Then back at Miriam. "OK... Since you're new, I'll let this go," he said. "But three strikes and you're out. I'll be watching you." He did the thing again where he put two fingers to his eyes and then pointed them at Miriam. *What a dork.* "I won't expel you from camp, but I will send you both home early today. And you can explain to your parents why. Got that?"

Miriam and Brad nodded, relieved.

"Now call whoever you need to call to pick you up because I don't want to see your faces for the rest of the day." And he marched off.

"OK by me," Miriam whispered to Brad.

"And me," said Brad. He imitated Steve, putting his fingers to his eyes. "I'll be watching you..." And the two of them started to giggle.

The more I know Brad, the more I like him...

Uncle Eddy

BRAD knew that his grandmother was at work and wouldn't be able to pick them up, so Miriam tried Grammy. She answered, whispering urgently, "Are you all right?"

"I'm fine," said Miriam. "Why are you whispering?"

"In a book meeting. Speak later. Love you," Grammy whispered and hung up.

So Miriam called Uncle Eddy. He and her mom had known each other since they were kids. And Eddy had been with her on that final trip to Greenland. "Could you come pick me and my friend up from camp?" Brad grinned. He loved that she said 'my friend.' " I'm really, really sorry cuz I know you're busy, but…"

"Don't apologize, Miri! Of course I'll come pick you up," said Eddy. "I'll be there faster than you can say…" "…tingisingajappat!" Miriam and Eddy said together. It was something Eddy and her mom used to say. He sounded so jolly and helpful, Miriam instantly felt better.

"Tingi…what?" said Brad, as they waited for Eddy.

"Tingisingajappat," said Miriam. "It's Greenlandic for 'surprised,' though technically it means 'almost flew away.'"

"So when you say, 'I'm surprised' in Greenland, you're actually saying, 'I almost flew away,'" said Brad thoughtfully. "Cool!" Then, "Is 'Krakey' Greenlandic for something?"

Miriam laughed. *Didn't expect that!* "I'll tell you later." *When I think of a good answer.*

While they waited for Uncle Eddy to arrive, Brad told Miriam about his family. About his parents who ran a big music festival, which is why they were always busy in the summer, and about Delilah, his older sister, whom he really didn't know that well because she never paid much attention to him. Last year, she'd been the one who'd driven him to camp, but this year, she'd gone travelling with friends. "Probably to avoid babysitting me," he sighed. *He's talking, but I'm not really listening. Sorry, Brad, but all I can think about is Krakey.* When Brad asked her about her family, though, she managed to stop thinking about Krakey long enough to tell him about her three brothers – Albert who was 13, Jeff who was 9 and Erik who was 6. And about how they were in France this summer with their dad who was working on a project. "And you didn't want to go because you wanted to go to camp instead, right?" said Brad. *Not really… but if that's what you want to think, go for it!*

Uncle Eddy arrived, and after Miriam introduced them, Brad immediately caught his finger in the seatbelt – "Don't worry, I do that all the time," he said to a concerned Eddy.

Reassured, Uncle Eddy started asking questions. "Why did you go into the pond? *Fair question.* I happen to know the water in that pond is pretty clean – after all, mayflies need clean water to survive – so that's not what bothers me. But did you see something? Something unusual? Is that why you went in?"

Miriam wanted to tell him about the Wateruba but decided not to because Brad was there. *Eddy's at least heard about the Waterubas from Mom, but Brad knows nothing, and explaining ancient aliens made of water is not something I want to do during a car ride.* But she didn't have to worry about it for long because once Uncle Eddy mentioned mayflies, Brad got excited – a fellow fan!

"You know, they've been around for more than 300 million years! And their order is Ephemeroptera which makes sense because of their life cycle, right?"

"Ephemeral! Yes, I guess it does!" chuckled Uncle Eddy. *Thank you, Brad!*

When they got to Grammy's house, Miriam hugged Uncle Eddy. "It was really nice of you to come and get us."

"Never worry about calling me if you need me, Miri. OK?"

"OK, thanks," said Miriam. *Mom isn't here for me, but Uncle Eddy is. I love knowing that.* Miriam called Grammy to tell her that she and Brad had been sent home and that Uncle Eddy had picked them up.

"Don't worry – I'm minutes away! Tell me about it when I get there," she said. "Eddy can go if he needs to get back to work." Miriam and Brad waved goodbye as Eddy drove off.

Miracle boy

MEANWHILE, across the world, Samir was putting his secret superpower to good use. He already knew how to puddle and unpuddle. He also knew that whatever you were wearing or holding would puddle and unpuddle with you, as if there'd been absolutely no molecular change. He'd puddled with the tools that he'd 'borrowed' from the construction camp. So when he unpuddled, so did the tools. He used them to repair the damage to the pipe, restoring the flow of water. Then he hid the tools, and ran back to the pump, arriving just as his sisters were filling their jerry cans. When the small but grateful crowd saw him, they called out "Miracle boy!" Samir proudly accepted the slaps on the back and the cheers, but he was worried. Those men and that resort weren't going away. "I just do what I can," he said, and then quietly, to himself, "until I can't…"

He believes me!

LATER, Miriam and Brad were washing the dishes, having just eaten Grammy's celebratory First Day of Science Camp Even Though You Almost Got Kicked Out meal. Grammy filled the sink up with soapy water, then left things to Miriam and Brad while she went up to her office to make notes on her earlier meeting. Miriam stared, mesmerized by the bubbly water swirling in the sink. *Are there any Waterubas in there?* "Look at it!" she sighed. "Isn't water amazing?"

"Absolutely!" said Brad, carefully drying a plate. "I mean, where would mayflies be without it?"

Miriam had just had the strangest day of her life and she felt almost fond of Brad. *He was such a big part of it.* "Can I tell you something before your grandmother picks you up?" she said.

"Shoot!" he answered cheerfully.

Brad is always cheerful. I like that. "It's just… I don't have a ton of friends – *none in fact* – so I don't talk about this stuff a lot." *Or ever.* Brad turned to her, listening. "Eighteen months ago, my… um… my…" *Just say it, Miriam!* She took a deep breath. "My mom died."

Brad's face flushed with sympathy. "Oh yeah. My nan mentioned that to me. I'm so sorry," he said.

"She was a glaciologist," Miriam ploughed on. "She disappeared on a research trip…"

"That's…" Brad started to say something, but Miriam held up her hand to stop him.

"Only I know she's still alive." *There. I said it.* Brad was confused.

"They never found her body," Miriam explained.

Then Brad got excited. "So, it's a mystery!" he said. If Miriam had had any doubts about Brad being her friend, they disappeared in this moment. *He believes me!* "Like maybe she's stranded or she's got amnesia!" Brad continued. "There's like <u>so</u> many things that can cause that!"

"Exactly!" said Miriam gratefully. "She's out there. I can feel it. And the real reason I didn't go to France with my dad and brothers is because I want to be here when she comes back."

"I get that," said Brad. *Oh thank you thank you thank you!* "Where was she when she disappeared?"

"In Greenland."

"Oh, so that's why you know words in Greenlandic!"

Miriam nodded. "She loved it there. But I don't have a lot to go on. Just some survey maps, her notes, and her camera. I have to do any research secretly because everybody else in my family thinks I'm nuts." Miriam dried her hands and headed to a closet in the hall. Brad followed. She opened the door, removed the top from a box on the floor, and gingerly retrieved the camera. Brad reached out for it.

"Nice," he said. "45-point cross-type auto focus. 10-fps. Sweet F-mount, too."

Amazing! "You know about cameras?"

"A bit," Brad said modestly. There was a click as he powered up the camera and scrolled through some shots. "My nan is a professional photographer, so... Whoa! Where is that??"

"In Greenland. It's the Jakobshavn Glacier." *So beautiful...*

"These shots are amazeballs!" Brad scrolled some more, then stopped at another photo. "What's your Uncle Eddy doing there?" he said, showing Miriam a picture of Ruth and Eddy.

"He's not really my uncle, you know. He and Mom have known each other since they were kids. They both studied watery subjects at university, and they used to work together. *It's hard talking about Mom.*

Breathe… He was my mom's research partner on this trip," she continued. "It was supposed to be her friend Edith, but she got sick or something and Eddy stepped in at the last minute."

Brad kept scrolling. "Last shot," he said, peering at it. "What's that?"

He showed the picture to Miriam. It was a funny angle – mostly ice and sky. Miriam couldn't see anything. "What's what?"

"Let's put these 32.5 megapixels to use," said Brad, zooming in. "There – in the ice."

Miriam looked, and then looked more closely. The watery shape… the glow. *Yes, I'm sure of it!* "It's a Wateruba!" she gasped.

"Cool!" said Brad. "What's a Wateruba?"

I'm going to find Krakey today

EARLY the next morning, Miriam jumped out of bed, wide awake. *I'm going to find Krakey today!* She rushed around the house, shoving everything she might need into her backpack: different-sized water bottles, ladles, compostable plastic bags. *No matter what happens, I am going to find Krakey.*

In the middle of her frantic packing, Brad called her on her tablet. "Brad – not now!" said Miriam when he appeared on the screen. *Brad's my friend now but he can still be annoying.* "I'm in the kitchen packing the stuff I need to find Krakey," she explained, trying to sound calm and friendly.

"That's what I figured, so I'm here to help! *See? Annoying.* You'll need waterproof sunscreen!" said Brad. *No.* "Waterproof band-aids! *Definitely not.* Waterproof underwear!" he shouted.

Miriam turned to the tablet, "Brad… Really?" she sighed.

"Really," he replied. "I'm going to pack some for myself. It would've come in handy yesterday, right?" Miriam smiled at him. *I don't think so…* Last night, she and Grammy had told Brad everything that had happened, from the moment Miriam saw Krakey in the same sink where Grammy had seen it sixty years ago, until the moment she discovered she was a Puddler. Brad was so fired up he couldn't even eat the gluten-free ice cream roll that Grammy had bought for him specially. He now understood why Miriam had gone into the pond shouting, "Krakey!", and vowed to do everything he could to help her find it. Brad continued with the checklist. "Obviously, we can't forget the most important thing: the asteroid!"

"Got it," said Miriam, carefully placing the Asteruba in her bag.

Despite what Krakey had said, she hadn't wanted to touch it again. But Brad had convinced her that if Waterubas were drawn to it, maybe it would be like a magnet for Krakey. *Good point.* To prove to her it was safe, he'd taken her hands and put them on the Asteruba. "See?" he'd said when nothing had happened, not even a little tingle. "One zap is all it takes, just like Krakey said. Trust me, that's how it works for a lot of superheroes." *OK — you win.*

"Miriam?" Grammy entered. "Isn't it about time for you to go? You'll be late."

"No, no, no! I want to be early today!"

"No problem!" said Brad from the tablet. "We're actually outside your house now! Nan, hit the horn!" This time the horn played Yankee Doodle.

"Why didn't you say so??" *Annoying, annoying, annoying!* Miriam quickly zipped up her bag, gave Bunster a pat on the head and headed towards the door. "Bye, Grammy!"

"Love you!" called Grammy.

"Love you, too!" said Miriam.

Grammy took Bunster into the back yard, leaving Brad on the tablet. As Miriam headed out, she heard his voice, "Love you three!" *Brad!*

The quest to find Krakey begins

MIRIAM and Brad got to camp early enough to have time before roll call to do the one thing they were absolutely forbidden to do – sneak off to Mayfly Millpond.

"Here begins the Quest to Find Krakey!" Miriam announced, pulling the asteroid out of her backpack and facing the pond. "So how's this supposed to work?"

"I have no idea," said Brad, circling Miriam to see the situation from all angles. He tripped and fell, but bounced right back up. "I'm OK!"

Annoying!! But funny… Miriam held the Asteruba out in front of her and closed her eyes. "What are you doing?" whispered Brad.

"I'm trying to feel if it's pulling me towards Krakey," said Miriam. "And you don't have to whisper." She held her arms out straight for a few minutes. She slowly turned to the right. Then to the left. "Nope. Nothing."

"Let me try," said Brad. He took the Asteruba and held it out. "You're right. Nothing." He handed the space rock back to his friend. "Confession: I was hoping I would puddle…"

"Win some, lose some." Miriam looked out over the pond. *Idea!* "Maybe I should walk into the water with it!"

But Brad held her back. "Do I need to remind you that rocks and water are a dangerous combination? And we both know from personal experience that the bottom of the pond is super mucky. If you drop the asteroid in there, it'll be lost forever. Guaranteed. *Annoying… but right.* Besides, since the camp gets its water from the pond, Krakey could actually be anywhere in the camp right now."

"I hadn't thought of that," sighed Miriam. *We'll never find it.* Discouraged, she put the Asteruba back in her backpack. "Come on – we'd better head back for roll call."

You took our water

WHILE Miriam and Brad hightailed it back to be treated like criminals by Steve, Samir was being treated like a hero by his neighbors. The villagers wondered how he'd managed to bring back their water. But to be honest, they were more interested in celebrating than in hearing any details. Pleased as Samir was that everyone was happy, the attention was too much. He had a particularly hard time with the women's ululations. They sounded like shrieking birds. Joyful – but loud. Samir needed to get out of there. Slipping away from the crowd, he sat on the ground by his house and closed his eyes to go to the peaceful oasis he had inside. But his inner stillness was cut short as a convoy of noisy vehicles barreled up the dirt road into the village. Angry men spilled out of the cars.

"You took our water!" they bellowed.

The villagers weren't buying that for a minute. Who were these people? "This is *OUR* water! Who are you?" they shouted back at the intruders.

Recognizing the men he'd seen at the construction site the day before, Samir ran. Intent on escaping, he didn't notice a mysterious figure dressed impeccably in white. But the man noticed Samir.

In the crowd, one of the construction crew turned on a little girl. He leaned down so that his big, menacing face was right next to hers. "Who did this?" he growled. When she didn't answer, the face roared again. "WHO??!?"

Frightened, the girl whispered, "Samir."

The shout went up: "Where is he? Where's Samir?" Everyone looked around. But Samir was nowhere to be seen.

Let the quest begin again

BACK at Science Camp, the most menacing face was Steve's, scowling at Brad and Miriam as they ran in to take their places with the rest of the campers. "Good to see you two," he said. "And why am I seeing you? Oh yes! Because I didn't expel you from camp yesterday, right?" Miriam and Brad nodded. *What an idiot...* "You're welcome."

Anu blew her whistle. "OK, campers! Free time! If anyone's interested, I'll be leading the camp choir near the Stone Stile!"

As the others dispersed, Steve came up to Miriam and Brad. "I'll be watching you two like a hawk." He did the fingers-to-the-eyes thing again. *Give me a break...* "You've had one strike – two more, and you're out!" *Thank you, we can count.*

Once Steve walked away, Miriam turned to Brad. "Let the quest begin... again!"

"The Quest to Find Krakey," said Brad solemnly. He pulled a piece of neatly folded paper from his pocket. "It's a map of the camp," he said. "I tried to remember all the places that have water. During free time, we should do activities that are near those places."

Whoa – impressed. "Brad," said Miriam. "You're a genius."

Brad blushed. "I just like being organized," he said modestly. *I still say genius.* Then he looked at his map. "Hokay! There's a sink in the Arts & Crafts cabin. Let's go there first!" As they headed off, Miriam looked back. Steve was following them. *Oh pooh sticks... Doesn't he have some counseling to do?*

Inside the Arts & Crafts cabin, Miriam headed for the sink. She turned on the water and watched it flow out of the faucet while Brad made meteors out of construction paper. His plan was to glue them to himself so he could run around as a meteor shower. Miriam laughed. *He's funny…* Then Steve shouted through a window, "TURN OFF THAT WATER NOW!"

"Sorry," Miriam said, quickly checking for any sign of Krakey before shutting off the faucet. She sighed and shook her head. "Come on, Mr. Meteor," she said to Brad. "Shouldn't you be outside?"

"Good idea!" said Brad. "Let's go to the outdoor showers!"

Once again, Steve followed. "We're never going to get rid of him!" Miriam groaned.

"Don't worry, we'll think of something," said Brad.

When they reached the showers, Miriam turned one on. "Are you planning on taking a shower now?" said Steve.

Of course not, you dingbat. "Maybe in a minute," said Miriam.

"Then you're just wasting water," said Steve, stepping forward to turn it off.

"I was just going to say the same thing myself!" said Brad. Miriam looked at him. *Whose side are you on?* But then he whispered, "Good cop, bad cop." *Right. I get it now.* He turned to Steve. "What's after free time?"

"For you two?" Steve looked at a list he had on his phone. "Ah ha. It's a hike. You're going on the Fern Hike, AWAY from Mayfly Millpond."

"Perfect!" said Brad. "Ferns are some of the oldest plants on earth. And they reproduce via spores. They don't have either seeds or flowers." Steve just glared at him. "Are we meeting the other Fern Hikers at the water station to fill up our bottles before setting off?" asked Brad. *Genius!*

"Yes…" said Steve, not sure where this was going.

"Oh, do we have to?" said Miriam. *Bad cop!* "I'd rather go set up my rock collection in the science tent."

"No way I'm letting you out of my sight," said Steve. "To the water station – now!" Miriam stomped off as if she was annoyed, giving Brad a big grin and the thumbs up when Steve wasn't looking. *Result!*

When they got to the water station, Miriam rushed to the front and volunteered to fill everyone's bottles, checking each one for Krakey before handing it back. Meanwhile, Brad helped by holding Miriam's backpack right next to the water station, hoping that the Asteruba would pull Krakey through the pipes. After all, if it had attracted Krakey to Grammy's house sixty years ago, even after Krakey had been in the ocean for a few thousand years, then it could pull Krakey from wherever it was in the camp. *I like his thinking.*

"What is it with you and water today?" Steve asked Miriam suspiciously.

If only you knew… "What do you mean?" asked Miriam. "This isn't wasting water, is it?" She held up the last bottle and stared into it. *No Krakey.*

"No…" said Steve. "But…" Before he could say any more, an eager hiker pointed out that it was time to go, and Steve scuttled off to be sure the Fern Hikers were heading towards the ferns and not towards the mosses.

Strike twO

ONCE Brad and Miriam were on their own, Brad suggested that they might be trying too hard, running around from place to place. "If Waterubas are attracted to the Asteruba, why not just leave your bag here? Give Krakey time for a vibe check. Then we could come back after the hike to see if it worked."

"Sounds like a plan." Miriam put her bag next to the filling station, covering it up with some branches.

As they set off to find the other Fern Hikers, Miriam and Brad passed a group of campers singing, conducted by Anu. "It's the camp choir," explained Brad.

"A science camp with a choir?!" asked Miriam. *Weird.* "I thought Anu was kidding."

"Oh no," said Brad. "She takes the choir very seriously. And I should know because…"

Jin, one of the singers, spotted Brad. "Brad! I said you'd be coming."

"Actually, I'm on my way to…"

"We were just getting to the part where you come in," interrupted Anu, pulling Brad into the group. "You know you love this song." She faced the choir and held up her hands. "Everyone! From the top. 1, 2, 3 and…" She brought her hands down and the choir started to sing.

"I am the ocean!
 I am the blue sky!
 I am the river!
 I am the rain!"
They're really good! Then Brad had a solo.

"I am the ocean,
So why do I
Fall asleep and dream that I'm a wave?"
Miriam's jaw dropped. *What a beautiful voice!*

As the last note died out, the singers broke into smiles. "Awesome!" "That sounded fantastic!"

As they crowded around Brad, Steve marched in. "You two!" he barked, pointing at Miriam and Brad. "Fern Hike. Now!"

"Fern Hike?" said Anu. "Are you serious? I thought we were having a water fight."

"Water fight! Water fight! Water fight!" Miriam and Brad joined the other campers in their chant.

The Fern Hikers surrounded Steve. "Can we do that instead please?" said the eager hiker from before. "We can hike later!" "When it's not so hot!" reasoned another.

Steve grimaced. *He knows he's lost.* "Fine. But under no circumstance are campers to get counselors wet."

Everyone ran around, filling buckets, water blasters, balloons and soaking sponges. Brad grabbed a couple of big sponges and handed one to Miriam. "Driest team wins!" announced Anu.

As Miriam looked for a place to soak her sponge, she heard a faint noise, and gasped. The Wateruba Tuba! *Could it be...?* She turned towards the sound and... there it was! Krakey! Floating on top of the water in a bucket! *Yes!!* "Hey, Puddler!" But as she rushed to get to it... it was sucked into a water blaster by Jin. *OH NO!!*

"Hey, Jin!" Miriam called, desperate. "Want to trade this first-class sponge for that blaster?"

"No thank you!" said Jin and ran off.

Miriam searched frantically for Brad and found him filling up a water balloon. "Brad! Brad! Brad! Brad! Jin's got Krakey in her blaster!"

Brad tied up the water balloon. "Leave it to me!" He headed towards Jin, holding the balloon over his head. "Hey Jin!"

"Brad! What are you doing? We're on the same team!" cried Jin, surprised.

"Not any more we're not!" laughed Brad and threw the water balloon at her. <BLOBBLE> It didn't break.

"Ha – Karma!" Jin screeched and gleefully drenched Brad with a mighty blast of water.

Miriam watched as Brad waddled back to her. "Well, that didn't work."

"What are you talking about?" said Brad. "We didn't need the blaster – we just needed the water in the blaster, right?"

"Hey there!" Krakey waved from Brad's shirt.

"Krakey!" *GENIUS!!!*

"I did good, right?" said Brad.

"Brad, you did better than good!" said Miriam, gently grabbing Brad's shirt. "Hold still while I wring Krakey into this bucket." Miriam carefully squeezed his shirt until she saw Krakey at the bottom of the bucket.

"I landed!"

Brad peered into the bucket. "So that's what Krakey looks like!"

Krakey waved. "Hi, Brad!"

"Hi, Krakey," said Brad, then turned to Miriam. "Miriam! I just saw a Wateruba! *I know!* An ancient alien from who-knows-where. *I know how it feels…* It knows my name! *It's heard it enough…* This is so cool!"

I hate to interrupt this moment of awe, but… "I need to get Krakey home. Now," said Miriam.

"Agreed," said Brad. He looked around and saw Steve and Anu starting to gather up the campers to see which team was driest. "But how?? Steve and Anu are coming!"

How how how? Miriam thought for a second. *This is so crazy, it just might work...* "If I puddle into the bucket, they won't see me."

"True…" said Brad.

He thinks that's a weird idea. I don't blame him. "Not only will I be able to hide from them, I'll be able to tell Krakey what's going on. *I'm not sure where this plan is going, but I'll keep talking.* Then, while I'm doing that, could you call Grammy to tell her I'm coming home and why?"

"Aye aye!" Brad saluted. "This is getting exciting! *I love that he gets it even when I'm not sure that I do!* Then, when everyone goes to lunch, you can unpuddle and go home with Krakey."

"Yes!" agreed Miriam. "It's a long walk, but it's possible."

"Or maybe your grandma can pick you up if she's not in a meeting," suggested Brad. "Either way, I'll cover for you. Believe me, I know lots of iron clad excuses for why you might need to leave early. Sudden onset diarrhea, nausea, vertigo…"

"Just pick one and stick with it," said Miriam, pulling the bucket behind a tree. She stepped into it, and as her feet touched the water, she relaxed… *Let go… flow… dissolve… liquefy… Mom…* When she thought of her mom, she felt her heart grow bigger and bigger… *Mom…* A big heart didn't feel like it had any edges… She puddled. *It gets easier…*

She looked around for Krakey but didn't see it at first. Then she heard, "Puddler!" She saw its two big ears appear out of the ripples.

"Krakey, I think a Wateruba was there when my mom had her accident."

"Do you know which one it was?" asked Krakey.

"No…" *How would I know that?*

Just then, she and Krakey were surrounded by a waterfall. "Oh yeah!" said Krakey joyfully.

"Help!!" *This is like being caught in a wave on the beach! Only I can breathe… I love that I can breathe, even when I'm water!* She heard Anu's voice.

"Full bucket! Steve, you won't be dry for long!"

Miriam felt herself being pulled up up up. "Wooo-hoooo!" shouted Krakey. "We're going to have a blast!" Then the pulling stopped.

Miriam looked around. "Where are we?" she gasped.

"We're in a water blaster! I love a water blaster!" cried Krakey, twirling its tentacle.

"What? NO!" Miriam saw the camp and Anu's face. It was like being inside a transparent spaceship. Then she saw Brad trying to grab the water blaster from Anu. *Brave!*

"Prepare to fly!" said Krakey. "I love this part!"

Krakey loves everything. Me, not so muuuuuuuch!! Miriam was pushed hard by a wall of water *Help!* then found herself soaring through the air. *This is not relaxing!!* "I'll see you when I see you!" called Krakey, just as Miriam unpuddled... at exactly the moment she hit a soaked Steve from behind, knocking him over with her now completely solid body. *No no no no no no no!* As she quickly crawled off him, she spied Krakey's flippery feet as it splashed into the underbrush before disappearing into the ground. She tried to chase after it, but Steve blocked her, wiping water from his eyes.

"Strike two."

Where was Samir?

BACK in Egypt: Where was Samir? The mysterious person in white was wondering exactly the same thing. As the fighting continued around him, he worked his way out of the pushing, shouting crowd towards the place where the young boy had disappeared. A set of footprints led him behind a building and stopped next to a large water barrel. Pulling a set of handcuffs from his jacket pocket, he loomed over the barrel… "Got you!" But it was empty - nothing but a small puddle of water. The man frowned and looked closer. Samir's face appeared. "I knew it! Don't worry. This won't hurt," the man said, replacing the handcuffs with a special, extra-absorbent sponge that he dropped into the water to soak up his prey. Or so he thought…

… "What do you want?" said a voice. It was Samir, standing right behind the mystery person. He'd been crouching in the eaves above the water barrel; the face in the water had been a reflection.

Before the man could retrieve the sponge, a mob of angry construction workers raced round the corner looking for Samir. "There he is!"

The mystery man regained his composure. "I want to keep you from getting hurt," he cooed, taking hold of Samir's arm. Samir doubted that very much, and squirmed to escape. The man tightened his grip and confidently turned to face the mob, which stopped advancing. "My team is on its way. They'll have everything sorted out in a minute." He pulled Samir back towards the cars. The workers were clearly confused. They didn't know this man, but he sounded like he knew what he was talking about, looked important, and he'd caught the culprit. "I said, my team is on its way. I suggest you get back to work." As everyone calmed down, the man bundled Samir into his car.

Kitchen – now!

BACK at Science Camp, it was lunch time. Everyone sat at one long table, and the cafeteria vibrated with talking, laughter, clinking cutlery, chairs scraping the floor. Miriam, sitting next to Brad at the end of the table, gulped down her lunch. "Slow down!" said Brad. "My stomach hurts just watching you. You'll get indigestion!"

"I don't care. We've got to get back out there to look for Krakey." *I can't believe I'm so hungry in the middle of a disaster!*

"Relax," said Brad, pushing his hash browns around his plate. "We found Krakey once, we'll find him, her, them, it – what is Krakey anyway?"

"Good question. *When you talk about water, you talk about 'it,' right? I'd say an it. The Waterubas are all its.*"

"Then 'it' it is!," agreed Brad. "By the way, would you mind eating my hash browns? I'm mildly allergic to potatoes." *Lucky for me cuz I love them!* Miriam forked the hash browns off Brad's plate, finished her food, bussed her tray, picked up her backpack, and was about to run outside when Steve stopped her.

"Where do you think you're going?"

"Um… to the bathroom?"

"Nope, not even close," said Steve. "You're going to the kitchen. Why? Because your punishment for knocking me over <u>and</u> getting me wet is to do the lunch dishes for the entire camp. Strike two, remember?" *Of course I remember, you… you… poo-head!*

"That sounds great!" said Brad, stepping between Steve and Miriam. "I love doing dishes! I'll help! *Is that really a good idea…?* With me by your side," continued Brad, "we'll be done in no time!"

"No no no no no no no," said Steve. "This isn't your punishment, Brad my boy… *He's not your boy…* It was Miriam who got me wet, so Miriam has to do it on her own!"

Brad then grabbed a glass of water off the table and dumped it on Steve's head. *Whoa, Brad! Surprising!* "How about now?" Brad was triumphant until he saw the look on Steve's dripping face. "Also sorry! So, so sorry!"

Steve angrily pointed towards the kitchen. "Both of you – kitchen – NOW!"

Arid

AS Miriam and Brad slumped towards the Science Camp kitchen, Samir was speeding away from his village into the sunset in a car driven by a mystery person who appeared to be kidnapping him. A convoy of vehicles, with tinted windows and official-looking insignia, passed them in the opposite direction. Samir craned his neck to watch. "They'll sort everything out," the man told Samir. "Trust me."

Trust him? No way. Samir was very sensitive to lying, and the man was clearly lying. "Sort what out?" Samir asked. "And who are you anyway?" The man presented Samir with a card. Samir read: ARID.

"Advanced Research in Innovative Demohydration," explained the man.

"Demohydration?" asked Samir. "What is that?"

"It is very innovative and advanced," said the man. "We're years ahead of anyone else on the planet."

"At doing what?" Samir asked.

The man smiled, though to Samir it was more of a wince. Even the man's face lied. "Doing what's good for everyone. And you have the chance to help us!" The man accelerated.

Samir didn't know who this was or what he was talking about, but he did know with every water molecule in his body that he was dangerous.

Research

MIRIAM surveyed the camp kitchen. *Ugh.* Every surface was covered with towering stacks of dirty dishes and food-caked pans. *Disgusting.* She moved her bag as far away from the mess as she could. "OK, so how are we going to do this?"

"I have absolutely no idea," said Brad.

"What happened to 'with me by your side, we'll be done in no time'?" *Don't bail on me now!*

"Listen, I'd never really washed any dishes before we did them last night at your grandmother's," Brad explained. *What?! You're twelve! How's that even possible?* "Nan won't let me do the dishes at her house. She says you can't spell 'cutlery' without 'cut'."

I guess it's up to me. But he did pour water on Steve. That was brave – and hilarious. "Look Brad, at least you're here, so don't worry. I'll get this done fast on my own, and then we'll look for Krakey." She picked up a scouring pad and started in on one of the pans.

Brad watched her scrub for a moment, then said, "You could do that. OR you could take a little bit of time to test your powers." Miriam looked at him, surprised. *Did not expect that.* "Come on, Miriam! Please? Look, it's the perfect place to experiment! Lots of water, tons of containers and <u>no counselors</u>."

Hmmm, not sure... "Maybe, but shouldn't we concentrate on finding Krakey?"

"Yes, but once we've found it, why waste time figuring out what you can and can't do as a Puddler? Wouldn't it be better to know, so you can hit the ground running – or flowing?" *He's got a point.* "Maybe one

58

of your powers will be to turn into a super-water-scrubbing- tornado that'll help us clean all these dishes!"

Unlikely, but hey… "OK – why not?" said Miriam. *Besides, I really, really, really want to know what I can do and I don't want to do it on my own.* "What should we try first?"

"Let's make this like a real scientific experiment and keep notes," suggested Brad. He looked around. *I bet he's going to ask me if I have a notebook.* "Uh, do you have a notebook?" Miriam retrieved her backpack and pulled out a notebook and pen. "Thanks!" Brad started to write. "I'm guessing that since you can turn into water, then you can fly."

Miriam was confused. "I know flying is a superpower, but what's it got to do with turning into water?"

"Are you kidding? Clouds fly! Well, actually, they float. But you get what I mean. *I do.* And they're made of water. *True.* I know! Steam flies out of a pan of boiling water, right?"

"Yessss," said Miriam. *Not sure I like where this is going.* "Are you going to boil me?" *Ha ha! As if!*

"How else are you going to evaporate and fly?" asked Brad. *He's not kidding!* He looked around the kitchen. "An electric kettle! Perfect!" He picked up a jug, still half-filled with drinking water. "Puddle into here, please."

I guess this isn't any weirder than everything else that's happened! Miriam jumped up onto a counter top. "OK, since you said 'please,' I will puddle into that jug." She relaxed, and started to breathe. In… out… *Be like water.* In… out… *Flow… Mom… I want to know what I can do… Relax… dissolve… I trust Brad… Mom would really like him… Mom… Heart getting bigger… I can't feel my skin anymore…* Miriam's feet dissolved first as she puddled and dripped off the counter.

"Gotcha!" said Brad, peering in at her through the glass of the jug. "How cool is this??"

Miriam tried to swirl like Krakey. "How do I look?"

"Like you, only watery. I'm going to pour you into the kettle now.

Ready?" *When do you ever hear the words 'I'm going to pour you into the kettle now'?!* Miriam gave Brad a watery thumbs up, then felt herself falling, falling. She landed in more water, surrounded by steel walls. *I am water inside a kettle! This is bizarre!! But also awesome...* "I'm turning it on now!" Brad shouted into the kettle. "You're water, so it shouldn't hurt!" *Shouldn't... not 'won't'!* Then he closed the kettle's lid.

It's really dark...! What's going to happen? Will it get really hot? Will it hurt? Do I even have nerves to feel the heat? No, no, don't get scared... I need to know! Miriam started to vibrate. It was like a little tingle at first, and then she vibrated faster and faster. *Hey! It doesn't feel hot – just jiggly!* Below her, bubbles were forming and, because they were trapped in by the colder water on top, they burst, filling the kettle with a kind of roar. *What a sound!* Miriam continued to vibrate, her watery body spreading out. *It doesn't hurt at all – not one little bit!* Her thoughts were all coming at once, fast and furious, like the bubbles in the kettle. *I'm evaporating! Evaporating! Turning into vapor! But I'm still me!*

Light poured in as Brad opened the top of the kettle and Miriam rose into the air. *Up up up! I feel so light!!* "You're flying!" he hooted, almost as excited as she was. *It's sort of more like floating. And... whoa... I can't control where I'm going. If I try to lead with my head, the rest of me doesn't follow. That's because the rest of me is all spread out! I hardly have a body anymore! Where am I going? Uh-oh! Wait!* She saw that she was heading towards an open window. But Brad was looking the other way. "Miriam? Miriam?? Where are you?"

Miriam tried to cry out "I'm here!" but unlike when she was a liquid, she couldn't seem to make any noise as a gas. She was getting closer and closer to the window. *No, no, no! If I float out the window, I might run into Steve!* The thought of running into Steve scared her so much that everything contracted. She unpuddled and landed in a heap, a solid girl once more, at Brad's feet.

"There you are!" he said. "I thought I lost you." He helped her up. "Are you okay? What was it like?"

"Amazing," said Miriam. "Weird, but amazing. And it didn't hurt at all."

"Weird but amazing," repeated Brad, writing it into the notebook.

"But I couldn't control where I was going, so that was scary."

"I bet," said Brad. He looked at her.

I bet he thinks I'm going to shut it down, but be prepared to be surprised, Brad my friend. "What's next? Turning me into ice?" *Mom would be proud.*

"Yes!" said Brad, fist pumping. *I knew he'd be surprised...* He spotted a pile of ice cube trays on one of the counters. "Ice it is. You've been water as a liquid and a gas – so time to be water as a solid. We can't leave out an important state of matter, right?" He reached for one of the trays and knocked over the whole pile. "Ooops."

"Right!" Miriam hopped onto the counter and puddled again into the water jug. *I'm getting better at this! The secret is to think of Mom... and let my heart fill up with her until I'm not scared.* This time, Brad carefully poured the water containing Miriam into an ice cube tray. Looking up from her section of the tray, Miriam watched the ceiling as Brad paced up and down the kitchen. *I bet he doesn't know where the freezer is.* Just then, Brad's face blocked her view. "Where's the freezer?" Miriam told him to look for a big steel box that opened from the top; he found it; in she went.

If boiling didn't make me hot, then freezing shouldn't make me cold... Everything slowed down. Even her thoughts felt heavier, calmer. *Look at me turning into ice! And I was right. I don't feel cold!*

Time almost stopped. It was incredibly relaxing... *I've heard that people who freeze to death just fall asleep, but I don't feel sleepy. I'm technically not a person, am I?* The voice in her head was getting lower and lower. *I'm... water... turning... to... ice. This... is w...i...l...d!*

Light poured in as Brad opened the freezer. He pulled out the ice tray and saw Miriam as an ice cube. "Coooool!" he said. "Or should I say 'cold'! *H...a... H...a...* Another experiment, while we're at it. If unpuddling means you get solid, what happens when you're already solid as ice?"

Good... question... Miriam tried to unpuddle. She imagined tensing her muscles. Nothing happened. She was already solid. She tried to call out, but couldn't. Even though she was scared, she still couldn't unpuddle. *I'm... not... a puddle ... I'm ice! I can't un-ice!*

"Let's talk about it after you melt," said Brad, bending the ice tray so the ice cubes fell out. He picked Miriam up and put her into a mug. "Hot water incoming!" he shouted. A torrent enveloped frozen Miriam. She started to vibrate. The crystals cracked as the vibration continued, and bit by bit she melted. *Phew!* She thought about being trapped in an ice cube and got so scared that she unpuddled as Brad poured her out of the mug onto the floor. "You're back," he said, sounding more than a little relieved.

"I couldn't unpuddle because I was already solid!" wailed Miriam. *I did not like that at all!!* Brad wrote down what she was saying in the book. "And when it all hit me that I could stay frozen forever, I tried to scream HELP!, but nothing came out. It was really scary." *Make that really **really** scary.*

"But here you are – unpuddled!" said Brad cheerfully. "Make a note to yourself: Avoid freezing when water."

"Noted," agreed Miriam. "Now, should we get back to the dishes?"

"Sure, but what do you think about taking the space rock out of the bag? So there's nothing between its magnetic vibes and Krakey? Not that that should make any difference, but you never know."

"Sure. Why not." *I'll try anything.*

Brad carefully took the Asteruba out of the bag. He looked around. "Where should I put it?" He took a step towards one of the sinks and promptly slipped on some of the ice from Miriam's tray.

"Brad!" cried Miriam. "Watch out!"

Brad skidded. The Asteruba flew into the air and landed in the sink full of dishwater with a

PLORP!

"Sorry sorry sorry sorry!" said Brad. "It was an accident!" Miriam opened her mouth to say something, but before any words came out, she was interrupted by a deep, powerful sound, like the one she'd heard before Krakey appeared in her sink. Only louder.

The Wateruba Tuba! "I've heard that sound before! It's the one the Waterubas make." She looked around. "Where are they? Do you see Krakey??"

Brad didn't see Krakey, but he saw something else. He didn't say anything, just pointed at the sink. Miriam looked. *What?? What is happening??* The Asteruba emerged out of the water, the deep sound growing louder and louder. *What is going on?* The Asteruba floated on the surface of the dishwater for a moment, then liquid cascaded from it as a geyser-like pedestal raised it into the air. *What the…???* Miriam and Brad gaped as the rock slowly spun. *How is this even possible?* Cool air, smelling like the sea, caressed their faces. Then the rock turned into… a globe! *WHAT??!* Water gently undulated on its surface. "Was that a good accident or a bad accident…?" whispered Brad, amazed.

"I'm not sure," said Miriam, cautiously edging forward for a closer look. *What is this??* As she reached out to touch the mysterious Globe, it abruptly stopped spinning and she pulled back. "Look!" she said to Brad who was now standing behind her. Pinpricks of light popped up all over the globe, each a different color. When Miriam and Brad leaned in for a closer look, they could see that some of them were moving.

"It looks like air traffic control or something," said Brad.

"Wait. *I'm thinking something so strange, I can barely say it.* Think about it, Brad." Miriam was whispering now. "Krakey glows. His color is bumblebee yellow, and he said that each Wateruba glows a different color. Could these little lights moving around be Waterubas?" *That's such a weird idea, but this is all weird…*

"Why not? *I love how Brad goes with it!* Maybe it's a tracking map." *Yes!* "Miriam, this is so exciting – and weird, in a good way." *Agree!* He looked closely at The Globe, then pointed. "I figure we're about here."

Miriam got as close as she could without actually getting her nose wet. She breathed in. *It smells ancient.* "There are a few little lights here. I wonder if one of them is Krakey." As she said the name "Krakey," one of the lights flared. *Whoa!* "Did you see that?!"

Brad nodded. "Krakey!" he said. Nothing happened. "You say it, Puddler."

"Krakey!" said Miriam. Again, a light flared. *And it's yellow. I can't believe this!*

"There!" said Brad.

"Krakey?" The light flared. Miriam reached out to touch it. *Wait! What's happening?? Something's pulling me! It has my finger! It's really strong! Help!* She jerked back.

"What happened?" asked Brad. "Are you all right? You look scared."

"The Globe tried to suck me in," said Miriam, rubbing her finger. "It was creepy and horrible." She shuddered. "Maybe this was a bad accident."

"Whatever it was, we're done with our research for now." Brad yanked the Globe off its pedestal. *Brave.* Water poured off of it and the mysterious Globe turned back into a rock. The pedestal disappeared into the sink with a splash, and the kitchen went back to smelling like onions with a hint of ripe banana. *What is that thing?* "You know my motto. *Do I?* Better safe than sorry. *Of course…* So don't you worry – that's enough for today. I'll take care of the Asteruba." He walked towards her bag, carefully avoiding the ice, then slipped on some water.

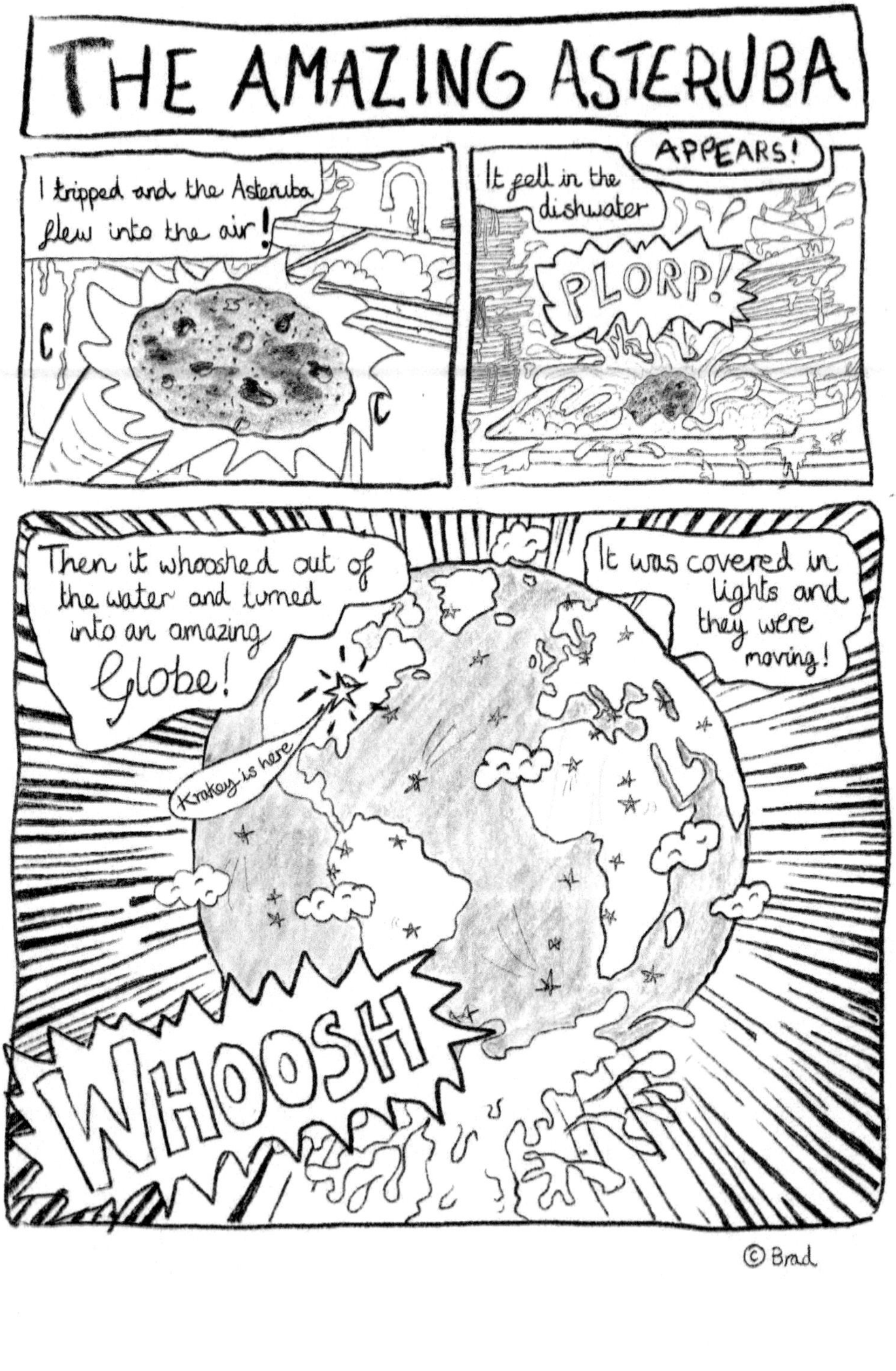

THE AMAZING ASTERUBA

"WHOAAA!!" As Brad fell, he dropped the Asteruba and it sailed through the air again. Miriam dove for it, but it slipped through her hands and went crashing into all the dirty dishes... just as Steve walked in.

"WHAT IS GOING ON IN HERE??" he roared. He strode over to the heap of now broken dishes and picked up the asteroid. Miriam hurried to Brad who was still on the floor. *This is a disaster.* Steve whirled round to face them. "Were you playing catch... with a ROCK?!"

Brad tried to get up but slipped and fell down again. "Ouch. It's not just any old rock," he said. "It's an asteroid that Miriam brought in for show-and-tell."

Miriam nodded. "It's super science-y and valuable." *Super science-y??*

Steve frowned. "Well, now it's confiscated." He tucked the Asteruba under his arm and headed for the door.

"What are you going to do with it?" Miriam called after him, alarmed. *We need the Asteruba!*

"I'm going to put it somewhere where you can't get your hands on it and do any more damage," snarled Steve. "I've had enough!" and he left, slamming the door behind him.

"He's angry," said Brad, getting to his feet.

"Y'think?" said Miriam, pacing. "Brad, this is a disaster. Where's he taking the Asteruba?"

"To his office in the counselor's cabin." Brad pointed out the window to a nearby building. They saw Steve coming out, without the asteroid, and locking the door.

"We've got to get in there and get it back!" said Miriam. *Now now now now now!*

"Agreed," said Brad, "But we've also got to do all these dishes."

Asteroid heist

MIRIAM looked around at the mess. *He's not wrong. Stinky poo and peepee! So frustrating!* A jaunty tune wafted in from outside. "There's the ice cream truck!" Brad rushed to the window. "I've got an idea! Let's get ice cream first! It'll give us more energy." Miriam just stared at him. *Ice cream? Now??* "I'll take that as a 'no'," he sighed. "But I'm hungry. I didn't have much lunch, remember?"

"Sorry, Brad, but there's no time." Miriam handed him a pair of rubber gloves. "While we stand here talking about ice cream, Krakey is getting further and further away." She squirted some dish washing liquid onto an industrial-sized scouring pad. "Now put on the gloves and use this to scrub that pan." She pointed to a pan thick with dried tomato sauce and cheese. "Please."

"Yes, boss," said Brad. "We'll have ice cream AFTER we've found Krakey!" He started to scrub. *That's better.* "Hey, this cleaning stuff really works!"

"Delivery!" The door opened as Anu backed in holding two ice creams cones.

Brad's face lit up. "Anu!"

Anu smiled. "And this cone is gluten free, specially for you, Brad."

"Thank you!" Without even taking off his rubber gloves, Brad reached for the cone – just as Steve burst into the room.

"Stop!!" he yelled. "Anu, these two are being punished! And being punished means NO ICE CREAM!" He grabbed the cones from Anu's hands and stuffed them both into his mouth as he stared at Brad and Miriam, ice cream dripping down his chin.

"Steve, what are you doing?" Anu looked shocked. His eyes widened. "Owowow!" "Brain freeze?" said Anu. *Serves you right.*

Steve recovered and wiped his face with his sleeve. "I'm being consistent. *You're being gross.* It's discipline 101, Anu – you should know that. Punishment is punishment." And he stomped out of the kitchen, slamming the door.

Anu sighed heavily. "I'm truly sorry about that. I think he's having trouble at home." *I think he's just an idiot.*

"It's not your fault," said Brad.

"Thanks for trying," said Miriam. She picked up Brad's scouring pad. "We'd better get back to it." Anu nodded and left. Miriam handed the pad to Brad while she grabbed the notebook. "Are you OK to keep doing the dishes while I plan our heist?"

"Heist??!" Brad was so excited he could barely speak. "Did you say heist??" He scrubbed pans as if he were trying out for the Pan Scrubbing Olympics.

"Yes. I've been thinking about it ever since Steve took the Asteruba." Miriam made a map of the counselor building and drew in two stick figures representing her and Brad. She showed it to Brad. "I'm calling this plan…"

"Please say 'Asteroid Heist'," whispered Brad. "Please say 'Asteroid Heist'…"

"Asteroid Heist," said Miriam. Brad did a little victory dance, knocking down a pile of dishes. *I suppose if we break them, then we won't have to wash them…* "Want to hear the plan so far?"

"Yes please!" said Brad. He stopped dancing and turned to give her his full attention.

"Keep scrubbing," said Miriam.

"Of course. Duh. What was I thinking?" said Brad, tackling a new pan with renewed vigor.

"OK, first some background information," said Miriam. "I've noticed that Anu keeps her stuff, including her keys to the office, in the cafeteria."

"That's so she can grab a snack every time she needs to get something from her bag," explained Brad.

"Smart," said Miriam. "And useful to us. The heist itself has ten steps."

"10. Good number," said Brad, approvingly. "If you're going to have steps, have ten of them."

"I thought so, too," said Miriam. *Until I met Brad, I never knew how much I liked making plans!* "Now, step 1: You will call a tow truck to tow the ice cream van."

"I will?? I've always wanted to do that!" He frowned. "Why should it be towed?"

"Uh, I don't know," said Miriam. "You can say it's parked illegally."

"Is it?" *Does it matter?* Brad felt Miriam staring at him. Then he had an idea and grinned. "Of course it's parked illegally! This is a camp site, not a parking lot! Continue!"

"Step 2: While the counselors are distracted, arguing that the ice cream van shouldn't be towed, I will grab the keys from Anu's bag."

"Genius."

"Step 3 – I will puddle into a bucket of water. Step 4 – when no one's looking, you'll grab a water blaster and suck me up."

"And is step 5 me squirting you under the door into the counselor's cabin?"

"Exactly!" *I love how he gets it!*

"Yes!!" Brad fist pumped, spraying dish washing suds all over the place. "Wait – why not use the keys to unlock that door?"

"Because it's quicker to squirt me under the door than it is for me to fiddle with the keys where everyone could see me." *Duh!*

"Good point," agreed Brad. "But how do you know the keys will puddle with you?"

"Fair question," said Miriam, grabbing a spoon. "Another experiment!" She breathed in... and out... relaxed... *Let go... flow... sink... Mom... Mom...* She dropped as her feet turned to water, then her legs, followed quickly by the rest of her body. *Such a strange feeling!* She puddled onto the floor. *And that time it was almost easy.*

"I will never get tired of watching you do that," said Brad admiringly. He leaned over to look at her. "Still got the spoon?" *Yep!* She rippled the watery spoon with her watery hand.

Now to unpuddle to finish the experiment. Ummm... Think of things that aren't anything like water. Solid things! Glass... rocks... bricks... reinforced steel... nothing's happening! Maybe I need to scare myself... Steve! Schwooomp! She was solid again, holding the spoon that was now also solid. "It works! So where was I?"

"Step 5 – we squirted you under the door. So Step 6!"

"Step 6 – I will unpuddle. Step 7 – I'll then unlock the door to Steve's office. Step 8 – I'll take the asteroid. Step 9 – I'll lock everything up. Step 10 – I'll sneak out. Done!"

Brad was pretty impressed with the plan. But most of all, he was thrilled to be asked to call the tow truck – he had always wanted to be part of a heist! They picked up the pace on the dishes.

VVVIP

BACK in Egypt: The car carrying Samir was still racing along the road. "We've had our eye on you, Samir," cooed the mystery man. "We're building a clear picture of your… skill-set, with a little help from that American woman who wrote a piece on you. I say 'a little' help because she actually didn't know that much. More hearsay than fact."

"So you've been spying on me." Samir said exactly what he was thinking. "I just want to help my village."

"Not a top priority, Sammy! Right now, there are some VIPs who think you're a very, very, VERY important person! That's VVVIP! And they have some simple questions that we need you to answer."

Samir stared at the back of this person's head. "Simple questions?" He knew the man was saying one thing while meaning another. "Where are we going?" Samir asked. "You're driving too fast."

"I don't want to be late," said the man. "We're going to a local facility. Hospital-slash-conference-center type place. It'll be fun. We'll ask our questions, run tests, and there'll be snacks."

"Tests?" Samir asked.

"And snacks!" the man said with false enthusiasm.

Samir had had enough. He started to roll down the window. "Don't do that," demanded the man. "It makes my ears pop." Samir didn't care. He just wanted out. Wind buffeted about inside the car. "Close that window NOW!" the man roared, slamming on the brakes. Samir puddled, was whipped into a mist and disappeared. The man stared at the empty seat. "Interesting…"

Steps
1 to 5

BACK at Camp: The Asteroid Heist was on! Step 1 – check! Brad had called the traffic police to report an illegally parked vehicle. They were very helpful and the truck would be there any minute. On cue, it rolled up. And as Miriam had predicted, an astonished Anu and irate Steve ran over to keep the ice cream van from getting towed.

While the counselors were otherwise engaged, Miriam grabbed Anu's keys and stepped into a bucket of water. *Breathe in... breathe out... Uh-oh... it's hard to relax when you're in a hurry...! Concentrate... Deep deep breath in... slowly out... Asteruba... Mom... Mommmm...* She puddled. *Phew. Steps 2 and 3.* It felt a little limiting to be water in a bucket. *I can only see what's directly above me. What's going on what's going on?* Miriam kept her watery hand near the watery keys. Brad looked to the left, then to the right, like people do in heist movies, then sucked his friend up into the water blaster – *Step 4 – Here we go!* – and squirted her under the door. <WHOOSH!> *Step 5!*

Now for step 6 Scary things... Monsters! Snakes! The dark! Steve! Miriam unpuddled, pleased to find herself inside the counselor's cabin and the keys still in her hand. *Phew. On to step 7 – unlock Steve's office door.* She tried one key, then another. *None of the keys fit! Of course! These are Anu's keys, not his! Why didn't we think of that??? Ohhh!!* She rushed to the cabin's front door and opened it. She grabbed the bucket and the water blaster, then frantically waved Brad inside.

"What's wrong?"

"We don't have the right keys, so I need you to squirt me under the door to Steve's office! It's the only way I'll get in there."

For the first time since the heist began, Brad wasn't so sure. "Maybe we should abort the mission and wait 'til after camp's done for the day."

"Abort?! *I can't believe what I'm hearing!* WHY?" cried Miriam.

"I'm scared we'll get caught," said Brad. "Steve's almost done convincing the tow truck driver there's been a mistake *and* to send her kids to this camp! He's good…."

"No," said Miriam. "There's no time!" She stepped into the bucket of water. *Breathe in… breathe out… let go… water flow… gush… tumble… Asteruuuuba… relaaaaxxx… Mommmmm…* She puddled.

Brad realized he had no choice. "Step 4 again!" He sucked her up into the blaster, then looked at his watery friend floating inside. "Ready for Step 5 again?" *Yes yes hurry!!* Miriam nodded so wildly that she made waves. "Good luck!" said Brad as he squirted her under Steve's office door.

Dribble

BEING in Steve's office made Miriam unpuddle immediately. *Steve scares me so much, he makes unpuddling easy.* The room had the same damp wood smell as the rest of the camp, with a trace of Steve's aftershave. She spotted the asteroid next to a big vase of flowers on the incredibly neat desk. *Yes! Now for Step 8 – take the asteroid.* But as she headed towards the desk, she passed a window and saw the tow truck driving off. Steve and Anu were walking towards the building. *No!!* She ran to the door. "Brad! Are you still there?"

"Of course!" said Brad.

"You've got to run! Steve and Anu are coming! If you go now, you can still make it out!"

"I'm not going anywhere," said Brad. "I'll try to buy you some time."

Brad is the best! Miriam watched through the window as he ran up to the counselors and stopped them. She couldn't hear what he was saying, but he was rubbing his stomach. *Must be telling them he feels sick, hoping they'll take him somewhere to lie down. Smart.* But before she could figure out her next move, she saw Steve put his arm around Brad to lead him back toward the counselors' cabin. *NO!*

"What kind of pain is it?" Steve was asking.

Brad did a big burp. "Hey! It's gone now – I think I'll be fine!!" *Brad's talking really loudly. Probably to warn me.*

Miriam stepped into the bucket. *Breathe in... breathe out... Aaaargh! Relax... Mommm... Mommmmmm... no, can't! Too scared!* She looked around. *How do I get out of here? Where does that door go?* She opened it. *Closet!! Now what now what now what??*

"I'D REALLY RATHER GO ON THAT HIKE NOW!!" Brad was practically yelling.

Miriam heard Steve open the door to the counselor's cabin. *They're in the corridor on their way to Steve's office. Hide!* Miriam tried to climb under the desk, almost knocking over the vase of flowers. Then she had another totally crazy idea. *Why not?* She took the flowers out of the vase and dumped all the water onto the Asteruba. *Will that work?* Nothing happened, and then… a low hum. Miriam held her breath as the Asteruba rose up on its watery pedestal *How is it doing that??* and magically turned into the Globe. The room smelled of the sea. *Better than smelling like Steve. Sorry, that's mean.* Miriam jiggled impatiently as she waited for the Globe to settle, *Hurry hurry hurry*! then jabbed her finger on the first light she saw. *It's pulling me! It's like undertow on the beach… Don't fight it… It's the only way out… Relax… Let go… Flow… Mom…* She puddled as she was pulled in.

Whoa whoa whoa! I'm falling into the Globe! Watery Miriam was whizzed out of the building and into the air. *Yi-yi-yikes!!! How did I get out here? What is happening?? Can anyone see me? No! I'm too small — and I'm water!!* She travelled so quickly that everything was a blur. *I'm not scared! Why am I not scared? I'm going somewhere, but where???* She was surrounded by water droplets. *Rain all around me! Am I in a cloud?!?* She was moving very, very quickly. *I'm still being pulled. Where am I going?? It's so loud! Is that wind? It must be wind!* She was dragged up. *Up up up! Body crystallizing! The higher you go, the colder it gets! Turning to ice! But that's okay… I've done that before!*

Then she started to fall. *Melting!* This time, she was surrounded by water droplets that were plummeting down, down. She hugged her watery knees with her watery arms to her watery chest. *I'm a raindrop! Woo-hoo!!* And then – plop. All movement stopped. She was floating. *What just happened?!* She heard a voice.

"Puddler!?"

She turned her head and saw … what could only be a Wateruba!

Its shape appeared and disappeared as the water moved. A long body, nose kind of like a platypus, and limbs that looked like a cross between flippers and liquidy paddles. *Look at that!* "Dribble here!" it said, waving one of the paddles. Before Miriam could say anything, she felt the bones in her feet, then her legs… her hips… her ribs… her head… she was a girl again. "Puddler!"

Miriam looked down. Dribble, with a violet glow at the center of its body, was part of the water near her feet. One of its liquidy paddles appeared and it waved again. "Are you a Wateruba?" she whispered. It nodded. *How can they be the same thing but so different?*

Miriam looked up. *Where am I?* The top of whatever she was standing in came up to her chest. *I'm in some kind of big barrel…* She looked one way and saw a house, but when she looked the other way… only sand. *Is that a desert?? Where am I??* A boy about Miriam's age ran in. *Huh. He looks familiar. Do I know him? But how can I? I've never been here before!* The boy stopped when he saw her. They stared at each other for a second. *Hide!* Miriam ducked down into the barrel.

"Go now!" said Dribble. *Go where? How did I even get here?* Dribble started chanting the Wateruba Tuba. *It's that pull again!* Miriam found the sound instantly relaxing. *So relaxing…* She puddled as Dribble drifted into her. Then… they were on a high speed trip into the sky with Dribble as tour guide!

"Ooooh! Cloud! Rain! Pling, pling, pling. Ooof!" Miriam and Dribble were plunged into darkness.

"What's happening now?" Miriam asked.

"Ground…" Dribble's voice came out of the darkness, right next to her ear. *Thank you, Dribble. Stay with me, stay with me!* They floated through something that would have been hard if you weren't water. But since they were water, they just slipped right through. Dribble's body elongated into a rivulet as it got absorbed. Miriam just went through. *This must be what it feels like to walk through a wall!* "Roots!" exclaimed Dribble. "Tree!"

"The roots of a tree?" *Amazing! I'm so glad to be with someone who knows what's happening! Someone who is water!! Water knowing where water is going! And I'm water too!! How how how how how?*

"Fast!" hooted Dribble gleefully, as they went up up up, still in the dark.

"I think travelling really fast is one of my superpowers!" shouted Miriam.

"Top tree," said Dribble. It was light again.

"Where are we going?"

Before Dribble could answer, they were lifted into the air. "Air…" Then they fell into more water. "River!" said Dribble. Miriam could see its flippers and watery paddles bobbing as they flowed along. Then, "Ocean!!" *Ocean?! We're in the ocean??* They jiggled and evaporated. *I'm vibrating again! And Dribble is coming apart. Can I still see its shape? Not sure.* "Sky!" Dribble appeared again – a bit more transparent, but still there. *Thank goodness.*

"We're in a cloud! I did this before!" said Miriam, as they were surrounded by water droplets.

"Rain! Rain! Rain!" cheered Dribble as they fell again. Then it got dark, as they were pushed along. "Drain!" announced Dribble. "Pipes!" *We're in the plumbing! I'm in the plumbing! This is wild!!*

Eventually they came out of the faucet in the Science Camp kitchen – Miriam first, landing in the sink like Krakey had landed in the sink in her house the day before. Then Dribble plopped on top of her. *What just happened?!?*

When Miriam unpuddled, holding Dribble in her hand, the first thing she saw was Brad standing there with the Asteruba. *Phew!* "There you are!" he said. "Where've you been? And what are you doing in that sink?"

"Long story," said Miriam. She fought to keep Dribble from slipping through her fingers, then spotted a bowl and let Dribble drip into it. "Look what I found."

Brad looked. "A Wateruba…? But how?"

"That's Dribble," said Miriam, climbing out of the sink. Dribble waved.

"Cool! Hey, Dribble! You look like a platypus with paddles! A paddlepus!" *He's not wrong.* Brad waved. Dribble waved again. Then Brad waved again. Dribble waved again. *Enough already!* Miriam tipped the bowl and poured Dribble into her water bottle. She turned to Brad whose face was going from confused to delighted to surprised back to confused. *Don't want to explain yet. Act normal!*

"I'll tell you all about that later. First, how did you get the Asteruba back?"

Brad told her it had all been fairly straightforward really. He and Steve had gone into the office. It was a big mess – water everywhere – and Steve was furious. Not so much because of the water, but the flowers that had been thrown everywhere were flowers he'd bought for his girlfriend who was about to move out.

"Ooops," said Miriam. *Though I don't blame her.*

"Yes, oops," said Brad. "Maybe that's what Anu meant when she said Steve was having trouble at home. So I told him I'd go get something from the kitchen to help clean up and he pointed to the asteroid and said, 'And take that rock with you!' I tell you, he was practically in tears."

"It's a good thing you had the Asteruba, though," said Miriam, "because if it had still been in Steve's office, I think I would've ended up there instead of here."

"Really? Why?"

"More research required," answered Miriam. "Shouldn't you be helping Steve?"

Brad grabbed cloths and sponges. "Okay. But where <u>were</u> you??"

"I'll tell you when you get back."

Another puddler?

WHILE Miriam waited for Brad, she tackled the dishes again. She wasn't quite sure what else to do. She even looked for some glue to see if she could stick some of the broken plates back together. *Can't find glue. Oh well! I'll scrub all the pieces so that maybe somebody who knows where the glue is could put them back together. Why am I even thinking about dishes??* She kept opening her bag to peer in at her water bottle. Sometimes it looked as if there was just water in there, but if she waited, then Dribble appeared and waved. *I can't believe it. Another Wateruba!* She closed the bag and continued scrubbing dishes. Then she heard a deep, echoey sound. She felt herself relaxing. *The Wateruba Tuba! It's coming from my bag!* She put down the scouring pad and broken bowl she was cleaning and opened her bag. "If you don't stop singing, I'll get so relaxed, I'll puddle!" she said to Dribble, laughing. This time, she took out the magazine that Grammy had given her the day before *Has it only been a day since all this started??* to get at the water bottle, clocked the photo on the cover, and gasped. "I *knew* I'd seen that boy somewhere before!"

Dribble stopped singing. "Boy." Miriam held the water bottle next to the picture of Samir, for that's who it was, and Dribble said, matter-of-factly, "Puddler."

"He's a Puddler? I saw another Puddler!" Miriam whispered.

"You saw what?" said Brad coming into the kitchen with an armful of wet cloths and sponges. He dumped them into the sink.

Should I tell him? Why not... Miriam pointed to the photo. "I saw this boy. Today." She flicked through the pages of the magazine and found a photo of Samir standing next to his house. And to the far right of the picture was the water barrel. "When the Globe pulled me in, I went incredibly fast, into the sky and into a cloud, and I went so high I froze for a bit, then I rained, then went back into the sky – and the whole time I was so busy wondering what was happening that I didn't have time to be scared. And then, I ended up here." She jabbed her finger at the picture. *There. I've said it.*

"Wait a minute," said Brad, reading the caption. "'Here' is in Egypt. You mean to say that you went to Egypt?!? And what do you mean the Globe pulled you in???"

"I was desperate to get out of Steve's office, so I dumped the water from the vase onto the Asteruba and…" She imitated the low hum.

"It turned into the Globe," said Brad, eyes wide. "With all those lights! I wondered why it smelled like the sea in there. You tried to touch one before, but it scared you."

Miriam nodded. "But this time getting caught in Steve's office scared me more."

"You brave brainiac! The Globe pulled you out of the office and all the way to Egypt!" whooped Brad, thrilled. "How does that work?? It shouldn't be possible, but you did it!!"

Brave brainiac – I like that! "I'm guessing that the light that I touched was Dribble's, and Dribble was in Egypt."

"Dribble," said Dribble, making little waves with its paddles.

"But touching a light is one thing. Suddenly ending up in Egypt is something else entirely. How did you get back?" Brad looked at Miriam, amazed.

"Dribble started chanting, and it made me relax and I felt the pull again so I puddled right on top of it and it told me where we were as we went along. Cloud… rain… ground… roots…"

"Tree!" said Dribble, floating to the top of the water bottle.

"Of course! You went up in the xylem," said Brad eagerly. "Then did you go into the leaf stomata where you were released into the air? It's called transpiration."

81

How does Brad know so much? "And then we rained into the ocean! The ocean!!"

"Yesssss!" said Dribble, disappearing in bubbles. It could make lots of them with its big snout.

"But we did all of that really, really fast," said Miriam.

"Really fast…" repeated Dribble.

Brad paced with excitement. "So you basically travelled to Egypt and back the way water would travel…"

"…only really, really fast," repeated Miriam.

"Fast," added Dribble. It kicked its flipper feet to whizz around the bottle to demonstrate the concept.

"Whooo-hoooo!" cried Brad. "Super speed! That's another superpower! Way to go, Miriam!"

Caught up in the joy of the moment, Dribble started to intone the Wateruba Tuba. Brad joined in. *What a voice!*

Then – another sound. "Shh shhh shhh! Listen!" Brad and Dribble stopped chanting. They all heard it – a rich, low note – clear as a bell… or a tuba. Miriam ran around, trying to find out where the sound was coming from. She practically dunked her head into the dirty dishwater to see if the sound was coming from there. *No. The pipes?* She turned on the faucet in one of the sinks. Nothing. Then she turned on another one. The sound got louder and out dripped a tentacle, then ears… then a bulbous body. KRAKEY!! *I'm so glad to see it!!!*

Miriam quickly soaked it up with a cloth, and squeezed it into the water bottle. When Krakey and Dribble saw each other, they sang the most joyous rendition of the Wateruba Tuba that had ever been sung by only two Waterubas. They whooshed around the water bottle – swimming through each other, around each other, undulating like over-excited eels.

"That must be the Wateruba version of a hug," said Brad, watching them, transfixed.

"We haven't seen each other since our asteroid crashed on this planet!" said Krakey, spiraling around Dribble.

"What? Four billion years ago??" asked Miriam.

"Dribble!" said Krakey.

"Krakey!" said Dribble.

"Dribble!" said Krakey.

"Krakey!" said Dribble.

"This could go on for a while!" *They're so funny! Just watching them makes me feel happier than I've ever felt.* She looked at Brad. *Hmm.*

"You're thinking. I can tell you're thinking," he said. "What are you thinking?"

"I'm thinking that Mom always knew deep down that Waterubas were real, even though she never saw one. So I want to show her these guys!" She held up the water bottle containing two ancient and exuberant aliens. "I need to find her."

Samir hides

MEANWHILE, back in Egypt, Samir was perplexed. Had he really seen a girl standing in his family's water barrel? Dark, curly hair? About his age? Big eyes? Then she'd disappeared. But how was that possible? He looked into the barrel – no water, no girl. Had he imagined it? No, it had been too real. And another thing that was real was that he was being chased by a mysterious person, someone who set off every alarm bell in Samir's sensitive internal security system. This person knew where he lived, so he was going to have to hide.

Promising himself that he'd think about the girl later, he ran into the room he shared with his sisters, and started to pack.

"Samir? What's going on?" asked his mother. She'd seen the brouhaha with the construction workers and heard people calling Samir's name. "Are you in some sort of trouble?"

"Not yet," said Samir. "Could I go stay with Father, just to be safe?"

"Good idea," said his mother. "I'll call him to let him know you're coming."

After she went to find her phone, Samir looked around to make sure he had everything. "My magic rock!" He grabbed his piece of the Asteruba from the window sill, threw it into his bag and left the house.

No more camp

MIRIAM and Brad were trying to get through the mountain of dishes they still had to clean. "I can't believe you're just washing dishes like nothing happened, when you've been all the way to Egypt and back – as water!" *I know I know but I just need something to be normal!*

Just then, Anu came in to tell them that Miriam's grandmother had arrived to pick them up. "Steve phoned her. I'm sorry, but he just wants you gone," she sighed.

"What about the dishes?" asked Miriam.

"What about them?" said Anu. "We'll just put them in the dishwashers!" She pulled open the doors to not one but three dishwashers.

"Dishwasher**sss**…?" said Miriam. "There's more than one??"

"You betcha!" said Anu. "This amazing appliance is for plates…" She gestured as if she were in a showroom. "This one is for glasses and cutlery…" Then she twirled and bowed to present the last one. "And this monstrous machine is for pots and pans. Yes, folks, we've got it all!"

"Who knew?" said Brad.

"Not you two, that's for sure!" said Anu, expertly loading dishes into the first machine. "And Steve wasn't going to tell you, was he?" Miriam and Brad started to help, but Anu waved them away. "Go on – your grandmother's waiting," she said. "And I have the feeling that once you tell her what's been happening here, you probably won't be back…" She hugged Miriam. "I won't miss you too badly because I hardly know you." Then she hugged Brad – "But you! I'm particularly going to miss your beautiful voice…"

Anu was right, but not for the reasons she thought. "What's been happening here" was far more incredible than what she imagined. Miriam knew Anu was referring to Steve, but she also knew that when she told Grammy about what had happened with the Waterubas and the Globe and speed-travelling to Egypt and back as water, life was going to change. Completely.

Life changes completely

WHEN Grammy found out "what had been happening," she got more excited than Miriam had ever seen her – including the day she got Bunster from the animal shelter. She declared that they would not be going back to camp. No way. "There's too much work to be done at home." Grammy immediately rang Eleanor to say that she needed Brad, please, for some experiments that she would be doing with Miriam for a new book she was writing – confidential for now. Would she mind if Brad worked with her this summer instead of going back to camp?

"Of course not!" said Eleanor. "As long as Brad is happy, so am I. A new book, Freida – how exciting! Let me know if you need photographs."

When Miriam pulled out her water bottle to introduce Krakey and Dribble to Grammy, Bunster took one look at the Waterubas and started to bark. But it was more of a squeal than a bark, as if he were saying, "Hello hello! Good to see you, arf arf arf!" instead of "Grrr! Growl! Go away!" Grammy burst into tears. "Yes, Bunster, they're real!" she said. "All these years I've tried to tell myself I imagined them, but I knew, KNEW way deep down where it counts, that they were real! And so did you!!"

"Hey, Bunster – how's it going?" said Krakey. "This is Dribble." Dribble lifted its flat, watery snout and howled like a dog, *Did not expect that!* and Bunster joined in.

This made Grammy laugh which then made her cry some more. She was sniffing and wiping her tears away when Miriam gasped. *There,* on Grammy's hand! *Billowing tentacles… big eyes… deep blue glow… Could that be another one?* "Grammy, look!!" She held Grammy's hand still, and as they watched, barely breathing, a wafty body underneath a wispy head – another Wateruba! – emerged from the water of her tears.

"Lutine!!" cried Krakey and Dribble when they saw it. They rippled around in the water bottle, colors vibrating.

"Krakey! Dribble!" whooped Lutine, glowing a beautiful blue.

Miriam couldn't believe what she was seeing. *THREE Waterubas! I'm so happy I could burst! Something is happening – really happening! Something magical! But what???*

"Do you guys have a bowl with a lid?" asked Brad, opening cupboards.

"Good thinking, Brad," said Grammy quietly, staring at Lutine. "There's one in that drawer down there." She gestured with her head in order to keep her hand still. Brad opened the drawer, found a bowl with a lid that fit, dumped Krakey, Dribble and the water from the water bottle into it and held it out for Lutine. Grammy tipped her hand.

"Wheeeee!" said Lutine, elongating to slide into the bowl to join the others.

"It's so weird to hear ancient creatures say 'Wheee!'" said Miriam.

"It's a good noise for joy, and joy has no age!" said Grammy. "Wheeeee!! *True…* Something big must be going on," she continued. *Yes, but what??* "Why all these Waterubas now? Is it because you touched the asteroid? Or because once you see one, you can see more? Or because of what's happening on the planet? *You mean how it seems we're trying to kill it?* What is it??"

Bunster did his squealy, excited dog yap again. Grammy picked him up. "Sorry, Bunster, but it's too much." She opened the door and put him into the back yard. "Won't be long!" Then she joined Miriam and Brad who were watching as the Waterubas ecstatically flowed into each other, swishing and undulating, while making gurgles and burbles and lots and lots of bubbles. *They're over 4 billion years old – words weren't even invented then! Neither were humans!*

"I guess they only use words when they want humans to understand," said Brad.

"I was just thinking the same thing," agreed Miriam.

"They're real – they're really real!" sighed Grammy. She couldn't get over it. "Let's put the top on the bowl so they don't evaporate away."

"I'll let them know what we're doing." Miriam picked up the cover for the bowl. "OK, everyone. Listen up!" The Waterubas didn't pay any attention. The gurgling and burbling continued. "Hello! HELLO!" Nothing. Then Brad opened his mouth and sang a beautiful low note. *The Wateruba Tuba!*

Grammy looked at him, amazed. "That boy can sing!"

"I know, right?" said Miriam.

The three Waterubas stopped moving around the bowl and chanted the Wateruba Tuba. As they chanted, they glowed. As they chanted and glowed, Miriam and Grammy stared, transfixed. Outside in the garden, Bunster stopped barking. "It's so relaxing," whispered Grammy.

"You can say that again…" said Miriam.

"It's so relaxing," said Grammy.

Very funny… but she's right… I love this… Then Miriam felt her feet get squishy. She looked down. *They're turning to water!* "No! Stop! I'm puddling!" Her feet became feet again. *Phew.*

"I'll take that, thank you very much," said Grammy, taking the cover and clipping it onto the bowl. "We're putting this here so you won't evaporate away!" she said into the bowl. Then she turned to Miriam. "So what was that about?"

"Well, I've noticed that…"

"Wait wait wait!" Brad interrupted. "Let me get our notebook. It's in your bag, right?"

Miriam nodded and waited while Brad went to find her bag, bashed his knee, hopped around, still looking for the bag, found the bag, got the notebook, and hit his toe on a chair. "Ow ow ow ow, that smarts," he said, opening the notebook to the last set of notes. "OK, shoot!"

"OK, so I've noticed that whenever I hear the Wateruba Tuba, I relax. And relaxing like that can make me puddle."

"What happens when you don't hear the Wateruba Tuba? Can you still puddle?" asked Grammy.

"Yes, but it's harder. I have to make myself relax and then be like water. It helps to think of Mom. Mommmmmmm…"

Grammy nodded. "It's kind of like Ommmm… the primordial sound of the universe." *I'm not exactly sure what that means, but the sound is relaxing.*

"So when you started to puddle because of the Wateruba Tuba, why did you stop?" asked Brad, pen poised to write the answer in the notebook.

"I got scared of puddling," answered Miriam. "It feels really weird. I mean, think about it – I'm turning into water! It's not a natural thing for a person to do."

"But it is natural for a Puddler," said Krakey.

"What's 'scared'?" Lutine asked. The Waterubas were lined up in the bowl, listening.

"Oh, er… It's when you think something bad could happen, and…" started Miriam.

"What do you mean 'bad'?" interrupted Krakey. The Waterubas were all looking at the humans, waiting for an answer. *They're the ancient ones. You'd think they'd know everything!*

"I get the feeling that being scared isn't something a Wateruba understands," said Brad.

"No…" said Grammy. *She's thinking, I can tell.* "They're water, so whatever is happening is just what's happening. Unlike humans, they don't make up stories about it. It just is. So they're never scared. Huh… Wouldn't it be great to be a Wateruba!"

"How is being scared just a story??" asked Miriam. *I'm confused!* "I was puddling – turning into water! – without wanting to and without knowing what was going to happen…"

"But you thought what was going to happen would be bad…"

"Bad?" asked Dribble. "What is bad?"

"It could be all sorts of things!" *Why am I the only one who understands this?*

"Think about it for a second," said Grammy. *I'm trying!* "Saying 'This-might-be-bad' is a story we tell ourselves. We could just as easily think, 'This will be great!', but we go to 'bad' first." *Because there's nothing great about turning into water and not knowing what's going to happen!*

"I get it," said Brad. "My grandfather is always going on about letting everything be as it is, not making anything a problem…"

But he's not about to turn into water! AARGH! I'm done talking about this. "Hey, do you think there are any other Waterubas around?"

"Let's find out!" said Krakey.

Flooso and splurdge

KRAKEY sang a low tone. Dribble joined in with another low tone. Then Lutine chanted a crystal clear tone on top of that. And finally, Brad sang. The sound was eerie and beautiful.

It sounds different each time they do it. Uh-oh! Uh-oh! Beginning to relax! Beginning to puddle! I know! Erik's headphones! Quick! Miriam's little brother, Erik, was highly sensitive to sounds, so had a collection of noise-cancelling headphones which their dad had left all over the house, just in case Erik needed them. Miriam was sure they hadn't taken all of them to France. She rifled through one of the big drawers in the kitchen and found a pair. *Thank you, Erik!* She put them on. *Ahhhh. Silence…* Brad still had his mouth open, singing, but she heard nothing. *These things really work!* Then Grammy waved her arms to get them to stop. Brad's mouth closed; Miriam took off the headphones. "What's going on?"

"Listen!" said Grammy. They heard a distant hum. "Is that my tinnitus or is it a Wateruba Tuba?"

"I hear it, too," said Miriam, walking carefully around the kitchen, leading with her right ear. "Where's it coming from?" She opened the back door, and the sound got a little louder.

Grammy looked into the garden and saw that Bunster was about to drink from a puddle, a puddle that could contain a Wateruba. She grabbed the biscuit jar where she kept Bunster's treats and shook it. "Bunster! Here boy!"

As Bunster ran to Grammy, Miriam picked up a glass and went into the garden to check out the puddle. She saw a shape in the water with a tell-tale glow. *YES!!* "There's a Wateruba out here!" *Have I seen that particular shade of red before?* The Wateruba waved. *Waterubas do love to wave! Maybe it's because waves are made of water! Ha!* She scooped up the Wateruba with the glass and carried it back into the kitchen.

"Splurdge!" cried Krakey, Lutine and Dribble when Miriam poured the Wateruba into the bowl. Then they all chanted and glowed and rippled and flowed and chanted some more. Miriam put the headphones back on and peered at Splurdge. She recognized the horsey snout and watery, wafty mane.

"HEY!" she shouted because she's couldn't hear how loudly she was speaking because of the headphones. "YOU'RE THE WATERUBA I SAW WHEN I FIRST PUDDLED ONTO THE FLOOR, RIGHT HERE!" Splurdge nodded and spread out its limbs and body, almost disappearing into the water again. "HOW DID YOU..." Then Brad pulled the headphones off her head and she heard that she was practically screaming. "Sorry – I mean how did you get into the puddle in the back yard? When I last saw you, you were disappearing under the sink."

"Wellll..." Splurdge spoke really slowly. *They each have a different way of speaking. Interesting...* "First.... I.... went... down... down... down... and... sunk..."

"Into the ground?" asked Miriam. *Splurdge speaks a little too slowly, but I guess that's just Splurdge.*

"Mmmm-hmmmm..." drawled Splurdge, pulling its limbs in next to its body. *Are those arms and legs?* It almost looked solid for a second.

"Then let me guess," said Brad, wanting to help out. "Did you get into a mycorrhizal network that took you along and then up into the puddle?" *What is he talking about?*

"Mmmmm-hmmmm..." drawled Splurdge again, twirling its body into a ripple.

Splurdge seems to know, but I don't! "Mycorrhizal network?"

"Fungi!" said Grammy. "The planet's great connectors."

"What? Like mushrooms?" said Miriam, confused.

"Exactly!" said Brad. He turned to Miriam. "Do you know that practically the whole world is connected up by underground mycorrhizal networks? And water can travel along them from place to place. I bet you'll be taking the old fungi express fairly regularly."

"Right," said Miriam. *I'd rather not think about that now.* "Are there any more Waterubas around here?" She turned to the Waterubas. "You guys are amazing – all so different – !"

"But all the same," said Lutine.

"Let's find out who else is here!" said Krakey. *Good idea! So exciting!* Miriam noticed that it waited until she put the headphones back on before it started to chant. *Thank you, Krakey!* Splurdge, Dribble and Lutine joined in, followed by Brad. Once again, Miriam watched until Grammy waved her arms to stop the singing, then she took off the headphones and listened.

"I think I hear something!" said Brad. He ran out of the kitchen, tripped over a rug, stopped to sing another low note, and listened. "It's coming from upstairs. Is it OK if I go up?"

"Be my guest!" said Grammy.

"I'll go with you!" said Miriam. She joined Brad at the bottom of the stairs. "But I don't hear anything…"

Brad sang a low tone. *When he does it, it's beautiful and relaxing but not enough to make me puddle. Maybe it's because it's not loud enough – or because he's not a Wateruba.* Brad took a breath, and sang another tone. He listened. Then he grabbed her hand and pulled her up the stairs. He slipped. "Ow!" They got to the top. "Hear it now?" whispered Brad. Miriam heard a low hum.

"It's coming from Grammy's office!" Miriam opened the door and they went in.

"Wow…" said Brad. "I've never seen so many books in one room!" They were piled on shelves, on the desk, on the floor, on the windowsills.

"I know," said Miriam. "Grammy loves books. But let's talk about that later. Sing!"

Brad sang, and they heard the hum, a little louder this time, coming from Grammy's coffee cup. It was a travel mug, so it was covered. Miriam lifted the lid, and out of the still surface of the coffee, a Wateruba appeared. It had long ears, kind of like Krakey's, and a body like a little ball, with a tail and two flippers. "Look at that," said Brad, eyes wide.

I bet no one else has ever seen anything like this before, not even in books. It waved. "We found another one!" Miriam called, covering the cup and heading back downstairs. *I always knew this was a magical place! It wasn't just because of Mom or Grammy that I didn't want to leave!* "I bet Waterubas have always been around here but we just haven't seen them," she said to Brad.

"Well, I'm glad we're seeing them now," said Brad. *Me, too.*

Under the floorboards

THE Wateruba in Grammy's coffee was Flooso. Krakey, Lutine, Dribble and Splurdge were overjoyed. Apparently, Krakey and Lutine had seen Flooso not so long ago because they'd all been pulled to this house again and again by the Asteruba (though "not so long" to a Wateruba could be decades). But they hadn't seen Dribble or Splurdge for eons! The five Waterubas plus Brad sang the Wateruba Tuba again. *I am so happy! Mom would love this so much! And that sound is really, really beautiful, relaxing, peaceful, calm…* Miriam was so caught up in her happiness and the sound that she didn't think to grab the headphones. And before anyone noticed… *Ahhhh… so relaxing… love that sound… Wait! I'm puddling!* She didn't really appreciate what had happened until she'd dripped through a crack in the floorboards into the small space between the kitchen floor and the ground.

Yuck!! I'm soaking into the dirt! Scared! Really scared! STOP! Her body tensed and ZOOP she unpuddled. But now she was squished under the floorboards, with her face in the mud! It was horrible. Miriam tried to move, but the space was too small. It smelled of worms and dead bugs. "Help!!" she whimpered, starting to panic. "HELP!!!!"

Up above her, Brad and the Waterubas stopped chanting. "What was that?" she heard Grammy say. Then "Where's Miriam??"

She sounds so far away. Miriam shouted as loudly as she could, which wasn't easy because her mouth was full of dirt. "HELP!! HELP!! I'M UNDER THE FLOOR! *Please hurry. I can't move. I can't breathe.* HELP!!!!"

"It's Miriam!" she heard Brad say. "Oh no! She must've puddled and dripped through this crack!"

"PULL UP THE FLOORBOARDS!" cried Grammy. "There's a crowbar in the shed!" Then Miriam heard footsteps above her. She took little gulps of air. *Am I trying to breathe or am I crying? Both!* "Miriam!" called Grammy. *Her voice is louder. She must be talking into the crack.*

"Grammy!" sobbed Miriam. "I'm scared!"

"We're coming, my sweetheart. We're going to pull up the floorboard, but we have to be careful so we don't bash you in the head with the crowbar."

"Just hurry," said Miriam. "Please."

She heard more footsteps, and the thud of someone falling. "I'm OK!" said Brad. Then there was a splintering sound as the crowbar was edged into the crack in the floorboard.

"Miriam? Is the crowbar touching you?" asked Grammy.

"No," said Miriam. *Please, please hurry.* Then a CRAAACK-CLUNK and a sudden burst of light as the floorboard was jimmied up.

"Miriam!" sobbed Brad. *Is he crying?* She felt herself being lifted out of the mud and gathered into her grandmother's arms. No one said a word, though Brad blew his nose. *Brad must be dying to know what happened, and I bet Grammy's giving him the eye to be quiet.*

When Miriam looked out from the comfort of Grammy's hug, she could see the Waterubas in the bowl, all five of them. For once, their shapes were clearly visible as each glowed a different color. *They're so beautiful… and strange. Maybe they want to know what happened, too.* As if it could read her mind, Krakey said, "Puddler? Maybe I don't read your mind so much as I read your heart. What happened?"

Miriam explained that the sound of the Wateruba Tuba with all of them singing plus Brad was so powerful that it unwound all of her knots and tensions and made her forget about headphones and before she knew it, she was dripping through a crack in the floorboards. "And when I realized what had happened and saw that I was about to seep into that smelly mud, I got scared."

"And terror triggers tension triggers immediate unpuddling," said Grammy.

Grammy does have a way with words. "If I'd been able to relax and stayed puddled, maybe I would've sunk into the ground and flowed onto the fungi express and ended up in a puddle, like Splurdge did."

"It's… ee… zee!" said Splurdge.

"Easy for you because you're a Wateruba. You never unpuddle. But I got scared and my bones came back and I was a girl again, stuck under the floorboards. I can't control it."

"That had to be nasty," said Brad.

"Very," agreed Grammy. "Miriam is human and humans get scared. From where I sit, at the grand old age of 73, I can tell you that facing your fear is no easy task. It's a life-long project. So while you work on that, how do you keep from puddling when the sound is so compelling that it makes you forget headphones and consequences?" *The thing I hate most about it is having no control.*

"Well," said Brad, "I could be a Wateruba Tuba Alert. A WTA. *WTA. That is so Brad!* If the Waterubas start chanting when I'm around, and let's face it, I'm around a lot now," said Brad, "then I'll make sure you're either covering your ears or wearing headphones, even if you think you don't need to. I'll also start carrying ear plugs in every pocket. And so should you."

"It won't be forever. I have the feeling you'll learn to control when you puddle," said Grammy. "I said the same thing to you when you were two, and look at you now – perfectly potty trained!"

Almost funny, but I get the point. "I'm OK being boiled or frozen if I want to be. But I do not want to puddle against my will, and that's that." Brad handed her some ear plugs. "Thank you."

Splurdge's story

NOW that they had five Waterubas, Miriam obviously couldn't stop thinking about them. But the one that kept floating into her imagination was Splurdge, the first Wateruba she saw as a Puddler. She'd seen Krakey in the sink, and that was mind-blowing enough. But then she saw Splurdge after she herself had turned into water! How much magic and mystery can a person take in one day? *The Waterubas all look weird, but I think Splurdge is particularly strange. I love it.* Miriam told Brad that she wanted to know more about it. She knew it would be difficult to get much information – Splurdge talked so slowly – but Brad was determined. *He's got a lot more patience than I do, though that's not saying much…*

Later, after Brad had talked to Splurdge for a while, *a really long while!* he told Miriam what he'd learned. He wasn't entirely sure about every single detail – "So I did a little improvising," confessed Brad. *You're forgiven. It's a great story. And now we know more than we did before.*

Apparently, Splurdge was on the other side of the world in New Zealand, splashing around in a natural spring. This was after it had been under the ground in an aquifer for about two thousand years. *It took over two hours for Brad to get that much out of Splurdge.* It got pumped out of the spring and was eventually put into a bottle. *That actually happens in New Zealand. In fact, according to Grammy, it happens all over the world. Companies take water that comes free out of a spring, put it in bottles, and sell it back to people. How does that make any sense?* The bottle with Splurdge in it ended up in Auckland Airport. (Auckland is a city in New Zealand.) A human bought the bottle, drank the water, including Splurdge, then got on an airplane to come to Chicago to visit his long-lost sister. Splurdge got peed out at the sister's house, and was flushed into the DuPage County municipal water system. *What a story! Splurdge knew about the aquifer and the spring and the bottle and getting drunk by a human and being flushed. Brad filled in the rest. I love the sister part!* When Splurdge was flowing along the pipes near Grammy's house, it got pulled into the smaller pipe that led to the kitchen sink – and the pull was because of the Asteruba. Splurdge came out of the faucet and got splashed onto the floor by Grammy when Miriam rushed in that day just after she'd seen Krakey in the bathroom sink. *Then I touched the Asteruba and the rest is history.*

"Asteruba!" said Dribble. "Boy."

"Wait a minute," said Grammy, leaning over the bowl to put her nose right next to Dribble's long snout. "Are you talking about the boy that Miriam saw? What's he got to do with the Asteruba?"

"Puddler," said Dribble, flipping its flippers.

Grammy grabbed the tablet and pulled up the issue of the magazine with her report on Samir. She scrolled through and found the photo of him standing next to his house near the water barrel. She pinched-and-spread to enlarge the window sill. And there was a piece of the asteroid. "Look!" she gasped. "Dribble's right. A piece of the Asteruba – it's right there." She showed the others.

"Maybe the boy touched it and it zapped him like mine zapped me," said Miriam.

"So where there's a Puddler, there's a piece of the Asteruba…" said Grammy. "Hmmmm… I wonder… *I love when she wonders.* Miriam has lived in this house since she was born. She's a Puddler. Her brother Albert was two when they moved in, and both Jeff and Erik lived here since birth. I wonder how many Puddlers we have in the family."

"I wonder if Mom was a Puddler only she never knew it because she never touched the Asteruba!" said Miriam.

"More Puddlers?" said Krakey. "Puddlers!" said Dribble. "Puddlers!" said Flooso and Lutine. "Puddddd…" started Splurdge.

The Waterubas rollicked around the bowl. And then they did what they usually did when they seemed to be overcome with joy, they sang the Wateruba Tuba. *Here we go again!* Miriam covered her ears.

"WILL MIRIAM'S BROTHERS BE COMING HOME FROM FRANCE ANYTIME SOON?" Brad shouted over the exuberant Waterubas. "I THINK THEY ALL NEED TO TOUCH THE ASTERUBA, DON'T YOU?"

"Puddlers!" said Dribble. They stopped chanting and Miriam took her hands off her ears.

"We need Puddlers," said Krakey.

"And Puddlers need Waterubas," said Lutine. *Why why why?*

"We need to know more about how it works," said Miriam. She turned to the Waterubas. "Do you know how many Puddlers there are? Or who's a Puddler and who's not? Do you know why you need Puddlers?"

"No," said Lutine, swirling around. "All we know is that we need Puddlers and Puddlers need us." And with that, it disappeared into the water.

"A ton of research required!" said Miriam.

"Agreed," said Grammy. "The boys aren't back until the end of the summer, so we've got some time." She picked up the bowl containing the Waterubas. "Now, I think we'd better figure out where we're going to keep these guys." She walked around the kitchen, hoping a place to put the bowl would wondrously appear. *She will end up putting that bowl back where it was.* She put the bowl back where it was. Then she opened the door leading into what she and Grandpa Albert used to call "the conservatory," though for as long as Miriam could remember, the only thing it "conserved" were things that had nowhere else to go. It was basically a store room. "I have a few ideas... But first we need to get someone in to fix that floorboard!"

Samir and his father

BACK in Egypt, Samir was just arriving at his father's apartment in Cairo. He let himself in with the key his mother had given him. His father had a good job there, so he lived in the city during the week, coming home on weekends. Sometimes Samir and his sisters and mother would visit him, in various combinations. But it had been a long time since Samir had come here. He went into the spare bedroom – just big enough for three small beds and a chest of drawers – put his bag on the bed where he usually slept, and started to unpack. He put the few clothes he'd brought with him into one of the drawers and slipped the faintly glowing piece of asteroid under the bed.

Samir found a note. "Home on time this evening – I hope! So glad you're here, habibi. See you later. Father xx" Samir loved his father but didn't expect to get much time with him – which was just as well because he didn't want to tell him anything about the mystery person. Exploring ARID's website using the address on the card the man had given him, he saw that it was a huge company dedicated to solving the world's water problems, from too much of it to too little of it. "Demohydration," according to ARID, meant getting water to people. "Water is what we do." It sounded good, but Samir wasn't sure. What kind of organization kidnapped children to take them in for tests??

Samir had no idea how much the ARID person knew about him. He had no idea if ARID would find him in Cairo. And he certainly had no idea that there was such a thing as a Wateruba. Yet.

The Wateroomba

WHILE Samir settled in to stay with his father, Grammy, Miriam and Brad were clearing out the "conservatory" and drawing up plans to turn it into something Grammy was calling "The Wateroomba." *Grammy loves making up words.* "Water is always moving, so it needs to be a place that will make it easy for the Waterubas to keep moving," said Grammy.

"Is it the Wateroomba because it's a 'room' for them or is it the Wateroomba because they can dance the rumba in there?" asked Brad. *He thinks he's hilarious.*

"Nice one, Brad!" said Grammy. And she did a little rumba box step. *Nice hip moves, Grammy!* "Want to dance?"

That wiped the grin off his face! "It's the Wateroomba – a <u>room</u> where they can easily keep moving but that they can't drift or sink out of," said Miriam. *He knows that…*

"I'll teach you the rumba another day, Brad!" said Grammy, humming to herself and *rumbaing* into the Wateroomba to pull out another box of stuff.

They'd put the five Waterubas they'd found so far into an old aquarium that Grammy had pulled out of the ex-conservatory. She'd even dug up a lid to put on it to keep them from evaporating out. If Waterubas needed Puddlers and Puddlers needed Waterubas, it made sense to try to keep the ones they'd found. *And there's no way we can let them go until we all know more about what's going on!* The aquarium sat on the big kitchen table so the Waterubas could see what the three humans, including one Puddler, were doing. They seemed to be fascinated, lining up to look out at them, making suggestions.

Brad started to draw a sort of Wateruba waterland with a river and puddles and a pond. "Oooh," bubbled the Waterubas, appreciatively. "He may not be able to rumba, but he makes good pictures!" said Krakey.

"What about a lake?" said Lutine, the tendrils coming out of its head wafting in the water like seaweed. It had recently spent time in a lake. Brad drew in a lake.

"And what about a waterfall? No – two waterfalls!" said Flooso. "I love waterfalls… whoosh!" It rolled up into a ball with just its two pointy ears sticking out and spun around the aquarium.

Brad added two waterfalls and a place where the sun could hit some rocks so the Waterubas could evaporate, turn into clouds and rain back into the pond or the river or lake. And there were pipes, tubes, hoses and even a wave-maker. Grammy and Miriam studied what he'd done so far. *Krakey's right – he makes good pictures.* "What about a cold place for any Waterubas who come from glaciers or ice bergs or ice caps?" suggested Miriam. *Mom would be glad I thought of that.*

"Good thinking, Puddler!" said Krakey, thrashing its feet and ears so vigorously that whitecaps appeared in the aquarium.

Brad drew a big freezer not unlike the one they'd had at Science Camp. "Only we'll decorate it to look like a glacier," he said.

"This is fantastic," said Grammy, grabbing her computer. "I'll start ordering all the materials we're going to need. Hmmmm… freezer first, I think. That can be delivered without anyone wondering what we're doing… Obviously, we have to keep this a secret, right?"

Duh!! "Right!" agreed Miriam and Brad in unison.

A visit from Uncle Eddy

JUST then, they heard the front door open. "Hello!"

"It's Uncle Eddy!" said Miriam. Bunster barked and ran to greet him. Uncle Eddy always had a doggy treat for him in his pocket. "We can tell him, can't we? He heard Mom talk about Waterubas. He'll be amazed that they're real!"

"NO!" shouted Grammy, hiding all the drawings. *Grammy never shouts. What's that about??* Grammy leaned over the aquarium. "Sorry about this, my ancient friends. It won't be for long," and she covered it with a towel. "Put that somewhere where he can't hear them if they start to chant. Garden shed! *Why??* Please," added Grammy.

"On it," said Brad.

"I'll head him off at the pass." Grammy ran towards the front door. "Hello, Eddy!" she called in her cheery voice. "Bunster! Leave Eddy alone!" Miriam watched her go. *I'm confused…*

Brad tried to pick up the aquarium, but it was too heavy. *Why can't we tell Uncle Eddy?* "Uh, Miriam?" said Brad. "A little help here?"

"Sorry." Miriam picked up the other end, and they headed out to the garden. "I wonder why we can't tell Uncle Eddy."

"I have no idea," said Brad, kicking open the door to the garden shed. "But your grandmother was adamant."

"I know," said Miriam. "She actually screamed NO. And who says, 'I'll head him off at the pass?'"

"Old people who can rumba," said Brad. "And your grandmother." *Boom. If there's one old person who isn't old, it's Grammy.* He looked around the shed. "Where should we put this?" Most of the boxes and broken furniture that they'd moved out of the ex-conservatory were now here.

"Behind Grandpa Albert's old rocking chair that doesn't rock anymore," said Miriam. They maneuvered the aquarium into place and carefully lowered it to the floor. Miriam lifted the towel. "Sorry about this, everyone. While we're gone, please do not chant, OK?"

"OK!" said Krakey, Lutine, Dribble and Flooso. "O….." said Splurdge, but they left before it got to the "K."

As Miriam and Brad walked back towards the house, they saw Grammy and Eddy in the kitchen. "What's Uncle Eddy even doing here? It's the middle of the day. Shouldn't he be at work?" *Grammy's put Eddy so his back is to the window. She clearly doesn't want him to see us until she wants him to see us.* When Grammy saw them and Brad gave her the thumbs up, she waved. *What is going on??* Miriam went into the kitchen, followed by Brad.

"Here they are now," said Grammy.

"Miri!" cried Uncle Eddy and gave her a big hug. She hugged him back. *It actually hasn't been that long since we saw you…* "Good to see you again, Brad," said Eddy, extending his right hand to shake Brad's, keeping his other arm around Miriam.

"Good to see you, too," said Brad, smiling. *He's good with grown-ups…* "I meant to ask you the other day, how are you Miriam's uncle? Are you her father's brother?"

"Actually, we're not related, but her Mom and I grew up together, so I've known Miriam all her life. Isn't that right, Miri?" He gave her an extra squeeze.

"That's right," added Grammy. "Eddy's family moved in down the street when he and Ruth were three years old. They were so cute together then…"

"And I still live there with my father," said Eddy. "It's a big house. We hardly ever see each other, in case you're wondering why a grown

106

man would still live with his father." *I'm pretty sure that's the last thing Brad would wonder…*

"Actually, I was wondering if I can call you 'Miri' too?" said Brad, grinning at Miriam.

"Absolutely not!" said Miriam. *Annoying.* "Only Uncle Eddy, my brothers and Mom are allowed to call me that."

"Anyway!" Eddy continued. "What happened to Science Camp? Did you guys wander into Mayfly Millpond again?" He gave Bunster another treat.

"No, I needed them more than they need camp," Grammy explained. "New book. They're my target audience."

"And my nan will be providing photographs," said Brad. *Nice detail. Makes it sound legit. Less annoying.*

"Oh, well if it has anything to do with water, you know who to call." Eddy turned to Brad because he was the only one in the room who needed the next bit of information. "I'm part of a giant organization that my great-great-great grandfather founded. It was tiny then, of course. But now it's huge. Global. It has to be because it's about making sure everyone on the planet has access to clean water. Water is what we do."

"Is it…?" said Grammy quietly. *Attitude!*

"Of course it is, Freida!" laughed Eddy. *He's laughing but he doesn't actually think she was being funny.* "You know that better than anyone!" *I'm not sure she does…*

"But when you say, 'everyone on the planet,'" said Grammy, "are you including animals? They need water, too."

"Yes…" said Eddy, "but do we sacrifice humans for animals?" *Sacrifice??*

Grammy just turned away. *I hate it when they talk to each other like this. Tetchy. Today's worse than ever. Something about Uncle Eddy is really bugging her. Is it still because he was with Mom when she had her accident?* She watched her grandmother wipe down all of the counter tops, none of which needed wiping down, to avoid making eye contact with Eddy.

Eddy turned his attention to Brad and explained that the organization was called ARID – for Advanced Research in Innovative Demohydration.

"Demohydration?" Brad frowned.

"Getting water to humans," explained Eddy. Then, to everyone's surprise, he sang a little jingle: "We know where the water is!" *Ugh! He sounds like a cheesy commercial. Even Brad looks amazed – and not in a good way.*

"Yes, well I've got to get back to turning the old conservatory into a workroom," said Grammy, wringing out her cloth. "My office has been taken over by books…" She left. *Rude!*

"Anything I can do to help?" Uncle Eddy called after her.

Grammy emerged with a box that she handed to Brad. "Not right now, thanks, Eddy. I've got all the help I need!" *She wants him out of here.*

"OK then." Eddy looked at his watch. "Oops, time to get to my office! I'll invite myself for dinner soon!" Miriam walked him to the door. "Is your grandmother all right?" he asked her. "She seems a bit off."

Only with you. "Does she? Maybe she's tired. She's running into a lot of memories clearing out the 'conservatory'." Miriam held her fingers up to put quotes around the word.

"I bet she is," Eddy said sympathetically.

"But she's all fired up about her new project," continued Miriam, opening the door. "It's exciting!"

"You'll have to tell me about it sometime. I was really interested in the article she wrote about that kid in Egypt. Does her new book have anything to do with that?"

Too many questions. "Not that I know of," said Miriam. *I'm not lying because there's not actually a new book! But I'm crossing my fingers just in case…*

"You'll have to ask her."

"As I said, I'll invite myself for dinner soon." He pulled her in for another hug. "Take care of yourself, Miri." He took one final treat out of his pocket, and held it up. "Sit Bunster!" Bunster sat and got the treat. And then Uncle Eddy left. *At last!*

A solemn oath

MIRIAM went back into the kitchen. "Well done," said Grammy.

"Grammy, what's going on? You barely looked at him. Are you still mad at him for not saving Mom?"

"It's not that." Grammy looked Miriam right in the eye. "No one could've saved your mom."

Yes, because she's not dead. "Then what is it?" asked Miriam. "You were almost rude – so not like you."

Grammy sighed. "Eddy's been bugging me ever since I wrote about that boy in Egypt who can find water and no one knows how. Asking all sorts of questions. And I don't know anything. I was just reporting on a local news story. I never went to Egypt; I never met the boy. But Eddy doesn't seem to believe me. And I don't like it. *I get that. Everyone, including Eddy, knows that Grammy hates lying more than anything.* I think there's more to it. He's never been interested in anything else I've written... Maybe he's worried that a kid like that could put ARID out of business. If he can find water at no cost to anyone, why use ARID for 'demohydration' or whatever they call it?"

"Yeah," said Brad. "Maybe that boy knows..." and Brad sang the next bit, "where the water is!" Miriam giggled. *He's funny...*

"If ARID is interested in this boy, it makes me nervous." Grammy shook her head.

"What do you mean 'nervous'?" asked Miriam. *Uncle Eddy says that ARID is all about doing good. Is ARID bad? Is Uncle Eddy bad? Does Grammy know something she's not telling us?*

110

"Well, that sounds mysterious…" said Brad.

"Yes, and it might not be good-mysterious," said Grammy. *She's being mysterious!*

"When you say 'a kid like that' you could mean a kid like me. *Now I'm getting nervous…* What if that boy's a Puddler?"

"I bet he is," said Brad. "For what that's worth."

It's worth a lot! "But wait – does that mean ARID would be interested in me?" *Bad thought. Bad bad thought.*

Grammy seemed unusually preoccupied. "I hate to say this about somebody I've known since he was a child, but I don't trust Eddy – not one bit. *She's right. This is bad-mysterious!* If he thinks I'm lying, then it makes me wonder what *he's* lying about."

"Projection," said Brad. "That's when someone says something about someone else when it's actually true about them."

"Exactly," said Grammy. *How does Brad know this stuff??* "I'm sure he's a good person – Ruth loved him … *We all love him!* But he's got ARID in his blood, and I've never, ever liked his father." Grammy turned to Brad to explain. "Eddy's father, Bertram, took over running ARID about ten years ago, when his father died. And let's just say that his management style isn't exactly supportive and encouraging. Eddy's terrified of him."

"I never knew that," said Miriam.

"There's a lot you don't know," sighed Grammy. "I think there's a lot that none of us knows."

"I love a good mystery…" said Brad. *Of course he does.*

"But what I do know is that we can't tell Eddy about anything we're doing here, anything we're discovering. And he must never find out that Miriam's a Puddler. Agreed?"

"Agreed," said Miriam and Brad together. *It feels like we've just taken a solemn oath.*

Grammy waved her arms as if to clear away the black cloud that had descended on the conversation. "Enough of all these dark thoughts! Back to work! Where are we on the experiments? How are you going to avoid getting stuck under floorboards – or anywhere else for that matter? And we need to learn more about that Globe."

Never too big for a hug

SAMIR was lying awake in his father's apartment. It was late, but how could he sleep? An organization he'd never heard of had tried to kidnap him. What was going on? What did they know? He heard his father come into the apartment, close and lock the door, and drop his keys into the key box. Light from the hall shone on Samir as his father cracked open the bedroom door. He was too tired for a conversation, but awake enough to want a hug. "Hello, Father," he said.

"I'm sorry, Samir," said his father. "Did I wake you?"

"No. I was just falling asleep." Samir yawned.

"Oh good. Then that means I can give you this." His father leaned down and gathered Samir up in his arms. "Never too big for a hug! I'm so glad you're here, habibi."

"So am I," said Samir, hugging his father back.

"I'm taking tomorrow morning off from work," said his father. "I'll make you breakfast, and we'll talk."

"Sounds like a plan," yawned Samir, letting go of his father and lying back on his pillow. More tired than he'd ever been in his life, he was asleep before his father left the room.

Shish

MIRIAM and Brad completely agreed with Grammy that they needed to know more about the Globe. As it was a beautiful day, they decided to take their research outside. Grammy found an old bucket and used the hose to fill it with water. While she was at it, she filled the old birdbath. "I haven't put water in there for years..." *Poor birds...*

Brad pulled the aquarium up to the door of the shed so that the Waterubas could see what was going on. *It's weird to think that creatures that are basically water and have been around for billions of years care what's going on now in our back yard!* "We care about whatever's going on wherever we are, and now we're here!" said Krakey. It watched as Miriam lowered the Asteruba into the bucket. The instant the rock touched the water, it bubbled and swirled. There was a low, tuba-type hum. Krakey and the other Waterubas joined in, creating a surround-sound Wateruba Tuba. Brad quickly put the headphones over Miriam's ears. *Thank you, Brad!* Hum... bubbles... swirly-swirls... then the Asteruba rose from the bucket. The Waterubas twirled and rippled as it morphed into the Globe and settled on its watery plinth. The air smelled of the sea. Little colored lights appeared.

Miriam took off the headphones. She saw her grandmother staring at the Globe, frozen in awe. *I'm not surprised. She hasn't seen it before.* "Grammy, are you all right?"

"What is this? Some kind of advanced technology? Or... magic?"

"Any sufficiently advanced technology is indistinguishable from magic," said Brad. "Arthur C Clarke." Grammy grinned. *That broke the spell.* Brad then gently spun the Globe to show the Waterubas where they were. They got excited when they saw their own lights. "Do you see any of your friends?" Brad asked. Krakey thought it saw Shish's Trout Gray light nearby. *Trout Gray? That's a color?*

And, sure enough, when Miriam said "Shish," one of the lights flared. *And it is gray, to be fair.* "There!" she said, pointing at the glow.

Brad took out the Book of Experiments. "So, when you say a Wateruba's name at the Globe, its light flares."

"Sorry, sorry, sorry – wait one second," said Grammy. "Mind boggled." *Not surprised!* She rubbed her face then tapped the top of her head. "OK. Proceed."

"Shish!" Miriam said again. The light flared. "That's a yes."

"So now what? Are you going to touch the light and see where it takes you?"

"No." *I'm scared.*

"Are you scared?"

Yes. "No…"

"Of course you are! This is scary stuff! But it's also really exciting."

"And you've already done it," said Krakey.

"With me!" said Dribble.

"You went all the way to Egypt and back," said Brad. "You never said it was scary."

"Well… it wasn't. Surprising, really fast, amazing – but I was more scared of being caught by Steve than of what the Globe could do. Right now, thinking about it is scary."

"Then don't think about it," said Grammy. *Easy for you to say!*

"Think about your mom instead," said Brad. "Wouldn't she want you to find out as much as possible?" *No doubt about it.*

"She would be so excited about all this," said Grammy. "And as Emerson said…"

"…knowledge is the antidote to fear." Miriam finished the sentence. *Mom said that all the time.* Miriam took a deep breath and faced the Globe. *Don't think about it!* "Shish!" she shouted. *Knowledge coming right up!* A light flashed. *Just go!* She reached out and touched it. As before, she was pulled in as she puddled. *This is so weird…!!*

"See you when we see you!" cried the Waterubas.

"Enjoy it!" called Grammy.

Whoa-oh-oh! I'm going so fast! And it's dark – and closed in! OOOH! Going in another direction! It's like being on a roller coaster! And I hate roller coasters! Miriam went up, up, up, *How high will I go?* then she was falling, falling, falling *AAAAAAH!!…* into warm water! Splash! She stopped moving. *Where am I? Still puddled…* "Shish?" She looked around… *Are those bubbles?? Hey!!* She was shoved by what could've been a hand and thrown back and forth. "Shish!!" *Quick, quick, quick! Where are you?* Though everything was moving and gurgling, Miriam heard the distinctive sound of the Wateruba Tuba. She looked towards the sound and saw a bubble with big eyes. "Shish?" The bubble popped, taking the shape of a Wateruba with fins coming out of its head.

"Hi!" it said and waved. *Let's go!!* Miriam quickly reached out for Shish and Whoosh! they were on their way back.

Was that a bathtub? I think that was maybe a bathtub! We must be in pipes now! Miriam did her best to keep hold of Shish as they raced back. *How do I hold onto something that's water when I'm water, too? Help! Stay with me, Shish!* Meanwhile, Shish seemed to be having a great time. "Wheeeeeee! Wahoooooo!" Then Miriam started to feel her bones… in her toes, feet, shins…. *I'm unpuddling! But I'm not scared, so that can't be why… Maybe we're close to the …* Before she even finished the thought, she was in the grass, near the Globe, a girl again. Shish was in a bubble in her hand. "SHISH!" When the other Waterubas saw their friend, they swirled around the aquarium. "Shish Shish Shish Shish Shish!" The Globe turned back into a rock, and dropped into the bucket as if nothing magical or wondrous had happened at all.

Miriam stood up to pour Shish into the aquarium. Just then, Bunster ran to greet her. Brad tried to stop Bunster from jumping, but lost his balance and accidentally pushed Miriam into the bird bath. Shish fell into the water. Before Miriam could find it, a bird swooped down, perched on the edge of the bird bath, drank Shish and flew away! "NO!"

"See you when we see you!" called the other Waterubas, waving towards the sky, completely unfazed.

"Well, that didn't work," said Miriam.

"It kind of did," said Brad. "I mean, you did find Shish…"

"…in what I think was a bathtub," added Miriam.

"Really??" said Brad.

"What?!" Grammy could barely contain her glee. "Was someone in it?" she asked, trying not to laugh, but not succeeding. "Did anyone see you?"

"No, because I stayed puddled. Thank goodness."

"No kidding," said Brad. "That is so interesting…"

Grammy stopped laughing and started pacing. "Incredibly interesting. The Globe is clearly magic. I mean duh. And all magic has rules. So far, the rules seem to be that the Globe shows us where Waterubas are by showing us their lights…"

"And if you call out one of their names, its light flashes," said Brad.

"Then if I touch that light, I'm taken to that Wateruba…"

"…and then back to the Globe," said Grammy.

"The one thing the magic doesn't do is help me carry the Wateruba back," said Miriam. "I found Shish and we travelled back, but I kept thinking I was going to lose it. *So frustrating!* And then when we got here, I did lose it."

"Yeah, but that was more Bunster's fault than yours," said Brad. "Not to mention the bird."

"True, but if Shish had been inside something, then it wouldn't have happened. It's hard to hold onto water – particularly if your hands are water." *Even I can hear what a weird thing that is to say - !*

"I can see how that would be a challenge," agreed Grammy. *She's trying to look all serious, but she can't hide how much she's enjoying this!*

"Maybe the Globe wouldn't let me lose a Wateruba while I'm still puddled," said Miriam, "but I'd rather not have to think about it." *And by 'think,' I mean 'worry.'*

"I don't blame you," said Grammy, no longer able to contain her excitement. "But it is a pretty amazing problem to be having, don't you think? We have so much to learn!" Grammy was so thrilled, she started to rumba again. *She makes all of this so exciting!* "So let's keep it going! I'll take the Asteruba inside. You guys bring the aquarium. We'll leave Bunster and any other thirsty wildlife out here." As she danced into the kitchen, she held the Asteruba in front of her. "I wish I could puddle… but I bet it's only kids who can do it – because more of you is water than we are. Your bodies are about 65% water, and mine's more like 60%."

"Oh, the difference 5% makes," laughed Brad as he and Miriam put the aquarium down on the kitchen table.

"And we're 99% water and 1% Ruba!" said Lutine.

"Really…?" said Grammy. She stopped dancing and peered in at the Waterubas. *All those different shapes and colors.* "I wonder what Ruba actually is… Some kind of light energy, I'm thinking…" Miriam could see her grandmother's science brain whirring. *This could turn into years of research. I love Grammy's curiosity, just not now.*

"Hello?" said Miriam, waving her hand in front of Grammy's eyes. "Problem of bringing a Wateruba back without me worrying about it getting lost or snatched by a bird? Focus, people!"

"On it!" said Brad, paging through the Book of Experiments.

"Look, we know that when you puddled with Anu's keys, they turned into water, but when you unpuddled, they were keys again. And your clothes stay clothes, right? So I bet you can take something to carry a Wateruba."

"Useful deduction, Brad!" said Grammy, rifling through the cupboards. She pulled out a plastic container with a flip lid. "I'm not happy that it's plastic…"

"But at least it's not single use," said Miriam. She took the container and flipped the lid a few times. "That's good. I won't have to twist or turn anything. But…"

"But what?" asked Grammy.

"But it would be better if I didn't have to hold it when everything is water. Is there any way of attaching it to me? Otherwise, it could get pulled out of my watery hand if I'm in a hurricane or something."

"Miriam, did you hear what you just said?" whooped Grammy, "'…if I'm in a hurricane or something.' IN A HURRICANE! AS WATER!! This is miraculous! Phenomenal! And so so exciting!" *She needs to calm down!*

"Hurricane!" said Dribble, twirling around the aquarium. The others joined in, creating a vortex.

Miriam watched the Waterubas tumble and twirl around the aquarium. *That is very cool, no two ways about it. You can't see each Wateruba, just the ripples they make. And you can hear them. "Shish! Shish! Shish!" If I didn't know I was hearing Waterubas, I'd think I was just hearing water swirling around in an aquarium. I wonder how many times I've heard Waterubas but just thought it was water… But back to my problem.* She turned to her grandmother. "It is exciting, Grammy, but how can I attach this Wateruba transport system to me so it won't get pulled off? Any ideas?"

"Wateruba Transport System!" exclaimed Brad. "You nailed it! WTS for short!"

What a team! "Grammy?" said Miriam. "Ideas?"

"As a matter of fact, I've got a solution," said Grammy. "It's in one of the boxes we took out to the shed." And she left the kitchen to go outside.

"She's usually full of energy, but I've never seen her like this," said Miriam as Grammy danced across the back yard. "She's super-charged!"

"Well, she's never watched her beloved granddaughter turn into water and then back into a girl in front of her very eyes, has she?" reasoned Brad. "And let's not forget that she's discovered that something she thought she'd dreamed up is actually real."

"We'rrrre… " started Splurdge.

"…REAL!" finished Krakey and Lutine.

"Exciting!" added Dribble.

Wateruba transport system

GRAMMY came back in, holding a sort of utility belt. She put it around Miriam's waist. "It was your mother's. *Say no more. I love it.* And I think we'll be able to attach the WTS with this thing." She took the container, positioned it on the belt, and pulled a flap to fasten it. She jiggled it. "That's not going anywhere soon." *So far so good.*

Miriam turned on the taps to fill the kitchen sink. "Where should I go to test it out?" *I can't believe I'm actually looking forward to this! It's so much better than being terrified. Maybe it's because I'll have something of Mom's with me.* She placed the Asteruba in the sink. There was the low Wateruba Tuba-like hum as it rose up on its watery plinth and transformed into the Globe.

"Unbelievable…" murmured Grammy, still awestruck.

"I see Smedley," said Lutine, the minute the little blinking lights appeared. "It's got a lovely, creamy, pink Ruba."

"Smedley," Miriam announced to the Globe. There was the flash they'd seen before that showed where a particular Wateruba was – but then a route from Grammy's kitchen sink to where Smedley was lit up, a thin thread of color. "Have we ever seen that colored line before?" Miriam turned to Brad and Grammy.

Brad leaned in for a closer look. "That's v v interesting." *V v interesting? I think it could be v v v v 'interesting'!* "The Globe doesn't just show you where Waterubas are. I think it also shows you how you get to them, as water." *Make that v v v v v v interesting!*

Grammy leaned in next to Brad. "Fascinating. And if you're right, the route to Smedley looks a little complicated."

"I'm v v not ready for complicated," said Miriam.

Brad turned towards the aquarium. "Can you guys see anyone else?"

"I… see…." Everyone waited for Splurdge to finish his sentence. "… Koink."

"Koink," Miriam declared to the Globe. Another flash, and the route lit up.

Brad grabbed the tablet and photographed the Globe before the route faded. "Do Smedley again."

"Smedley!" said Miriam. Again, Brad photographed the Globe. He positioned the two photographs side by side and started to study them. "Hmmmm," he said. Grammy put on her glasses to have a better look. "Hmmmm," she hmmmed. "Hmmmm," they hmmmed together. *Not helpful!*

"You know, it doesn't really matter how complicated the route to a Wateruba is because I get there really quickly," said Miriam, trying to interrupt their hmming. "It's one of my superpowers, remember?" More hmmmming. "I think I'll just go find Smedley to see if the WTS works, OK?" *If I think too long, I might not go at all!*

But Grammy and Brad still weren't paying any attention. They were totally focused on the pictures. "I'm not sure how to read this, but it looks as if this route goes through a storm," Brad said. "The Globe isn't giving us ordinary images, but that looks stormy to me. What do you think?"

"I think you're right," said Grammy. "It's giving us water routes, but we'll have to learn how to interpret them."

Beginning to feel the fears… but I've got to find out if this belt works! Quick! Go! Miriam checked to see that the WTS was firmly attached to the belt, which was firmly attached to her body. *All set! Now GO!* "Bye!" she called.

"See you when we see you!" said the Waterubas.

"Smedley!" Miriam shouted at the Globe, and when Smedley's light flashed, she reached out to touch it. *On my way!* Miriam felt her skin liquefy and her bones dissolve *Gooshy!* as her body turned into water, and she was sucked into the Globe. *Wheeeeeee!!!*

Smedley

THIS time, Miriam was pulled up and up. *Am I in the sky? I wish Dribble were here to tell me!* All she could see was thick fog, and her watery body vibrated with a deep rumbling. *That must be thunder! Sounds like the sky to me. Brad was right. There's a storm!* She was tossed around, twirled, smashed in with other drops of water and whirled out again. *I should be scared. Am I scared?*

No! Why not? Maybe it's the magic of the Globe. Or it's because water doesn't get scared – and I'm 99% water and only 1% Miriam! I'm water in a storm!! Nothing's bad – it just is! Woo-hooo!! Miriam fell and fell and then stopped falling and was pushed along. *Where now? A river maybe?* The pushing stopped and she drifted until she couldn't go any further. *End of the route?* She began to feel her bones again. She felt her toes… feet… legs… she unpuddled. *Yes. End of the route. Travelling as water – fast – has got to be the strangest thing ever.* She touched the WTS. *Good. Still here.* She looked around. She was in water, right by a tree. *Is this some kind of swamp?* "Smedley?" she shouted. At first, nothing – and then the distinctive sound of a Wateruba chanting the Wateruba Tuba. She turned towards the sound and saw Smedley wafting near the surface.

123

It seemed bigger and more complicated than the Waterubas she'd seen so far, with large eyes and bulgy bits. It glowed a creamy pink.

Smedley waved. Miriam reached towards it and the second she touched it, she puddled, and the return journey started. "Wait!" she cried. As she and Smedley joined the river, she fought to guide Smedley into the container attached to her waist. "Go in go in go in go in!!" Smedley waved again, shrank a little, and Miriam was then able to maneuver it into the WTS. *Thanks, Smedley!* She clicked the lid closed. *Success!* Now that she didn't have to keep track of a Wateruba, she closed her eyes. *I'm going to relax and enjoy the ride! Will there be another storm? Who cares? I'm water!! I go with the flow!* She was just getting into it when she felt her bones, and SCHLOOMP! she was in the kitchen, a solid girl with a container holding a Wateruba attached to her waist. "I'm back!"

"It worked!" cried Grammy.

"And it took you hardly any time at all," said Brad.

Really?? "How long was I gone?"

"A minute… maybe two," said Brad.

Weird!! "It felt much longer to me. I mean, under an hour, but much more than two minutes. I think time does a funny thing once I get sucked into the Globe. Kind of like dreaming. You know when you feel you've been asleep for hours, but it turns out to be only minutes? It's like that."

"There's dream time and 'real' time," said Brad. "That's a thing."

"To be fair," added Grammy, the scientist, "no one really knows what time is. But it's interesting that your normal sense of time is distorted when you're puddle-jumping."

"Puddle-jumping!" Miriam and Brad exclaimed. "I love that!" said Miriam.

"Well, that's what it is, isn't it? You puddle, and jump from here to there and back again."

Brad wrote in the Book of Experiments: "Normal sense of time is distorted during puddle-jumping."

"And here's something else for the book," said Miriam. "Once I touch the Globe, there's nothing I can do to control how puddle-jumping works, including if or when I unpuddle."

"Explain?" said Grammy.

Miriam continued. "So, 1) I puddle-jump. 2) I get to where the Wateruba is and stop travelling. Sometimes I unpuddle. Sometimes I stay water. This time I was in some kind of swamp, and I unpuddled. Whichever way it goes, it just happens. It doesn't seem to have anything to do with what I do or how I'm feeling. 3) I touch the Wateruba. 4) Puddle-jump back, and 5) unpuddle."

"So it's kind of like breathing," said Grammy. "Breathe in – puddle-jump. Stopping to find the Wateruba is the space between the inbreath and outbreath. Then you touch the Wateruba, breathe out, and puddle-jump back. Elegant..."

"I like it because I don't have to do anything. Just be," said Miriam.

"And there's really nothing more relaxing than just being," said Grammy. *Agreed.*

Miriam poured Smedley into the aquarium. "Smedley Smedley Smedley Smedley!" The Waterubas swirled around the latest addition until its knobbly bits dissolved and they were all just one shimmering eddy of water. Before they started to chant the Wateruba Tuba, Miriam put the headphones on. *I still feel bad about losing Shish, but I'm sure I'll find it again. Look at them go!* Every now and again, Krakey emerged out of the swirl and waved. "Hey Krakey!" She waved back. Then Lutine, Dribble... even Splurdge slowly drifted in to wave. *They're so funny. Mom, I can't wait until you can see this. You will not believe your eyes!*

Brad tapped her on the shoulder, interrupting her thoughts. He signaled for her that it was OK to remove the headphones. "What's up?" said Miriam.

"Did you say that when you unpuddled, you thought you were in some kind of swamp?" Miriam nodded. "Let me show you your journey."

"What do you mean?"

"This is so exciting, I can barely stand it.," said Grammy. *It must be good because she's doing the rumba again!* Brad showed Miriam a photographic version of the route on the tablet. "Look! Brad found a way of combining the photos from the Globe with a live weather map app!"

"What?" *I'm confused.*

"You know how there are maps on your computer and you can push in on them until you can actually see what's on the ground – a street or a forest or whatever?"

"Yes…"

"Well, I found out that when I pushed in on the photos I took of the light threads on the Globe, I could see what was on the ground – like the swamp."

"No way!"

"Yes way!"

"But listen to this!" squealed Grammy. *Not sure I've ever heard her squeal before. She might actually burst with excitement!* "Go on, Brad! Tell her!"

"I figured out how to put a weather app on top of the Globe photo – so I could see what the weather was on your journey. And as we know, weather is all about water. Let me show you." *Yes, please!* "So, what was the first thing that happened when you touched the Globe?"

"I was pulled up and up and up."

"That's because you went up into the sky, and then got mixed up with these cumulonimbus clouds…" On the screen was a picture of dark clouds.

Look at that! This is amazing! "I thought I was in a storm!" said Miriam. "I got smashed and twirled and spun around."

"Of course you did! That storm was a doozy!" Grammy hugged Brad. "And this extremely clever person figured out how to make a photographic account of your route as water!"

"I think I'll call it 'WaterView'," said Brad.

"Or… wait for it… WaterViewba!" said Grammy. Brad and Miriam groaned. *Grammy…*

"This is great because when I'm puddle-jumping, I can't see where I am – I can only feel it," said Miriam. "So I felt myself getting pulled up – and then I was tossed around, and I couldn't see anything but fog and then I vibrated when I heard a low rumble…"

"Thunder!" said Grammy.

"Then, I fell… and I thought maybe I landed in a river."

Brad swiped to the next picture. "Yep, you did. You fell, or should we say you rained, into this river. Then you went along, along, along, along until you veered off into this tributary which took you into these wetlands." He swiped again. It was a picture of a tree coming up out of the water. "And you stopped by this tree." He swiped again, but the screen went black. "See? That was your journey as water. No more pictures."

"My mind is officially blown," said Grammy. *Same!* She picked up the Asteruba which was back to being just a rock. "How does this thing work?? And why? What kind of intelligence is behind it?"

"Magic," said Miriam. "You said so yourself."

Cairo

IN Cairo, Samir's father was having breakfast with his son. Hearing how the resort construction workers had blamed Samir for taking their water, he was confused. "Why you?" he asked.

Samir so badly wanted to tell his father everything – about being able to turn into water, so he could find problems in the pipes if it wasn't flowing, and about how a mysterious person from a group called ARID had tried to kidnap him. But something told Samir to keep quiet. If his father didn't have any information, then he couldn't give it away, even accidentally.

"I know people think you have some kind of magical powers, but it's not like you could divert water away from a major building site," his father laughed. Samir tried to laugh too, but none of it seemed funny and he wasn't good at faking something he didn't feel. "Look, your mother told me how everyone turned on you. That is very unfortunate. We think you should stay here as long as you like."

"Thank you, Father," said Samir.

"She talked to your teachers. They're happy for Asmaa to get your schoolwork and email it to you. You're such a good student, no one is worried about you keeping up."

"Good," said Samir. But the last thing he was worried about was his schoolwork. He was much more worried about ARID finding him. "Do you think I'll be safe here?"

"From the construction team?" snorted his father. "They're far too busy destroying the environment and gutting local resources to chase a young boy." You didn't need to be highly sensitive like Samir to pick up how angry all this made his father. "This silliness will soon pass. No one will look for you here."

But Samir wasn't so sure.

Ruba
colors

GRAMMY was feeling a strong sense of urgency. She couldn't say why exactly, but Miriam didn't need an explanation. *Grammy trusts her feelings and so do I.* "There are two things I know now with all the water in my body," she told Miriam. "The first is that we have to hurry and the second is that we have to keep it all secret. There's so much to learn, and what we're discovering is enormous, so we need to do our research quickly without anyone interfering." *And by 'anyone', I'm guessing you mean Uncle Eddy.*

To help with both speed and secrecy, Grammy asked Brad if he wanted to stay in Jeff and Erik's room instead of going back to his nan's every evening. Brad was thrilled. So was Miriam. And once he'd checked it out with Eleanor, and she'd agreed, Brad moved in. *There is no question about it. Brad is now officially my best friend.*

Miriam hadn't had a best friend since her mother disappeared. Before that, she used to hang out with Bella and Niko at school. The three of them would have sleep-overs. But once her friends thought her mom had died, they didn't know what to say to her. Miriam didn't want to leak her sadness all over them, so she'd gone into herself and stayed there.

Now that Brad was living in Grammy's house, Miriam had to get used to his strange habits, like his nightly body check for scratches and bumps. She could hear him recording his discoveries on his phone. "Hangnail, third finger, right hand. Weirdly splotchy bruise from tripping on throw rug, second toe, left foot." *Gross! But the upside is that if I wake up in the middle of the night and go downstairs to watch the Waterubas in the aquarium, I bet I won't be alone for long.*

The aquarium was still on the kitchen table. *We'll have to move it tomorrow so we can have breakfast. And we'll need to put it somewhere it can't be seen if somebody drops by, and by 'somebody,' I mean Uncle Eddy.* The kitchen was dark, and if Miriam didn't know better, she'd have thought there wasn't anything in the aquarium except water, though there was a faint glow. *That must be the Ruba. But I don't see any shapes... but then again, you don't see the shapes until you do...* Not wanting to turn on all the overhead lights, *Too bright* Miriam ran back up to her room to get her desk lamp. On the way to the stairs to go back down, she bumped into Brad, who'd just been in the bathroom. Actually, he was the one who bumped into her because he wasn't looking where he was going. "Hey!" said Miriam. Brad's pajamas were decorated with UFOs.

"Hi," he yawned. "You OK?"

"Perfect," said Miriam. "I'm just checking on the Waterubas."

"Good plan!" said Brad, fully awake now. *I knew he'd be up for it!* He followed her down the stairs, grabbing the banister to keep from falling when he tripped on his overly long pj bottoms.

There was enough moonlight to set the lamp up next to the tank. "It doesn't look as if anything's in there," said Brad, peering into the water. "They just look like water, until they look like themselves."

"I was thinking the same thing," said Miriam, "It's all part of the deep, dark, ancient magic." She flicked on the desk lamp. Six Waterubas appeared as the water morphed into the shapes of Krakey, Flooso, Lutine, Dribble, Splurdge and Smedley. *Magic...* When they saw Brad and Miriam, they waved.

"Hi!" whispered Miriam. *Phew! I knew they were here, but it's good to see them.*

"You guys are so cool!" said Brad. "And so ancient..." He turned to Miriam. "Isn't it weird to be looking at something that's billions of years old..."

"Water is billions of years old," said Lutine, matter-of-factly, "and you look at water all the time. The water with us in this tank could've been part of a dinosaur's blood."

"Or… part… of… Panthalasssssssssa…" said Splurdge, disappearing into bubbles.

"That was the first ocean," said Brad. *How does he know this stuff??* "All water is ancient. I never thought of it like that before." *Me neither.*

Krakey came right up against the glass. "Questions?" he asked.

"Not really," said Miriam. "We just wanted to look at you."

"Do you want us to sing the Wateruba Tuba?" asked Flooso. "Then you can puddle and join us!"

"Good idea!" said Brad. "Right, Miriam?"

"Wrong, Brad," said Miriam. "I'd really rather watch them from out here." *I'm still not totally sure about puddling.* She stared into the aquarium. "I love how you move."

"We're primeval like water, and we move like water," said Lutine. "You're new like humans, and you move like humans."

"Except when Miriam puddles," said Krakey. "Then she moves like water."

"It's amazing how you seem to disappear, and then the water takes your shape again," said Brad.

"You mean how our shape comes out of the water," corrected Lutine. Brad wasn't exactly sure how that was different than what he'd said, but never mind.

"I do have a question now," said Miriam. The Waterubas all lined up next to the glass to listen. Except for Splurdge who floated up to the top of the tank until his snout stuck out of the water and then dripped back in. "When I'm water, do I disappear into the water like you guys do?"

"From what I've seen, you never completely disappear," said Krakey, "Your Miriam shape is always there."

"I've noticed the same thing," said Brad. "I wonder if that's because you're a Puddler – a human who turns into water – and not a Wateruba who's water all the time."

"Exactly," said Lutine, who seemed to be the expert. *I have to admit, Lutine does look very wise.* "I've met a number of Puddlers, so I've seen how it works," it added.

"You have?" said Miriam. *I would love to meet another Puddler.*

"I've met a few... I think..." said Flooso.

"Two!" said Dribble.

"One!" said Smedley. "You!"

"None," said Splurdge floating down to join the others.

"But you've met Miriam, Splurdge," said Smedley.

"One," said Splurdge, rolling around and around in the water.

"Puddlers don't have a Ruba, at least not that we can see like ours," said Krakey. They chanted the Wateruba Tuba so that their Rubas glowed. Miriam quickly grabbed Erik's headphones. She and Brad stared wide-eyed into the aquarium. "KRAKEY TOLD ME THAT EVERYBODY'S RUBA IS A DIFFERENT COLOR!" Miriam was yelling again because she'd forgotten that she was wearing headphones. The Waterubas stopped chanting, and Brad motioned for her to take them off.

"That's right," said Krakey. "Each Wateruba's Ruba is a different color, and it never changes, which is how we know who's where when we see all the colors on the Globe."

"Do you know the names and colors of all 81 Waterubas?" asked Brad, amazed.

"Krakey doesn't, but I do," said Lutine flowing through Krakey to get right up against the glass. "And so does Dribble."

Dribble whirled up next to Lutine. "Dribble here!"

"Dribble?" said Lutine. "What color is Voda's Ruba?"

"Apricot," said Dribble.

"Vesi?"

"Scarlet."

"Fishman?"

"Grape."

"Emoto?"

"Baby blue," said Dribble.

It sounds like they're speaking a foreign language. "Who knew there were so many colors?" said Miriam.

"Trust me, there are," said Brad. "And they have weird names like eggplant."

"Ploop," said Dribble.

"So Ploop's Ruba color is eggplant?" asked Miriam.

"Exactly," said Lutine.

"What about mellow yellow?" said Brad.

"Chawaga," said Dribble.

"Flamingo pink?" said Miriam. *Is that a color? I just made it up.*

"Tinkle," said Dribble. *Bingo!*

"Wow," said Brad, clearly impressed. "Dribble doesn't say much, but it sure knows its Ruba colors."

Then Miriam gasped. *I've just thought of something amazing!* "Brad, Brad, Brad, what about the photo in Mom's camera? The one of the Wateruba?" *This is so exciting I might start to rumba!*

"Good thinking!" said Brad.

"Dribble, Lutine. If we show you a photo of a Wateruba, could you tell us who it is?"

"Indubitably," said Lutine.

Indubitably. Right answer! I love that word! Miriam ran up the stairs to her room to get the camera. *If Lutine and Dribble can identify the Wateruba by its color, then they can find it on the Globe! And if they find it on the Globe, then I can jump to it and find out what happened to Mom.* Miriam was in such a hurry, she almost pulled a Brad and fell down the stairs. *Close one!* But she got back to the kitchen without injury and handed the camera to Brad. He scrolled through the pictures until he got to the one of the crevasse with the Wateruba in the ice. He enlarged the

Wateruba and showed the picture to Lutine and Dribble.

"Vesi," they said in unison.

That's the Wateruba who saw my mom's accident! I've got to puddle-jump to Vesi NOW! "I've got to puddle-jump to Vesi now!" she said aloud.

"That is a terrible idea," said Brad.

"But Vesi will know what happened to Mom!" *I need to go now now now!*

"I know," said Brad. "And Vesi will still have that information tomorrow. It's very late. You need sleep. WE need sleep."

When did you become my dad?? "We'll sleep after I get Vesi."

"We also need your grandmother," said Brad. *True.* "Miriam, this is huge."

"I'll go wake her up!" said Miriam. But Brad grabbed her before she could go anywhere.

"No you won't," said Brad. "She'd hate that. We'll make the Globe tomorrow." And then he yawned. A big, jaw-cracking yawn. Miriam couldn't help it. She yawned, too. *I'm so so tired... Brad's right – I need sleep...*

"Okay. We'll do it tomorrow." She yawned again and went up the stairs. "I'll use the bathroom first. Will you turn off the lights? See you tomorrow..." She waved at the Waterubas who all waved back.

Azizi

IN Cairo, Samir spent his days doing his schoolwork, making meals for his father, noting any stranger who looked at him for more than four seconds, and wondering about that girl he'd seen in the water barrel.

Samir felt it was safer to stay inside the apartment. But he was used to being outside most of the time, so he was getting a little squirrely being cooped up all day. The only person he spoke to was Mr. Amin who had always lived across the hall from Samir's father. A couple of years ago, Mr. Amin had rescued a street dog – a beautiful dog called Azizi that Samir and his sisters loved. Whenever he heard Mr. Amin open his door to take Azizi out for a walk, Samir went into the hall to say hello. He was only allowed to give Azizi one treat – a bit of leftover food – but he could give him as many hugs as he liked. Mr. Amin saw how much Samir loved Azizi – and vice versa. "Samir, why don't you come out with us for a walk?" Mr. Amin said every day.

And Azizi always barked as if he agreed (though Samir knew he was probably only barking because he'd heard the word "walk.")

And every day Samir said, "Thank you for asking, Mr. Amin, but unfortunately, I have an essay to finish." Or extra math problems to do. Or an article to translate into English. He would have loved more than anything to go for a walk with Mr. Amin and Azizi, but it was too risky.

"Maybe next time then," said Mr. Amin. And Samir watched Mr. Amin and Azizi go down the stairs. Sometimes he ran to the window to watch them leave the building and head toward the park, Azizi pulling on the lead as he sniffed his way along the pavement.

The quest to find Vesi

WHILE it was afternoon in Cairo, in Illinois, Miriam was just opening her eyes. *I'm awake! Is it morning?* She looked at the clock. *It's early, but morning enough. Time to start the Quest to find Vesi!* She jumped out of bed and quickly got dressed. *I'll puddle-jump to Vesi, and when I bring it back, we'll find out what happened to Mom. Finally, finally we'll know for sure that she's alive.* She picked up the Asteruba and headed for the stairs. As she passed Brad's door, she knocked. "It's the Vest to find Quesi!" She giggled. *Not awake yet!* "I mean the Quest to find Vesi!"

"What time is it?" came a sleepy voice from inside the room.

"Time to get up!!" whooped Miriam. *Brad's a morning person, so maybe it's too early even for him. Tough!* When she got into the kitchen, she put the Asteruba down next to the sink, then turned to the aquarium. "Hello, Waterubas!" she said, and watched as the water morphed into their distinctive shapes, shimmers becoming limbs, reflections becoming faces. *I love seeing them so much.* They waved. She waved back. "We're going to find Vesi today!"

"Vesi! Vesi! Vesi! Vesi! Vesi!" sang the Waterubas, whizzing the water around. Miriam put on the headphones that she'd left on the table in case they started to chant the Wateruba Tuba. *Don't want to waste time puddling too soon!*

Grammy came in, yawning. She waited a second, then signaled that it was safe for Miriam to remove the headphones. "What's going on?"

"Last night, the Waterubas told us that the Wateruba in that picture on Mom's camera is Vesi."

"So, today is the Quest to find Vesi!" said Brad, coming into the kitchen and turning on the computer.

"Oh, Grammy, I'm so excited!" Miriam hugged her grandmother. "Vesi will tell us what happened to Mom!" *I love today.*

"Sweetheart, we know what happened to your mom." *Oh why did I say that out loud? Now I'll get a lecture.* Grammy put her hands on Miriam's shoulders and looked her right in the eye. *Here it comes.* "Please, please don't expect the impossible."

"I won't," said Miriam, turning away. *Because it's not impossible!*

"Vesi! Vesi! Vesi! Vesi! Vesi!" sang the Waterubas. Miriam put her headphones back on. *Vesi is the only one who can tell us all what I know is true.*

Grammy wouldn't let anyone do anything until she'd made her coffee, of course. *She loves her coffee almost as much as she loves her books.* She ground the beans, boiled the kettle to just the right temperature, and filtered the coffee into a special mug that Albert had made for her. "OK, go!" she said. While Grammy savored those first few sips, with her usual "Mmmm-mmmm-mmmm!" Brad filled the kitchen sink with water. Miriam picked up the Asteruba and turned to the Waterubas who were all lined up next to the glass of the aquarium.

"Is everybody ready?"

"Vesi!" said the Waterubas.

"Yes-i!" said Brad.

"Mmmmm!" said Grammy.

Miriam lowered the Asteruba into the water. The deep hum that came from the sink was so strong, the dishes vibrated. As Miriam, Brad and Grammy watched, mesmerized, the Asteruba slowly rose on its geyser-like pedestal. When the pedestal was about a foot high, all the water ran off of the Asteruba, and, spinning slowly, it transformed into the Globe. The air felt cooler, and smelled of the sea. *I don't care how many times I see this, it's still mind-boggling.* The Globe settled with a quiet whoosh, and the Wateruba lights appeared, dotting it with pinpoints of color.

"Vesi!" said Miriam. She waited. But there was no flash – no nothing. *Maybe I just didn't see it.* "Does anyone see Vesi?" *Please please please see Vesi.*

No one said anything for a moment, then Lutine piped up, "Could you bring me and Dribble closer?"

"Closer," said Dribble.

Miriam's belt with the WTS was hanging over a chair. Brad detached the container from the belt and scooped up Dribble and Lutine. Splurdge came along for the ride. Normally, Splurdge and Dribble seemed bigger than the other Waterubas, except maybe Shish – but like water, they fit the space they were in. *I love how they can be any size they need to be. All three are in that WTS and they fit perfectly.* Brad closed the lid – "Just in case I trip," he said to Miriam, *Smart* and he carried the Waterubas over to the Globe. He handed the WTS to Miriam, who held it up so that the Waterubas could see, while Brad slowly turned the Globe. After they'd studied it for three turns, "No," said Dribble. "No Vesi."

"That's right," said Lutine. "Vesi's Ruba light isn't here. But Vesi is definitely somewhere on the planet. Where else would it be? Our Ruba is pulled here by the pieces of the Asteruba."

"Just like the Asteruba was pulled to Earth when we first came," said Krakey.

"You mean billions of years ago?" asked Grammy. "You came here on an asteroid that was actually pulled to the Earth?"

"That's right," said Krakey. "It pulled us and pulled us and pulled us until…"

"… it CRASHED!" said all the Waterubas together.

"That was the last time I saw Dribble until you brought it here from Egypt," said Krakey.

"I'm sorry, but you are remembering something that must have happened not long after the Earth was formed," said Grammy.

"Billions of years ago… Ouch!" She shook her head. "Way too much for our limited minds to grasp…"

I hate to ask this at such an amazing moment but "What about Vesi…?"

"Sometimes Waterubas find themselves deep underground, inside rocks," said Lutine. "I've been there. Very relaxing."

"Or maybe it's in a Pseudoliparis swirei," said Brad. *What is he talking about??* "That's a fish that lives in the Mariana Trench, almost 8000 meters down. Very cool."

This isn't helping. "But I could still get to it, right?"

Grammy put her arm around Miriam. "We just don't know. The Globe is inexplicable, baffling, mysterious," said Grammy. "More research required. Maybe it only shows us Waterubas that you can get to as a Puddler."

"And I bet not even a Puddler could handle the water pressure in the Mariana Trench," added Brad. "The pressure down there would be like having one hundred grown-up elephants standing on your head." He thought for a second, calculating. "Or one thousand two hundred baby elephants!"

First of all, how does he know this stuff? Second of all, I give up. For now. Miriam poured Lutine, Dribble and Splurdge back into the aquarium. "Waterubas, like water, keep moving, right?"

"Right," said Krakey. "Sometimes fast, sometimes slow – but Waterubas always keep moving."

"Always," added Smedley.

"So we'll keep checking the Globe to see when Vesi appears." *I will ignore the fact that if it's stuck in the middle of a rock it could be there for centuries. I will find that Wateruba!*

"We will find that Wateruba," said Brad. "The Vest for Quesi continues!"

I really, really, really like Brad…

Pirta and Jala

"IN the meantime," said Grammy, "let's have breakfast and then get on with constructing the Wateroomba!" She put some boxes of cereal on the table as well as a loaf of bread and a variety of nut spreads. "We need a place where we can put Vesi when we find it, right?" She handed Miriam a bowl and a spoon. *Always trying to get me to eat, even when I'm way too sad to be hungry.* "The fact that you have the strange and wonderful ability to collect Waterubas says to me that that is what you should be doing. And it's no good collecting them if we have nowhere to keep them." *But I was so sure I was going to find out what had happened to Mom! Today! I can't believe it's not happening.* She stared into the empty bowl, feeling Brad watching her.

"You may not be able to get Vesi today," he said gently, "but you can start finding other Waterubas, and maybe one of them will have seen Vesi." *He's got a point. A very good point.*

"Brad, that's a plan!" said Miriam and, feeling better, she poured cereal into the bowl and started to eat.

"And you know how much I love a plan!" said Brad, taking the Globe off its watery pedestal and putting the Asteruba in a safe place. *It's so great to have Brad and Grammy doing so much to help.*

Miriam watched as Grammy took her coffee into the Wateroomba to start pacing off where the various elements would go. *Grammy loves a project like this! I remember when she turned the downstairs bathroom into a mini-rainforest. The boys don't like peeing in there, but I do!* The Wateroomba was a huge undertaking, and Grammy worried that it might be tricky getting help from people like Lucas, the local plumber, without giving away any of the secret. "I've got to make sure Lucas doesn't guess what I'm doing!" *As if! Who would ever guess that she's building a place to house some mysterious and ancient creatures made out of water?* Lucas, like everyone else, accepted Grammy's not entirely untrue story that she was building a laboratory for her water experiments – just like the bathroom rainforest, only bigger!

"And to do those experiments, I need a scaled-down river and a miniature lake and various wetlands, like a bog, a marsh, a fen and a swamp, plus lots of plants and two waterfalls. We need to find out as much as we can as quickly as we can." *Agreed.*

Brad helped her install a bright light that came on at regular intervals to heat the water below, so it could evaporate and turn into little clouds. The clouds were then blown across the room by a strategically placed fan and, when they reached the area where the air was colder, the water in the clouds condensed into rain. *I love that bit!* "It's a thing of beauty, if I do say so myself," Grammy sighed.

"A masterpiece!" said Brad. *I can't wait to see it filled with Waterubas. I can't wait to bring Vesi back here.*

There were pipes and a waterwheel. There was no place where water could get stuck for very long – except maybe in the freezer. And it was all self-contained, so that the Waterubas couldn't accidentally drift, float, sink or flow away.

Grammy was so engrossed in the Wateroomba that all the space in her head and heart usually filled with worrying about Miriam was overflowing with building mini eco-systems instead. Now that Miriam had done it a few times, Grammy understood that puddle-jumping was like breathing – something that happened naturally at its own rhythm. She decided to be confident that every time her precious granddaughter touched a light on the Globe and disappeared, she would safely return. Grammy surrendered to the wondrous power of the Globe, and with her full approval, it officially became Miriam's job to go out there and bring back Waterubas. Not just her amazing gift, but her job. *When you think about it, it couldn't be anyone else's job. But I'm happy she's not worrying about it. It is what it is! And if Puddlers need Waterubas, then I need to find them!*

Miriam, however, still got scared. But since it didn't seem that puddle-jumping required her to make any decisions that she could mess up, she told herself to focus on what she would learn, rather than on what could go wrong. *What's 'wrong' anyway? No matter what happens, we're learning. The more I do it, the more we find out about how the Globe works. So that's good, right? I seem to be the only one who can do this, so it's more than a job. It's actually a responsibility. I can't wait to meet someone else who can puddle!*

Miriam learned something new every time she went – like discovering that it didn't matter what she was wearing. When she puddle-jumped for Pirta, she was wearing shorts, a t-shirt and the WTS. She was ready to go, so she didn't wait for Brad's WaterView. *If I wait, I think – if I think, I get scared. Better to just go.* "Pirta!" she shouted at the Globe, touched the light and was sucked in. When she stopped travelling, as she always did when she'd reached the Wateruba she was jumping for, she unpuddled. She was in a blizzard. Yes, snow whirling around, wind howling, visibility zero, just like in her Mom-dream. But unlike in her dream, she wasn't cold. *Weird. How am I not freezing? I'm wearing flip-flops! And shorts! But I'm not cold at all. This is wild! Better not think about it too much. Where's Pirta? Will it hear me over this wind?* "PIRTA!!" Fortunately, Pirta's Ruba color was candy apple red, so its glow was soon visible in the middle of all the white. Then Miriam saw its long, skinny limbs and its head like a puddle. *I couldn't even imagine something looking like that! Every Wateruba is a complete surprise.*

143

Pirta waved. Miriam reached out to touch it, and was so glad to get home and away from the wind and the snow and the thoughts of her dream that she hugged both Grammy <u>and</u> Brad (much to Brad's surprise). Then she remembered Pirta. "Oh no! I just wanted out of that blizzard and forgot to put Pirta in the WTS!" Brad, still recovering from the hug, noticed a snowflake on Miriam's t-shirt, glowing red. Then the snowflake formed a body, two long arms and two long legs, and they heard the faint sound of the Wateruba Tuba. "Pirta!" cried Miriam and guided it into the WTS before handing it over to Grammy. "Here's something for the Book of Experiments: even though I was in a blizzard, I wasn't cold."

"And it was a proper blizzard – wind howling, zero visibility?" said Grammy, trying to get her head around this.

"Absolutely," said Miriam.

"Of course, if you hadn't unpuddled and stayed water, you would've frozen," said Brad. "Oooh, I wish I hadn't said that…"

Snap. "But I did unpuddle, and wasn't cold at all," said Miriam. "It was really strange."

"And wonderful," said Grammy, shaking her head with amazement. "The miracle that is the Globe…"

The next time Miriam faced the Globe, she was dressed in warm clothes and boots, just in case. *It was just too weird being in a blizzard in shorts and flip-flops.* The Waterubas still couldn't see Vesi, but Lutine told her that the glowing cinnamon light was Jala. *They look amazing and their names are really interesting!* "Jala!" said Miriam.

The route lit up, and Brad photographed it. "No storms that I can see – and certainly no snow." He peered at the image. "Hey! You're going to the Galapagos!"

"Oh, the Enchanted Isles…" said Grammy, dreamily. "I've always wanted to go there."

"Where is it?" asked Miriam. *Even though it doesn't really matter because I won't really know where I am, I kind of want to know where I'm going. Does that make sense?*

"It's a group of islands in the Pacific, west of Ecuador," said Brad. *I wish I'd paid more attention in geography...* "They're on the equator. It'll be hot. Are you sure you want to wear those clothes?"

As usual, Miriam was in a hurry. *Don't make me think! I just want to go! Besides, we've already discovered it doesn't matter what I'm wearing.* "Jala!" she said again, touching the light that flashed. It went dark as she was pulled into the Globe. The dark was soon followed by light as she soared into the sky, then falling, falling as she rained into water, *A river? The ocean?* then up, up, up, then joining up with more water. *A cloud?* Then falling again... then dark as she was pulled down. *Into the ground?* When she stopped, Miriam wasn't exactly sure where she was. She was inside something greenish that smelled plant-ish. She didn't unpuddle. *I wonder what would happen if I unpuddled now. Stop! Don't even think like that! I probably can't anyway because the Globe is more powerful than anything I can do. I hope...* She then heard the Wateruba Tuba, looked around and saw Jala, glowing a cinnamon brown. It had a pudgy, watery body, a long, long tentacle coming out of the top if its head, and big, bulgy eyes.

It's completely different to all the others, but they're somehow all the same! I love them! Miriam reached out; Jala reached out. They touched and Miriam just managed to get it into the WTS before they sped towards home.

"I ended up inside something that was kind of green and orange..." Miriam said, once she'd delivered Jala to Grammy.

"Inside a cactus," said Brad, looking at the photo replay on the computer. "I think it was a lava cactus."

"So-called because it grows on lava fields. The Galapagos Islands were formed from volcanoes," said Grammy.

"Cool!" said Brad.

Miriam interrupted them. "Whatever it was, I didn't unpuddle. I stayed water like I did in the bath."

"Too bad," said Grammy dreamily. "It's a shame you couldn't get out and walk around. You were in the Galapagos!" *What?! Grammy you know that's not how it works! I was there to get Jala, not sightsee!*

"She was inside a cactus, so that makes sense," said Brad. "Though, when you think about it, does being inside a cactus really make sense…?"

"It does if you're water," said Miriam.

"It's all so brain-bending!!" said Brad, rubbing his face and shaking his head. "It's awesome…"

"Thanks to the wisdom of the Globe, you didn't unpuddle in such a small space," added Grammy. *Yay, Globe!* "It seems that if you can be your normal size, as in a blizzard or a swamp, you will be. But if you need to be small, you stay puddled. It's beyond fascinating…"

"And we'll find out more, the more puddle-jumps I do," said Miriam. *Right, Mom?*

"That we will!" said Brad, writing it all in the Book of Experiments.

Miriam's other job was keeping Uncle Eddy happy. *Easier said than done.* Eddy was clearly curious about what was going on, and sensitive to being fobbed off. He was asking a lot of questions, like "Why does Freida need so many pipes? *That's fair. He was here when the pipes arrived and there were a lot of them.* Is she learning to be a plumber now?"

"She's a woman of many talents!" laughed Miriam. *But I assure you, plumbing isn't one of them!* Normally, she would have answered any question Uncle Eddy asked, but since Grammy had said she didn't trust him, Miriam was having a re-think. *He's coming over so often that Bunster's getting fat from all the doggy treats. He always wants to see what we're up to. I'm sure my excuses are making him suspicious. But his questions are making me suspicious… I wish I knew what was going on.* "We'll have to show him something," Miriam told Grammy and Brad. "Soon." So they decided to accept Eddy's latest attempt to invite himself for dinner. It was time to give him a tour of the laboratory.

The mystery person

IN Cairo, Samir was staring out the window, trying to figure out how to translate the complicated English sentence "He would have told the truth if he'd known it" into Egyptian Arabic – when he saw a familiar black car pull up outside the apartment building. Samir quickly stepped back from the window. He watched through the curtains as the mystery person got out, checked the address, and entered the building. This was the moment Samir had been dreading. He hid. The doorbell rang. Then the man knocked. Loudly. Samir stayed perfectly still. He could hear Azizi barking from Mr. Amin's apartment. The man eventually went away. But Samir knew that he wouldn't have gone far.

It was time to go. Samir wrote his father a note. "I have to leave. It's better if you don't know where I am. That way, you won't have to lie. Please don't worry about me." Fat chance. Of course his father would worry, but it would be a much bigger worry if that ARID person got hold of him. Samir packed his clothes into his bag and shoved it under the bed.

He put his shard of asteroid in a special hiding place in a corner of the room under a loose bit of the vinyl flooring. But how would he get away without the man seeing? Samir had seen enough movies to know he was probably being watched. Just then, he heard Mr. Amin call for Azizi. "Time for a walk!" An idea fizzed through Samir like an electric shock. He grabbed a piece of chicken from last night's dinner, ran into the hall, put it down outside Mr. Amin's door and puddled beside it, just as Mr. Amin and Azizi came out of the apartment.

Azizi smelled the chicken right away and gobbled it up, licking up the watery Samir.

Mr. Amin looked around and saw that the door to Samir's father's apartment was open. "Samir? Samir??" When he heard no answer, he shut the door. "I'm sure he's not far away, Azizi – he left the door open! We'll see him when we get back." He was right about one thing – Samir wasn't far away. He was going down Azizi's esophagus, heading towards his stomach. As Mr. Amin led Azizi down the stairs, little did he know that, for once, Samir was coming with them on their walk. Mr. Amin didn't notice the black car parked in front of their building until Azizi stopped to sniff a tire. Seeing someone sitting in the driver's seat, Mr. Amin quickly pulled the dog away.

Distraction, diversion, digression

THERE were now twenty two Waterubas circulating in the Wateroomba. *Twenty two down, fifty nine to go – including Vesi!* "How are we going to give Uncle Eddy a tour of the "laboratory" without him seeing what's actually in there?" asked Miriam.

"For one thing, we'll keep the lights up so he won't notice the Ruba glow," said Grammy.

"But what if he does?" said Miriam. *This whole thing makes me really nervous.* "If he sees a glow – or several glows – and says, 'What's that?', we can't all be standing there, looking fatuous, with our mouths hanging open. *Fatuous – my new favorite word. Right up there with indubitably.* We have to have a plan that doesn't involve lying. Indubitably."

"We use distraction, diversion, or digression!" said Brad. *What??* "It's what spies use." *I guess he'd know.*

"Tell us more," said Grammy. *A lot more!*

"I'd be happy to," Brad grinned. "Imagine we're in there and Eddy sees a Ruba glow or even a Wateruba and says, Freida? Miri? What is that glow? *He does a pretty good Eddy imitation, it has to be said.* We distract by going right up to the Wateruba he sees, pulling a plant out of the water and saying, 'You mean this? Oh, it's just a bit of limnobium laevugatum. Isn't it pretty?'"

"More plants in the water – genius, Brad!" said Grammy. "Even we sometimes have a hard time telling the difference between a plant and a Wateruba."

"OK…" said Miriam. "That's distraction. What about diversion?"

"Pretend I'm walking along with Uncle Eddy." Brad mimed

walking. Miriam got the giggles. *He's funny.* "'Hey, Uncle Eddy, how's it going?' I say, all friendly-like. I then see a Wateruba, but Eddy hasn't seen it yet. So I stop and point at the floor. 'Careful – you're about to step on the pipe that takes the saltwater into the desalination system.' So he looks down and by the time he looks up again, no more Wateruba! I diverted his attention!"

"That's funny because the pipes for the desalination system aren't on the ground." Miriam was still laughing.

"We know that," said Brad, "but Uncle Eddy doesn't."

"And digression?" asked Miriam. *This is actually pretty interesting – and it's hilarious!*

Brad fanned his hand in front of his nose. "'Oooh, is that your aftershave I'm smelling?' or 'Where did you get those dope shoes?' We digress to anything that has nothing to do with the laboratory or water."

Pop quiz! "OK, just to make sure I get this. What if he thinks he hears the Wateruba Tuba?" said Miriam. "Do distraction!"

"'What is that sound? Is it coming from the pump? That's no good – they advertised it as 'whisper-soft!'"

"Diversion?"

"'It's the refrigerator, isn't it?' And you take him into the kitchen."

"Digression?"

"'Want to see me and Miriam dance the rumba?' and then I start singing a rumba tune."

"I don't know the rumba!" laughed Miriam. *And neither do you!*

"Or I could say, 'What time is it?'" said Grammy, "then look at my watch and gasp. 'Sorry, but there's something I really need to hear live on the radio,' and then turn it on full volume."

"Better," said Miriam.

Do you know any sea shanties?

THEY were as prepared as they could be to wrangle Uncle Eddy's curiosity. *We're Eddy ready!*

He arrived on time *He's always on time* and brought Grammy a bottle of red wine. When she asked him if he wanted a glass, he said he'd wait until after the tour. "I can't wait to see what you've been doing!" he said, rubbing his hands together. *Is he rubbing his hands like a villain does or is he just excited? His face looks excited…*

They entered the 'laboratory' and Eddy took a deep breath and looked around. *There's Dribble, Krakey and Flooso! Plain as day!* But Eddy didn't seem to see them.

"My goal," Grammy explained, "was to create as many ecosystems as possible – still pond, lake, wetlands, riverbed, so that I can study…"

"Mmm-hmm," said Eddy. *Rude! He doesn't seem to be listening. Oh no! There's Smedley!* Brad noticed Miriam staring at Smedley, so he picked up a piece of limnobiam laeviatum. *Distraction!*

"And I've helped identify the plants you'd find in these systems," said Brad. *Good one, Brad!*

"Ah yes. Limnobiam laeviatum," said Eddy. "Nice…" He looked up at the ceiling. *OK, OK, here comes a question… NOT!* It was then that the Waterubas started to chant the Wateruba Tuba. *No! No! Shh shh! There's no way he won't hear that!* Brad then started to sing 'My Bonnie Lies Over the Ocean' as he pointed out the largest body of water Grammy had built.

Digression! Brilliant! "An ocean. Of course! Very good!" said Eddy.

"I even tried to replicate some of the ocean currents," said Grammy, flicking on a switch that moved the water around.

"Nice touch," said Eddy, then turned to Brad. "Mister, you have a beautiful voice. *That's the most enthusiastic he's been the entire time! And... 'Mister??'* Do you know any sea shanties? *What kind of question is that??* I've been wanting to add them to the soundscape we have at ARID in our ocean display." As Brad broke into 'You Can't Hold a Good Man Down': "I set to sea as a country lad to make a dream come true..." Eddy took one final look around. "Impressive lab, Freida," he said and left the room.

What just happened??? Miriam and Grammy looked at each other, totally bewildered, *She's as confused as I am* then followed Eddy and Brad into the kitchen. When they got there, Brad was still singing and Eddy was doing some kind of dance. *What is going on??*

"Is that the hornpipe?" asked Grammy.

"Sort of!" Eddy laughed. *Shifty bad guys don't do the hornpipe...do they?* "Pick up the tempo, please, Brad!"

Brad switched to a faster song. *How can he sing without laughing?* "Now try this!" said Grammy to Eddy. She joined him, expertly executing the steps. *I love watching Grammy dance!* "You and Ruth used to do this dance when you were little, remember?" Eddy tried to do a fancy step but fell over, laughing his head off. *This is more like it!*

So after all the preparation to be Eddy Ready, Uncle Eddy seemed to accept that this was a laboratory that Grammy had built for her water experiments, no questions asked. *Does he believe that or is that what he wants us to think he believes? Confusing.* After the hornpipe, the four of them had a lovely dinner. *This is almost like the happy times before the accident.* Eddy told funny stories about when Ruth was a little girl, and Grammy talked about Eddy's mother who'd been a good friend of hers. Eddy ate two helpings of dessert *Grammy's homemade blueberry cheese cake – mmm, so good!!*, and then left.

He thinks we're onto something

ONCE Eddy had gone, Miriam, Brad and Grammy went over the evening as they did the dishes. "The only question he asked was 'do you know any sea shanties?'," said Miriam, filling the sink with soapy water.

"After all the times he's tried to get in there to see what's going on, he didn't seem all that interested," said Brad. He started scrubbing one of the pans. *At camp, he couldn't scrub a pan to save his life. Now look at him!*

"Oh, he was interested, all right," said Grammy. "There was something almost professional about the way he was looking around, as if he were making assessments."

"Assessments," said Brad, thoughtfully scratching his head, forgetting that he was holding a scouring pad. "Ow. That's the kind of thing that teachers or people who sell you insurance make."

"Or someone from ARID who's up to no good," sighed Grammy. "I'm really not happy about feeling so suspicious, but I don't trust Eddy as far as I can throw him. I mean, Advanced Research in Innovative Demohydration... ?" She picked up a pencil that Eddy had left in the pencil can ages ago. It had the ARID logo on it. "Give me a break." She snapped the pencil in two. *Dramatic!* "Advanced Research in Making a Killing more like. In more ways than one." *Go, Grammy!*

"ARIMAK," said Brad. He picked up the lead-end of the broken pencil. "Hmmm – this is a good pencil for drawing... I'll ignore the ARID bit, don't worry."

"I believe he thinks we're onto something." Grammy closed the dishwasher and turned it on.

"Onto something?" said Miriam. "We're just two kids and a grandmother!"

"I know, but… he would've heard about Waterubas from Ruth for years, though I never got the impression he even remotely believed what she was saying. *You have to admit, the idea of Waterubas does sound insane.* But now I'm wondering if I was wrong. I remember Ruth once telling Bertram, Eddy's father, about the Waterubas. She was about eight years old and full of fantastic stories she'd made up about them, and he shut her down. Not by laughing and changing the subject. Oh no. He practically bit her head off. 'Don't be so ridiculous, young lady! You must never speak such nonsense!' He actually raised his voice and made Ruth cry. It was so over the top that Alisha, Eddy's mother, grabbed Bertram's arm and told him to calm down. That Ruth was just a child. I didn't think much of it at the time – Bertram was often mean, still is – but now, I'm not so sure there wasn't something more sinister behind it."

Sinister – good word. "Like what?" asked Miriam.

"Like maybe they know more than they're letting on?" asked Brad.

"Exactly," said Grammy.

"It really bothers me that we can't trust Uncle Eddy," said Miriam. "It makes me feel sad…"

"It makes me feel like I'm in a spy movie," said Brad. "I can't wait to find out what happens next."

Azizi pee

THEY didn't know yet what would happen next in Riverside, Illinois, but Samir knew what had happened next in Cairo, Egypt: Azizi had peed him out by a tree in a park, nowhere near the street and the black car. That wasn't the sort of thing that usually happened next, but Samir, like Miriam, wasn't having the kinds of experiences that usually happened at all, never mind next. Being spotted by Mr. Amir and Azizi was not what Samir wanted to happen next to him. Fortunately, he was one of the world's most experienced and proficient Puddlers, so he managed to hold off unpuddling until his friends had walked far enough away from the tree not to see him. Once he did unpuddle, he looked around – no one. Then, hoping he didn't smell too much like Azizi pee, he disappeared into the shadows.

People destined to meet will do so

AS much as Miriam loved Grammy and Brad and their unwavering involvement in the Wateruba project, she was lonely. Their experience was nothing like hers. How could it be? *They can't puddle, and I can. I really want to see that boy again. Another Puddler – imagine meeting another Puddler!* She knew that going back to where she'd found Dribble didn't mean she would miraculously run into the boy, of course. *But what is it that Grammy and Mom used to say? Emerson again: 'People destined to meet will do so, apparently by chance, at precisely the right moment.' I love that. I'm destined to see that boy again, I know it. But if not, at least I'll find another Wateruba. And maybe it will know where Vesi is…*

When Dribble saw Awa's light in the part of the Globe that was Egypt, Miriam decided that that was close enough to where she'd been before, even though it was, in fact, miles away. *Geography isn't one of my strengths.*

Brad photographed her route. "There's not a lot of rain in that part of the world, so it looks as if you'll be travelling more via rivers and streams. You may get caught in a fog net, which people put up to collect the fresh water that's in fog, *Clever!* but you go so fast you'll evaporate out before someone drinks you."

Miriam didn't care. She just wanted to try to find the boy, even if it was a longshot. She slowed her breathing, which was more difficult to do than usual because she was so excited. She let go of her worries and doubts and tried to be like water, by trusting everything, relaxing, thinking of her mother. "Awa!" she said to the Globe. When Awa's light flared, Miriam touched it and off she went.

156

The whoosh of two puddlers

AWA was in Lake Qarun, which was part of Fayoum oasis, in a quiet little inlet where boats were moored. There was an anchor sticking up out of the water, and Awa was floating right next to it.

As luck or destiny would have it, Samir was hiding in the bottom of one of the small boats moored in the lake. It was dusk and there were hardly any people around. He'd been on the run for days and he was exhausted.

Miriam arrived in the water near Awa, and this time, she unpuddled, which meant she could see where she was. *Thank you, Globe!* She slowly stood up in the shallow water and looked for the boy.
The chances are practically zero, but hey – if there's a right moment out there somewhere, why can't it be this one?
Because Samir and Miriam were, in fact, destined to meet, Miriam was near the boat where he was hiding. She didn't see him, but he saw her. "It's that girl!" he whispered. *What was that?* Miriam looked around. *Did I hear something?* The sun had set, so it was getting dark. No sign of a boy. *Guess not.* But she spotted Awa, floating near her on the surface of the water, waving. It had big eyes and long, droopy things that dangled from the side of its head.

Miriam reached out for it and puddled. When Samir, who hadn't taken his eyes off of her, saw this, he was absolutely amazed – and excited – and knew that he had to meet her. Someone else could do what he did! He quickly slid into the water and puddled. He was practically on top of her, but as she was focusing on what looked like some kind of plant, she didn't notice. Samir stayed as close to Miriam as he could without gliding into her. Then surprisingly, he found himself travelling at speed. He'd never gone so fast before – not even in a speeding car. Help! Where were they going? He had no idea. Why would he? He was simultaneously exhilarated and terrified. "What is happening???" he shouted, but the words were drowned out by the whoosh of two Puddlers puddle-jumping.

You're that boy from Egypt!

WHEN Miriam unpuddled back in the Wateroomba with Awa safely in the WTS, Grammy and Brad didn't even look up – not even to examine the latest Wateruba. *And it's amazing!* Miriam studied the tendrils that came out of Awa's head, which looked like ears. They were so long, they drooped down into its puddly body. Grammy was totally absorbed trying to see how Waterubas react to pollution. (Spoiler alert: They don't. It is what it is, and Waterubas never wish anything to be different than what is. Waterubas, like water, are easily polluted. Water is known as a "universal solvent" because it can dissolve more substances than any other liquid on earth. This is great when the substances are harmless – but water, and Waterubas, also dissolve and mix with toxic substances. Grammy, needless to say, was not polluting the Waterubas with toxic substances.)

Meanwhile, Brad was busy cataloguing all the Waterubas Miriam had found. They were up to 37 now. 38 with Awa! He wrote down name, Ruba color, where Miriam had found them, and any extra notes about that particular puddle jump. And he made drawings of each Wateruba using the top half of the ARID pencil that Grammy had broken. It was a particularly good pencil for sketching the differences between Waterubas – some had tentacles, some had big eyes, some had seaweedy appendages, some had bulbous bodies, etc. – even though they were all water.

As Grammy and Brad didn't notice that Miriam had returned, they also didn't see Samir, at least not right away. Samir was so flabbergasted about what had just happened, and bewildered by what he was seeing

Wateruba Names	Glow Color	Where we found them	Travel Notes
Lutine	Egyptian Blue	Miriams House Chicago	Grammy laughed and cried out a Wateruba in her tears
Dribble	Violet	Samirs House Egypt	Dribble was in the water barrel and Samir saw them but they flew into the clouds then turned into rain
Jala	Cinnamon	Islands near Ecuador	Miriam found Jala inside a cactus

© Brad

now, that it didn't even occur to him to hide. Besides, he was tired of hiding, and these people, as strange as they looked, didn't feel like the kind of people he needed to hide from. As if to prove the point, the boy went to put the pencil back behind his ear but missed and poked himself in the head. "Ow!" Not the move of a shady thug.

I can't believe they have no idea I'm back! "Ahem!" Miriam loudly cleared her throat. "I found Awa." She took the WTS off of its belt, and held it up for Grammy and Brad to see. Awa waved. They waved back, and then Miriam carefully poured the Wateruba into the water as far away from Grammy's experiment as possible. "Awa!!" cried all the Waterubas joyously, and, as usual, they started to do the Wateruba Tuba with Awa joining in.

Miriam quickly covered her ears to avoid puddling, but Samir didn't. "What is that sound?" he said, stunned. He looked down and saw his feet and legs turning into water without him doing anything to make it happen. What was going on? This was too much! "Awwww!!" he howled.

The Waterubas immediately stopped chanting. Samir stopped puddling. Grammy stopped polluting. Brad stopped drawing. Bunster started barking. Miriam, who still had her hands over her ears, had no idea what was happening until Brad tapped her on the head and pointed to Samir. She turned and gasped. "You're that boy from Egypt!" she said, baffled. "How did you get here?"

161

Where is here?

EVERYONE stared at Samir, and he stared back at them. Grammy was the first one to think of something useful to say. "Do you speak English?" she asked.

Samir nodded. "I am learning at school," he said. "I understand more than I can speak."

"I'm like that with German," said Brad. *Irrelevant!*

"How did you get here?" Miriam repeated the question.

"With you," said Samir. "I was hiding in a boat. And suddenly you were there. I saw you turn into water, so I did too – very close to you. Then something happened – we travelled so fast! And now we are here." He looked around. "Where is here?"

Miriam, Grammy and Brad all looked at each other. *Where to begin?*

Grammy picked up the tablet. "You're in Illinois, in the middle of the United States – in a place called Riverside. Here." She showed him where they were on a map. "Our nearest big city is Chicago, about 16 miles away."

"I have heard of Chicago," whispered Samir. *And I bet he's also thinking, 'HOW CAN I BE IN CHICAGO?!?!?'*

"And the Des Plaines River runs through the town, here," Grammy pointed. "And over here is the Brookfield Zoo."

"Zoo?" Samir stared at the map. Then he looked up and stared at them.

I can practically hear his brain whirring trying to make sense of this. Miriam approached him. "You and I can turn into water." She paused. "We're Puddlers."

162

"And it sounds like Puddlers can puddle-jump together," said Brad to Grammy.

"Still a hypothesis. More research required," said Grammy.

"Point taken," said Brad.

"Puddlers?" Samir gazed at Miriam, trying to understand. *Whir whir whir goes his brain.*

"PUDDLERS!!" cried the Waterubas from wherever they were in the Wateroomba. Samir saw them for the first time. McKibben and Krakey were in a cloud; Smedley, Amanzi and Doris tumbled down a waterfall; Flooso, Vasser, Burble and Ploop swirled in a river. Gurgle, Hydros, Jala and Tinkle drifted among the plants in the wetland area. Wherever he looked, there were Waterubas waving. A menagerie of watery creatures. His eyes widened. *I guess he's never seen a Wateruba before – or if he has, he didn't know what it was. As if puddling isn't hard enough to understand, let's add Waterubas!*

"Meet the Waterubas!" said Miriam. And once again, the Waterubas started to chant the Wateruba Tuba. "Cover your ears!" cried Miriam, as she covered hers. Samir did as she said. *He looks both freaked out and delighted. I can't believe there's another Puddler standing right there... RIGHT THERE!*

Brad gave Miriam the nod when the Waterubas stopped chanting. She took her hands away from her ears and indicated to Samir that he could do the same. "We've got a lot to tell you. What's your name?"

"Samir," said Samir.

"I'm Miriam," said Miriam.

"Miriam," said Samir.

"I'm Brad," said Brad.

"Brad," repeated Samir.

"And I'm Freida," said Grammy.

"She's my grandmother," said Miriam.

"Grandmother," said Samir.

"Now, before we go any further," said Grammy, "let's get you something to eat." She handed the Asteruba to Miriam. "Put that somewhere safe." *Yes, ma'am!* Then she ushered everyone out of the Wateroomba and into the kitchen. "If Samir's been hiding in a boat, he's got to be starving!"

While Brad helped Grammy pull together a meal of rice and vegetables with tomato sauce – she even made hummus from scratch thanks to a couple cans of chickpeas she found after she remembered there was pita bread in the freezer – Miriam showed Samir Albert's room, where he'd be staying, and the bathroom. Bunster followed them. "I love dogs," Samir said without smiling. *Normally people smile when they say things like 'I love dogs.' I'm smiling like a fatuous fool, but nothing back from him. He's so serious!*

"And it looks like Bunster loves you, too!" said Miriam. *Me still fatuous... Him still nothing.* Then she showed Samir Grammy's room and Jeff and Erik's room where Brad was staying. He said nothing else until she took him into her room and put the gently glowing Asteruba down on its table next to her bed.

"I have a piece of rock like that. It is flat, but it glows."

"That's right," said Miriam. "And when you first touched it, is that when you turned into water?"

"Yes," whispered Samir, staring at Miriam. *I bet I'm the first person he's met who understands what happened to him.*

"As I said, we're Puddlers," said Miriam.

Arid actually lives nearby

IT was a good thing Grammy thought to offer Samir food – he was famished, just as she'd guessed. He ate three helpings of rice and vegetables, most of the hummus and several flats of pita bread. During the meal, Grammy, Miriam and Brad talked about the James Webb telescope and about how Brad's grandfather had moved to a monastery ten years ago to become a monk after he'd left the CIA, *What?! Note to self: Find out more about Brad's grandfather!* and the fact that Miriam's old friend, Lenita, had just won a national spelling contest. *Of course she did. She's the only kid at school who can spell 'chiaroscurist.'* Anything, as long as it had nothing to do with Waterubas or puddling. Brad asked Samir about the lovely old watch he was wearing. "It's a really good one!" said Brad. *I guess he knows about watches.* Samir stopped eating long enough to say that his father gave it to him. *Samir clearly needs to eat, not talk. I've never seen anyone concentrate so hard on putting food in his mouth!*

When everyone was finished, Samir thanked Grammy and cleared the table. *Good manners.* Then Brad took over doing the dishes so that Miriam could bring Samir up to speed. She began by telling him about the day not so long ago *Has it only been two weeks?* when she'd seen a Wateruba in the sink. Samir said nothing until she got to the first time she'd puddle-jumped to get out of Steve's office.

"So that <u>was</u> you in our water barrel, right?"

"Right," said Miriam. "I hid, but I knew you'd seen me."

"Yes, I saw you," said Samir, smiling. *Yay! A smile!*

"Well, I got there because of Dribble. It was Dribble's light I touched on the Globe."

"Dribble, Dribble, Dribble…" Brad flipped through the pages of the Wateruba book he was making until he got to the drawing of Dribble. "Dribble's got fingers on its paddles, and these long… hang on, this isn't quite right yet…" He took the pencil out from behind his ear and added a watery finger – and that was when Samir noticed the ARID logo.

"ARID?" he gasped, pushing his chair away from the table. Bunster, who'd planted himself on Samir's lap, yelped as Samir stood up, dumping him on the floor. He faced them. "Are you from ARID?" He started to breathe heavily. *He's scared!*

"No, no, no, no, no, no, no, no, no!" said Grammy, alarmed. "Please, sit. Calm down, my love. We're not from ARID. We're your friends. I promise you. What do you know about ARID anyway?"

Samir pulled out the card that the mystery person had given him. "Where did you get this?" asked Grammy.

Now it was Samir's turn to bring them up to speed. His story finished when he puddle-jumped with Miriam and landed in the Wateroomba. "At least the mystery man can't find me here," he said.

"Yes, well…" said Grammy. *I feel sick.* "You're safe here from the person who tried to kidnap you in Egypt, but you're not safe from ARID. I hate to tell you this, but ARID actually lives nearby." Samir said nothing, so she continued. "A man and his father live here in Riverside. The father, Bertram Calhoun, heads up ARID. His son, Eddy, is also part of it. It's complicated because I've known Eddy since he was a boy. He's an old friend of my daughter, Ruth – Miriam's mother."

"Is he the man who was there when she had her accident?" asked Samir. Miriam nodded. *He did not say "died." I like him.*

"Eddy never paid any attention to the work I do until I wrote this little piece about you," continued Grammy. She showed him the article on the tablet.

Samir nodded. "Yes, my teacher showed this to me. You wrote it?!"

"It was only a short report," said Grammy. "I wasn't allowed to do any kind of research. The magazine didn't have the money to send me to Egypt…"

"But that article has a picture of Samir, so Eddy will know what he looks like," said Brad. He looked at Samir and smiled. "You get to be another secret we have to keep." *He said that as if Samir should be thrilled.*

"Sorry," said Samir.

"It's not your fault!" said Miriam. "We're so glad you're here. But how <u>are</u> we going to keep all these secrets? Uncle Eddy just drops in. It's almost like he's trying to catch us out."

"There's nothing 'almost' about it. He's definitely trying to catch us out," said Grammy.

"What does he think of the Waterubas?" asked Samir.

"He seems to believe my story that the Wateroomba is a laboratory for my water experiments," said Grammy. "He apparently knows nothing about the Waterubas."

Samir shook his head. "Not true." *Snap.*

Treats for Bunster

AS if on cue, the doorbell rang. "Anybody home? I forgot my key!" Eddy called from outside. Bunster barked and ran to get his treat.

"He knows damn well we're home," muttered Grammy. *Grammy! Language!* She quickly gathered up Brad's drawings. "Brad, quick! Take Samir upstairs. And be very, very quiet. I'll tell Eddy that you're off seeing your nan." She pulled an old picture of Eleanor out from under one of the fridge magnets and handed it to Brad. "Here's a picture of her that you can look at so I'm not technically lying."

I guess that works—! "Clever," said Brad. "Nice picture, too." He put it with the drawings.

"Miriam – let Eddy in, but take your time!"

Miriam called out, "Coming, Uncle Eddy!" then stepped out of the way as Samir leaned past her to grab the ARID card he'd left on the table. *He smells like the beach.* The boys scurried out of the kitchen and ran up the stairs. For once, Brad didn't trip. Miriam was impressed by Samir's agility. *He's used to running.* Miriam picked up the over-excited Bunster and answered the front door. "Uncle Eddy! No key? I hope you haven't lost it."

"No, no, no," said Eddy. "I'm pretty sure I left it at the office. I've been working from home. Here you go, Bunster!" He reached into his pocket and pulled out a doggy treat. Miriam put Bunster down to let him chew in peace and followed Eddy into the kitchen. "Freida!" he said. "Could I be brazen and ask for a cup of your excellent coffee? It's already been a long day, and I've been dreaming of a mug of Freida-coffee for hours."

"No problem!" said Grammy, pressing a button on the coffee grinder.

"SO WHERE'S BRAD?" Eddy shouted over the noise.

"He's seeing his nan today." *In a photograph, but still true!*

Miriam turned to Grammy. "What time's he supposed to be back?"

"Not sure," said Grammy, pouring hot water over the coffee grounds. "Soonish."

Oooh. We are good! "Then I'd better get back to cleaning out my drawers. It's useless doing it while he's around because he keeps asking if I'm sure I want to keep this or how could I possibly throw that out. Annoying!" She left the kitchen and went upstairs to find Brad and Samir crouched on the floor in her room, listening to the conversation in the kitchen through the vent. Brad picked up an old hat that she'd left on the floor.

"Are you sure you want to keep this?" he whispered.

"Ha-ha," Miriam whispered back. *Annoying!*

Samir put his finger to his lips to shhhush them and drew their attention back to the muffled words coming up through the vent. *Intense.*

"I was wondering if you guys would like a tour of ARID," Eddy was saying to Grammy. *Did not see that coming.* "I thought with all your creative research on water, you might want to see what we're doing these days." *You mean we might like to see what you want us to see. What about the part where you kidnap Puddlers?* Grammy must've handed the coffee to Eddy because they heard him loudly breathing in the aroma. "Mmmm, proper coffee…"

"Nothing but the best!" said Grammy. *She sounds like a commercial.*

"So what exactly is the research you're doing now, if you don't mind me asking?" Eddy slurped a mouthful of coffee.

Miriam looked at Brad. *We know she absolutely does mind you asking!*

"I'm researching how various pollutants move through different eco-systems," said Grammy. Brad smiled and mouthed the word 'perfect.' *I want to be like her when I grow up.* Samir continued to listen intently.

"We've got several projects like that on the go, if you're interested," said Eddy.

"He lies," whispered Samir. "I know from his voice."

"They're not researching pollution?" whispered Brad. Samir shook his head.

Then Eddy suddenly changed the subject. "I noticed when I was last here that you've replaced some floorboards. Were they rotting?"

"Exactly," said Grammy. "They're old boards, and I figured it was better to replace them than face a huge insurance claim one day when someone breaks a leg."

"I hear you," said Eddy. "When they took the old boards out, did you get a look at what's underneath? Are there pipes? Being a water man, I'm always interested in how the plumbing works in old houses like this, and it's not often you get to see behind the scenes, as it were."

"That is why he came," whispered Samir.

"I don't get it," said Brad. Legs stiff from crouching, he shifted his position and in the process knocked over a little table Miriam had with pictures of her mom on it. CRASH! *Brad!!*

"What was that?" said Eddy. Then they heard him calling up the stairs. "Miri? Are you all right?"

Miriam grabbed one of the pictures that now had a broken frame, and ran out the door. "I'm fine! I just put too many things on one of my tables." She went downstairs with the picture. *I'm sad about this but not sad enough to cry, but I'll pretend. Distraction!* "Look what happened," she said, showing the picture to Eddy.

"Aww, Miri," said Eddy. "Don't cry." *It worked. I'll sniff for effect.*

Grammy came out of the kitchen, took the picture and examined the frame. "Don't worry, sweetie, I can fix this with some glue," she said.

"Thanks, Grammy. *Another sniff.* I love this picture. Can we fix it now?" *Then maybe Uncle Eddy will leave.*

"Of course," said Grammy, pushing past Eddy to open a drawer in the small table near the door. "The last time I saw the glue it was in here… I think…"

"Well, I'd better love you and leave you," said Eddy, taking the hint. "Thanks for the coffee – and think about my invitation for a tour. Bring Miriam and Brad – come into the city – make a day of it!"

"It could be fun," said Grammy. She held up a tube of glue. "Ah, here it is!" She opened the door. "I'll let you know." *Wow. Just this side of rude.*

"I'll call you when I get to the office," Eddy said as Grammy closed the door behind him.

That's no doggy treat

MIRIAM went into the kitchen and called up towards the vent. "Coast is clear!" She noticed that Bunster was still busy chewing. "Uncle Eddy gave you an extra-chewy treat this time, eh Bunster?" She reached down to pet him, just as the thing he was gnawing fell out of his mouth. *Wait a minute… that's no doggy treat.* Miriam picked up the chewed whatever-it-was as Brad, Samir and Grammy came back into the kitchen. "Bunster was chewing on this. Uncle Eddy gave it to him. What do you think it is?" She took the glue and broken frame from Grammy and dropped the blob covered in Bunster-spit in Grammy's hand.

Grammy peered at it. "It's no doggy treat…"

"That's what I thought," said Miriam.

Then Brad picked it out of Grammy's hand with his thumb and forefinger and held it up for a look. "You guys… it's a microphone. It looks pretty destroyed, but just to be safe…" Brad placed the mangled microphone on a chopping board, opened a few drawers until he found a rolling pin, smashed the microphone with the rolling pin, then picked it up and dropped it in a glass of water. "Better."

Grammy stared into the glass of water. "So do you really think Eddy is trying to bug us?" *No!*

"Not anymore," snorted Brad.

"Definitely," said Samir.

"You can't say that!" said Miriam. *I don't know why but that really makes me angry!* "You don't know him." Samir flinched. *Oh no. I hurt his feelings. But he has no right to say anything about Uncle Eddy.*

"Miriam, let's find out what Samir is thinking," said Grammy gently. *She's right. That wasn't fair. Rein in the anger, Miriam.* Grammy turned to Samir. "Samir, why do you say that?"

"It is his voice," explained Samir. "He says one thing but he means another thing. Just like the person who tried to kidnap me." *Interesting... but why would Eddy lie?*

"I'm sorry I yelled at you, Samir," said Miriam and he nodded. "I'm just really hating thinking of Uncle Eddy as a bad guy." Samir nodded again.

"Of course you are, but think of all the things that have changed recently," said Grammy. "We know Waterubas are real; you can turn into water; you can travel around the Earth as water; you met Samir; Eddy's a bad guy... all part of the 'new normal'!" *I guess so...*

"Do you think he came over today to plant that thing?" asked Brad. "This is getting more like a spy movie every minute!"

"Definitely," said Samir. "He also asked about the plumbing. Maybe he thinks it is a way of getting into the Wateroomba?" *Samir's not wrong. We all heard him ask Grammy about it. This just keeps getting worse and worse!*

Grammy started to laugh. "As discombobulating as it is to think Eddy is trying to bug us, it's hilarious that he put the microphone in his pocket with the doggy treats and accidentally gave it to Bunster!" When Bunster heard his name, he barked and Grammy went to get the biscuit jar to give him a proper treat. She couldn't stop laughing. "If he came to plant it, he must be wondering what happened to it. Eddy makes a terrible spy!"

"Do not underestimate him," said Samir. Grammy stopped laughing. *Ominous.*

Just then, Grammy's phone rang. "It's Eddy," she said.

"If he's calling about the invitation to tour ARID, let's go," said Brad. "I'd like to make some assessments."

"Bad idea," said Miriam.

"No, good idea," said Samir. Miriam just stared at him. *Really? Why?*

Grammy shushed them and tapped the phone. "Hello, Eddy! Did you find your key?"

While she talked to Eddy, Miriam signaled for Samir to follow her out of the kitchen into the hall and into the living room. Brad came, too. "Why do you think it's a good idea?" Miriam asked.

"He wants you all to leave the house," said Samir. *I hadn't thought of that.* "If you go on a tour, he will know where you are. *Maybe he's trying to lure us away. I really don't like this.* But he does not know about me. I will be here if something happens."

"Genius!" said Brad.

"You're right, Samir. Good idea." *Glad we figured that out!*

Grammy came out of the kitchen. "I've organized the tour of ARID for tomorrow."

Brad then excitedly told her about how Samir would stay behind so he could "spy on the spy…!" *I wonder if Samir is as happy about this as Brad is…*

"That's all very well," said Grammy, "but if something does happen with ARID, we can't just leave Samir here to deal with it on his own."

"You're right," said Brad. "I'll stay behind with Samir tomorrow." *Oh, no no. Not an option.*

"What about your assessments?" asked Miriam. *There's no way he's staying behind with Samir. It would be like leaving a rhinoceros in the school cafeteria.*

"You and your grandmother can do those," said Brad. "All the real spy work will be happening here."

"Uh-huh. And what about how bad you are at hiding and/or being quiet? What about knocking over the table upstairs?"

"I don't know what you're talking about," said Brad, indignantly throwing himself into a chair, which he missed, landing on the floor. "OW!"

Miriam laughed. Grammy tried not to. "Are you all right, m'love?"

Samir helped Brad up. "It is better if I stay here alone," he said.

"Agreed," sighed Brad. "I don't know who moved that chair, but it's NOT FUNNY!" *Yes it is!*

"But we still need a plan," said Miriam. *Grammy's right. We can't just leave Samir here all by himself.* "Let's say that someone from ARID comes here to poke around. How's Samir supposed to stop them?"

"Well, we could booby trap the kitchen," said Brad. *Really? You call that a plan?*

"What do you mean exactly?" asked Grammy. *Diplomatic.*

"We could rig it up so that when someone walks through the door on the way to the Wateroomba, a frying pan would come flying through the air…"

"So it would be a flying pan," said Miriam. *Couldn't help it.*

"Yes, OK…" said Brad. "And it would brain whoever's come into the room."

"Knocking them out?" asked Grammy.

"Obviously," said Brad.

"Then Samir would be stuck with an unconscious ARID operative." *Call me crazy but how is this a plan?*

"OK, OK, I'm not finished yet." Brad started to pace, banging his knee on the coffee table. "Ouch." He inspected his leg. "Didn't break the skin. Good. Where was I? *Exactly nowhere.* I know. What if we get Samir a burner phone…" *What is this – a cop drama on TV?*

"A burner phone?" asked Samir.

"A burner phone is a cheap pre-paid phone that we can get rid of when we're finished," explained Grammy. Samir nodded. "Go on, Brad." *She's acting as if this might actually be a plan!*

"And we program the phone so that Samir can send us a message if someone comes," finished Brad. *He's clearly proud of himself.*

"The thing is," said Grammy, "we'll be in the city, and it would take us a good 45 minutes to get home, and that's after we catch a train…"

"Good point," said Brad. *Of course it is.* He paced some more. This time he hit the coffee table with his other knee. "Ouch." He rubbed his leg. "I know! Samir can send a message to my nan!" *To your nan?!?*

"Yes yes yes…" said Grammy, warming to this idea. "She just lives minutes away." *True.*

"And if we ask her to drop whatever she's doing if she gets a text message from Samir and to get over here to start banging on the door to find out what's going on, to take photos of any vehicle, to threaten to call the police…" said Brad, clearly excited.

"That would scare anyone off!" agreed Grammy.

Actually, this could work. "Would she do that?" asked Miriam.

"Guaranteed," said Brad. "Even though Gramps now lives in a monastery, she's still married to him, and she was with him the whole time he was in the CIA. I secretly think she misses the intrigue…"

"Then Samir would have back-up." Grammy turned to Samir. "What do you think?"

"Sounds good," said Samir.

Tour
of Arid

SO Grammy got a burner phone and Brad programmed in his nan's number so Samir could send a text. Brad even wrote it – it just said "Now" – so that all Samir had to do was push the send button.

Grammy talked to Eleanor, telling her that she was sponsoring a young immigrant who was waiting for paperwork, but who was being hounded by some anti-immigration protestors, would Eleanor mind helping out? *It's not strictly true, but we can't tell her about the Waterubas and ARID, can we?* As Brad predicted, Eleanor was on it. No questions asked except "What do you want me to do?" *I like Brad's nan almost as much as I like Brad!*

Meanwhile, Brad insisted on booby-trapping the kitchen. *He's the booby. Sorry, but it had to be said.* The main feature of this trap was the flying pan. In setting it up, Brad himself got bonked on the head a number of times, but to him that just meant that it worked. *No comment.*

Before Grammy, Brad and Miriam left for the city to tour ARID, they made sure Samir was comfortable – mainly that he had enough food. *Grammy does not want him to be hungry. She also doesn't want him to go into the kitchen and get hit by a pan.*

Grammy checked that the Wateroomba was working properly – the pumps all pumping, the heat lamps heating, the timers timing, etc., etc. Miriam walked around the house carrying the Asteruba, trying to find the best place to put it, and ended up hiding it deep in a closet. No one thought that ARID would have time to rifle through drawers and closets with Eleanor pounding on the door, but who knew? "Even if they see the asteroid," said Brad, "to them it's just a rock."

True. "But as you've said yourself, better safe than sorry," said Miriam, and Brad gave her the thumbs up. She then went into the Wateroomba to wave goodbye to the Waterubas. *I can't really see them, but I know they're here. I can feel them!* "See-ee-ee you when we see-ee you-ooo!" called McKibben, waving as it swirled around and around in a whirlpool.

Finally, Brad set his trap, and they left the house, triple-locking the door. "Eddy officially has one key so he can get in when we're home. I've triple-locked, so if someone gets in, we'll know that Eddy somehow has all the keys," said Grammy.

"Or that they brought a locksmith along to jimmy the locks," said Brad.

"Good point," agreed Grammy. "Did you learn this kind of stuff from your grandfather?" Brad smiled and narrowed his eyes. *He's trying to look mysterious.* "I couldn't possibly say…" *Meaning 'yes.'*

They were going to leave keys with Samir in case he had to get out, but he said he'd puddle to escape if he needed to. *How does that work?? I really need to talk to him about puddling!* Grammy, Brad and Miriam took the train from their quiet suburb into the city *I love the train! I love the city! It's been ages since I've been here!* and arrived at ARID's impressive building a little early, giving them time to look at the window displays, publicizing their mission to demohydrate humanity. And there were big signs. "We know where the water is." *Do you?* "Water is for everyone." *Duh.* "We make life flow smoothly." *Pa-leeze.*

"The dioramas are pretty cool," admitted Brad.

"But 'demohydrate' is not a word," muttered Grammy. "I can't believe I've never been here before, considering all the years I've known the Calhoun family…"

I just want to get this over with. I'm not happy we had to leave Samir on his own. It's my fault he's even in Riverside. "Shall we go in?" said Miriam, pushing through the revolving door. It opened with a watery swishing sound effect, like waves on a beach. *This is almost like a theme park…*

"Nice touch," said Brad.

They signed in with the receptionist. "Mr. Calhoun is on his way down." She suggested they look around while they waited. And there was a lot to look at. *Not so much a theme park as an interactive museum...* They roamed from display to display, each with its own soundscape, showing how ARID was digging wells, how ARID was building desalination plants, how ARID was cleaning up the ocean, how ARID was re-instating wetlands, how ARID was 'getting water to everyone.'

"Yes, but can ARID make a decent cup of coffee?" muttered Grammy.

"No," said Eddy, who had arrived just in time to hear the question. "But we make sure the coffee farmers have the water they need to grow the beans. It takes 18,900 liters of water to produce 1 kg of beans."

"What? That's about 80,000 cups of water," said Brad. *How how how does he know this stuff??* "How many cups of coffee can you make with one kilogram of beans?"

"Between 120 to 140," said Eddy.

"Let's say 140 – which means it takes over 570 cups of water to make one cup of coffee," said Brad. *And he did all that in his head. Really quickly!*

"I'm impressed," said Eddy. "One day, you too could work for ARID!" Eddy laughed, but Brad didn't, which confused Eddy, so Grammy jumped in.

"It's probably way more than 570 cups because you're not counting the water it takes to harvest the beans, package them, fly them around. I almost wish I didn't love coffee so much..."

"We use water for everything," said Eddy. *And by "we" you mean humans. What about plants and animals?!* "It's the most amazing substance... *Particularly when it's filled with Waterubas!* Which is exactly why ARID is so important. *Is ARID really important or do you just say it is?* We can protect and distribute all this water, but we don't have the talent to make coffee that tastes good, no matter how pure the water is."

OK! Let's get this show on the road. "So when do we start the tour?" asked Miriam.

Eddy looked at his watch. "Are you in a hurry?"

Yes. "No. I just want to see this place I've heard so much about all my life!"

Eddy put his arm around Miriam to lead everyone into the first part of the tour. "Speaking of something you've heard about all your life, do you remember your mom talking about… what did she call them? *Nice fake.* Waterubas?"

Miriam tensed. *Organize your face so you don't look suspicious.* "Of course!" said Miriam, organizing her face so she didn't look suspicious. "She told me and Albert and Jeff and Erik stories about them and even drew pictures. The boys weren't that interested, but I was."

"Me, too," said Eddy. *I bet you were.* "My favorite story is the one where Freida actually saw one when she was young. *He is definitely trying to find something out. Maybe he's guessed we found his microphone.* What exactly did she see?"

"By 'she' do you mean me?" asked Grammy, having heard her name. *Help!!*

"Uncle Eddy asked me what you saw when you thought you'd seen a Wateruba," said Miriam.

Grammy chuckled. *Nice touch.* "The story about how I thought I saw one was Ruth's favorite. She also loved the stories about the city of trairies in the back garden," said Grammy. "Trairies are a combination of trolls and fairies. Very rare." She looked right at Eddy. "I see things, you know."

Things like what he's up to. Eddy laughed. *I think she makes him nervous. Good.* "Well, let's see what's behind this door!"

Eddy showed them the areas of the building that were open to the public, "to raise awareness of how important water is." Brad asked a lot of questions; Grammy barely said a word, except occasionally mumbling things like "Nonsense" or "I don't think so" or "pull the

180

other one" or "demohydration is not a word." Miriam noticed that Eddy kept an eye on the time and wondered if it had anything to do with what might be happening back at Grammy's house. Whenever it seemed the tour was finished, *What else can he show us??* Eddy suddenly remembered something he wanted to demonstrate or a person he wanted them to meet. *I bet he's keeping us here so that whatever's happening at our house has enough time to happen. At least that's what he thinks. He doesn't know anything about Samir or Brad's nan, of course.*

At one point, Eddy even took them up to his father's office. "I'm sure he'll want to say hello," he said.

As they approached the executive wing, they could hear someone bellowing, "I don't care what you have to do, get me the power I need!"

"That's Bertram," Grammy whispered to Miriam. *Terrifying...*

Then a door opened, and a man backed out of the office. "Yes, Mr. Calhoun. Right away, Mr. Calhoun."

"NOW!!" His face contorted with fury, Bertram Calhoun appeared at the door, and slammed it.

"I think we'd better come back another time," said Eddy. *He's embarrassed. And scared. I don't blame him.*

Drain the system

BACK at Grammy's house: soon after Grammy, Miriam and Brad had left, Samir decided to do a little research. He'd noticed that there were photographs on the bookshelves in the living room. He took the blueberry muffin that Grammy had left for him and went to have a look. There were pictures of Miriam with her three brothers. And pictures of Miriam and her brothers with their parents. And there was a really nice photo of Miriam with her mom. "They look alike," Samir whispered to himself.

Then he heard a car drive up. This was it – the moment he'd been waiting for. Samir rushed out of the room and crouched in the shadows on the way up the stairs. He'd already decided this was the best place to be in order to see and hear without being seen or heard himself. And if anyone turned on a light, he'd puddle. He'd had a lot of practice hiding, and he was very good at being quiet. Thanks to the muffin, he knew his stomach wouldn't rumble. He heard a key go into a lock and then some scraping and fiddling until all three locks were open. Brad was right. They'd brought a locksmith. He reached for the phone to send the text as planned… but no phone! Oh no! Where was it? Samir patted all his pockets, then saw it sitting on the bookshelf near the photos – where he'd left it. He felt sick. He was about to run to get it when the front door opened. Quickly retreating into the shadows, Samir hunkered down to watch as two men in hazmat suits walked into the house. They were each pushing a water tank on wheels with tubes attached. Trying not to cry with frustration – how could he have been so stupid?? – Samir made himself as small as possible.

The men seemed to know exactly where they were going, expertly briefed by Eddy, no doubt – which meant they headed straight for the Wateroomba without even glancing up the stairs.

The men approached the kitchen door. "Duck!" one of them cried as he opened it, and the flying pan soared towards their heads.

"Is this their version of a burglar alarm, or were they expecting us?" laughed the other. "We better get a move on. This way!" They quickly pushed their tanks into the Wateroomba.

"Drain the system!" Samir heard water gushing into a tank. Making sure the men weren't looking, he flitted back across the hall into the living room. As more water sounds came from the Wateroomba, he grabbed the phone and was just about to send the text when the men hurried back through the hall, pushing the tanks past the stairs. Samir ducked behind a chair. As they headed out the door, he heard the Wateruba Tuba echoing from one of the tanks. It wasn't loud enough to make him puddle, but when the men heard it, they stopped and took off their hoods. "Don't tell the boss, but I love that sound," said one.

"So relaxing," agreed the other, yawning. "I wonder where it comes from…"

"Let's go before we fall asleep!" They pushed the tanks out the door and closed it. Samir put the phone in his pocket. It was too late.

That means they got 31

WHEN Miriam, Grammy and Brad eventually got home, Samir was sitting on the floor in the Wateroomba. "Samir, are you all right?" Miriam knelt down beside him.

"Not really," said Samir. "I went to look at the pictures of your family, and left the phone on the bookshelf. So stupid! When the men came, I could not keep to the plan. The Waterubas are gone."

"Gone?? All of them??" *I can't believe it!*

"It's not stupid, Samir," said Grammy. "These things happen."

"They happen to me all the time," said Brad.

Miriam looked around. *This is terrible!* "They can't have got all of them. Krakey? Lutine? Flooso?" she called. Silence. No sign of them.

"No, wait! Last night I took Krakey, Lutine and Flooso upstairs!" said Grammy. When everyone looked at her, *You did what!??* she explained that she couldn't sleep. She'd been worried about Samir. So she took the Waterubas up to chant the Wateruba Tuba so she could relax. "Next thing I knew, it was morning! Forgot all about it 'til now."

Miriam ran up to Grammy's bedroom. The glass of water was still next to her bed, covered. She looked in, and Krakey, Lutine and Flooso appeared – first Krakey's head, Flooso's ears and Lutine's seaweedy tentacles, soon followed by the rest of their watery bodies. They waved. *Thank goodness!* Miriam waved back. She called downstairs, "They're still here!" She took the glass back to the kitchen. "So they didn't get all the Waterubas."

"Let's hear if there are any others around," said Brad. He turned to Miriam and Samir. "Puddlers? Cover your ears, please. Wateroooo-ooooo-ooooo…" He started off the Wateruba Tuba, and Krakey, Lutine and Flooso quickly joined in – and so did Awa and McKibben.

"Two more!" said Grammy, pointing at a cloud.

"What about the freezer?" *I bet those ARID guys didn't think to look in there.* Miriam opened up the freezer and found the special Wateruba ice tray that Brad had made. She could just make out two shapes in their ice cubes, gently glowing. *Hurrah.* "Nope! They didn't get Fishman or Pirta!"

"We have seven Waterubas here, so that means they got 31," said Brad. *Getting one was too many.* "And if you're interested, I can look in my Waterubas log to tell you exactly which ones." Brad holds up a notebook with a log drawn on the front of it. *Very funny.*

"I'm so sorry," said Samir. *He looks as if he's going to cry.*

"Samir! None of this is your fault!" said Grammy, handing him a glass of water and a muffin. "Take a few deep breaths and tell us what happened."

"Did anyone get hit by the pan?" asked Brad.

"Almost, but…" Samir smiled and shook his head. *Oh good. He's smiling.*

When Samir told them about the tanks and all the water sounds, Grammy said, "They drained the system, then replaced the water."

"Maybe that's so we wouldn't notice right away," said Miriam.

"To give them time to take the Waterubas wherever they've taken them," said Brad. "They're probably still driving down the highway now." His face lit up. "Should we chase them? Every good spy film needs a high-speed chase!" *Except this one. Down, boy!*

"No need," said Samir. "We will know where the Waterubas are because of the Globe."

"They didn't go upstairs, right?" said Miriam. Samir shook his head. "So the Asteruba will still be there."

"One more thing I can say is that when the men heard the Wateruba Tuba they said how much they liked it. They even took off their hoods to listen. It made them sleepy. That sound relaxes everyone, not just Puddlers."

"I could've told you that," said Brad.

"Why do you think I took three of them up to sing me to sleep?" said Grammy. Then she asked about the hoods. "So they were wearing hazmat suits… Hmmmm…" *What's she thinking?*

"They also said, 'I wonder where it comes from.'"

"Really?" said Grammy.

"So they don't know Waterubas make that sound…" said Brad. *Why would they? The idea of a Wateruba is weird enough, but the Wateruba Tuba??*

"From the way they've been chasing Samir, they know something about Puddlers," said Grammy, "but they don't seem to know much about Waterubas."

"And since the Asteruba was in your cupboard for years, they won't know about the Globe," said Miriam.

"If they're wearing hazmat suits," said Grammy, "they're thinking 'dangerous space aliens' rather than 'life-enhancing joy buckets'. *Life-enhancing joy buckets' – I love that!* Why do they want them? What do they even think they are?"

Grammy suggested that Miriam and Brad put the remaining Waterubas, including the two that were in the freezer, back in the aquarium, and put it on the kitchen table. "That'll give me time to purify the water in the Wateroomba – just in case – plus it means the Waterubas will be able to join in the conversation." She also suggested that they get rid of the burner phone.

"Good idea," said Brad, breaking it up to take out the SIM card. "We don't want anyone getting their hands on Nan's number."

I wish we didn't have to think like this! Miriam looked into the aquarium to see the Waterubas floating, drifting, and gliding, except for Fishman and Pirta who were bobbing at the top, still frozen. *Water is so weird.*

Ice is solid, but it floats. "They look so peaceful," she said. "Why would they want to hear about the bad stuff going on?"

"Hey, Puddler!" said Krakey, and they all waved (except for Fishman and Pirta who were still ice).

"How is stuff 'ba-a-ad'?" said McKibben.

"Isn't it just stuff?" asked Flooso.

"You keep saying 'bad.' What is 'bad'? What does that mean?" asked Awa.

Waterubas really are different from us... "We are and we aren't," said Krakey. Miriam looked at it. *Can you really hear what I'm thinking?!?* But all she could see was a bumblebee yellow glow.

Please give this message to Mr Fouad

IT was clear that Samir wouldn't be going home anytime soon. He insisted on staying to help. *He knows there's too much to do and too much for me to learn before I can do any of it.* Grammy, though, wanted to let his family know he was OK. But how? Since ARID knew where Samir's family lived, both in the country and in Cairo, Samir was assuming that they'd be watching both places, possibly even monitoring communications. That was why he couldn't even send an email. "If I send a message from here, they will know where I am," he said.

"Not if you use a VPN," says Brad. "We can make it look like you're anywhere in the world. *Smart.* But what should the message be?" *Good question.*

"We just need to let your mother know that you're safe," said Grammy.

Samir shook his head. "If we send a message to my mother, she will tell everyone. In our village, people love to talk." Samir concentrated. *He looks so serious when he's thinking.* Then his face brightened. "I have an idea!" he said. *Yes!* "My father's neighbor, Mr. Amin. He does not speak English, but my father does. So if we get a message to him to give to my father, it will not travel the world."

"And why would anyone monitor Mr. Amin's messages?" said Grammy.

"No reason I can think of," answered Samir. *This sounds like a plan.*

"Oooh, I've always wanted to send a secret message," said Brad, sliding the computer over in front of him. *Of course you have.* "A note that says enough but not too much." Samir nodded. "And you need something that'll show your father the message is really from you – not someone pretending to be you." *That's creepy but I guess that's how it is now.*

Samir thought for a second, then said, "Rock in safe place." As Brad typed it in, Samir explained. "My father is the only one who knows where I keep my special rock so no one else touches it. If he sees that, he'll go to the place and find the rock. He will know the message is from me." *Are we really in the middle of some kind of real-life thriller, all because of some goofy Waterubas?*

"Done!" said Brad.

Samir nodded. "I will write in Arabic to please print the message and give it to Mr. Fouad, my father. My father will know what to say to Mr. Amin to answer any questions."

"Won't Mr. Amin think it's weird for your father to get a message in English?" asked Miriam.

Samir shook his head. "He knows my father works for an international company in Cairo. They do business in English. Sometimes I translate documents. Last month, Father got one in English from Denmark."

"Perfect," said Brad, tapping into the computer. "I'll create a new email address, and use a VPN to send this message from an IP address in Denmark. *Go, technology!* So what's Mr. Amin's email address?" Samir told him; he typed it in and hit send.

"I feel better knowing there's a message on its way to your father," said Grammy.

"So do I," said Samir. "Thank you."

One plan down, one to go. The big one. How do we get the Waterubas back?

Operation Wateruba retrieval

"SO what do we call our mission?" asked Brad. *I don't know, but I'm sure you have an idea.* "I know! *Told you!* Operation Wateruba Rescue!"

"Technically, we're not rescuing them," Grammy pointed out. "Because Waterubas never want anything to be different than it is, they don't need rescuing."

"They can't want to be imprisoned in ARID!" *Who would want that??*

"Think about it," continued Grammy. "Basically, the Waterubas ARE water, right?"

"Right…" said Miriam. *Where is this going…?*

Grammy turned to the aquarium. "Waterubas!" she called. "Does water ever want anything?"

"What is wanting?" asked Lutine, its big eyes and pointy head taking shape out of the water at the front of the aquarium. *I love love love how you don't see them and then you do.*

"If you're evaporating, do you ever try to stay liquid?" asked Grammy.

"Try to stay liquid? What for?" It started to laugh, creating a burst of bubbles.

"And if you're in a storm, do you ever <u>try</u> to go somewhere else?" asked Brad.

"No way! Why?" Krakey appeared next to Lutine. "There's nothing like a storm! Besides, why try to go somewhere we aren't? If we're in a storm, we're in a storm."

"So if you were floating on a boring old pond," said Miriam, "you wouldn't try to be in an exciting storm instead?"

"What is 'boring'?" This time it was Flooso who pitched in. "We love ponds!"

"And we love storms!"

"And evaporating!"

"We love whatever's happening," said Krakey. *That sounds great, but who can live like that?*

"Waterubas can," said Krakey. *What??* By the time Miriam looked at Krakey, it had disappeared into the reflections.

"You know, I sometimes think Krakey can read my mind."

"Well, your brain is 75% water," said Grammy, "so that makes some kind of sense." *Yes, I guess it does...*

Grammy then turned to Miriam, Brad and Samir. "So, my fellow humans, we have just had an important lesson in how to be happy. Love everything. Have no preferences. Can you imagine water ever wanting anything, the way a human does?"

"Or a dog," said Brad, responding to Bunster yipping at the back door by opening it. "When a dog's gotta pee, a dog's gotta pee."

"Waterubas don't even know what 'bad' means," Grammy continued. "So they don't think 'this is good and that is bad.' Wherever the Waterubas are, whatever is happening, they're content. *I wish I could do that.* And that includes being wherever they are with ARID. So we're not rescuing them, we're..."

Brad interrupted. "...retrieving them! Operation Wateruba Retrieval. *Sounds good to me!* Or OpWatRet for short!" *Not so good...*

"I'll get the Asteruba!" Miriam ran out of the room. *We can't retrieve them until we know where they are!* She dashed up the stairs to get the rock from her closet. When she got back, Grammy had finished filling the kitchen sink with water, Brad and Samir were standing on either side of her, and the Waterubas were lined up in the aquarium.

"Here goes," said Miriam, squeezing in between Grammy and Samir to get to the sink. Samir watched closely as she gently lowered the glowing Asteruba into the water. The second it was submerged, the water started to bubble and out of the bubbly gurgles came a deep hum. The Waterubas added the Wateruba Tuba. Brad quickly handed both Miriam and Samir some earplugs. The Asteruba rose up out of the kitchen sink on its watery plinth, turning into a Globe as it reached the apex.

"OH!" said Samir, his eyes wide with wonder. "HOW DOES IT DO THAT?" He was speaking loudly because he was wearing earplugs. *Good question, Samir. How is any of this happening?* The air filled with the smell of the sea. *Deep and mysterious.* The Globe took a moment to settle. When they saw the lights, Brad signaled that it was safe to remove the earplugs.

"Look, there!" said Miriam, pointing to a cluster of lights.

"Who do you see?" asked Brad, grabbing the notebook. "I'll check them off so we can keep track."

Lutine swirled forward and drifted up and down in the aquarium as Miriam pointed out the lights. "I see Dribble, Splurdge, Smedley, Amanzi, Plink, Jala, Taneer, Agua, Burble, Chawaga, Goutte, Gurgle, Ama, Doris, Fons, Origo, Ploop, Rano, Rajendra, Swoosh, Tiktik, Tinkle, Vasser, Yami, Pitter, Hydros, Mizu, Patter, Splatter, Vatura and Gleik."

"Wow," said Samir.

"Wow is right," said Grammy. "Impressive."

Brad counted the checks. "Yep. Thirty one. Just as I thought."

"While we're here," said Miriam, slowly turning the Globe, "any sign of Vesi?" She repeated the name, directing it right at the Globe. "VESI!" *No flash…*

"No," said Lutine.

Brad meanwhile took a photo of the cluster of lights. He zoomed in. "Those Waterubas are on West Madison and North Franklin, right where the ARID building is."

"Why am I not surprised?" said Grammy.

"Because it is not surprising," said Samir, completely seriously. *He always says it like it is.* "We have to go there to get them." He turned to

Miriam. "You need to puddle jump to find out exactly where they are."

"I agree," said Miriam. "But I'm not ready."

"You came to Egypt – twice! – but you cannot travel a few miles?"

Once again, Samir says it like it is. "No, because I'm not good enough yet at puddling and even worse at unpuddling. *I feel upset. Why am I upset? I'm just saying what's true. And I am not content!* When I go to find out where the Waterubas are, I'll have to be able to control when I puddle and when I unpuddle, and I can't do that yet. I just can't. I get too scared. I don't want to ruin our chances of getting the Waterubas back because I'm scared." She looked up at Samir who watched her intently. "Will you help me?"

"Yes," he said. "Please do not be upset."

Needing leads to wanting

BRAD made a space in the kitchen for what he was calling the Puddling Workshop. *If he had a whistle, he'd be like a camp counselor. More Anu than Steve, I'm hoping.* He was taking notes, and Grammy gave him a special notebook for the purpose. *Brad has amazing handwriting. If I were taking notes, we'd never be able to read them!* He covered the floor in a waterproof tarp so that no one accidentally dripped through the floorboards. *And by 'no one,' he means me.* He and Miriam put the aquarium with the Waterubas in it on the counter so they could watch what was going on. Brad knew that Samir was good at puddling, but he didn't really know what that meant. Was Samir good at puddling because he was confident? Or was Samir confident because he was good at puddling? *Does it matter?* "So, Samir, show us what you can do," said Brad.

"I can puddle when I want to," said Samir. *And I know that I can't.* And with that, Samir puddled. *Whoa! That's the first time I've seen it from the outside! Is that what it looks like when I do it? So cool! And weird!!* Brad leaned over the little puddle. "I can see Samir in the water, the way you can see Waterubas, only Samir is a little bit more solid, like you are when you puddle, Miriam."

"So when I'm water, I look like a me-version of that?" *It's freaky-deaky to think of a watery me!*

Brad nodded. "Like Lutine said, you're more solid because you're Puddlers, and not Waterubas." Miriam waved at Samir. He waved back. Brad leaned over the puddle. "Samir? Can you unpuddle now?" Suddenly, the water all came together to form a liquid boy who got filled in with bones and muscles and became Samir!

How can humans do that? What is all this about? "That was amazing," said Miriam.

Brad started to pace. *Uh-oh. He's being more like Steve than Anu.* "You say you puddle when you want to," he said. "Is that true even when you hear the Wateruba Tuba?" And at the mention of the words, the Waterubas started chanting. "Samir, try not to puddle!" said Brad just before he joined in. Miriam puddled immediately. *I can't help it!* And she wasn't puddled for long before Samir appeared next to her.

"I guess the Wateruba Tuba can make any Puddler puddle, whether you want to or not," Miriam said.

"Yes," said Samir. "I have never talked to anyone when I am water before."

"I've talked to Waterubas, and to Grammy and Brad," said Miriam. "It's weird that it just sounds like talking, isn't it? No bubbly sounds." *It's so nice to have someone who understands all this!!*

"Hello? Miriam? Samir?" They looked up and saw Brad waving at them.

"Should we ignore him?" Miriam giggled. *A little mean but funny…*

"Why?" said Samir. "He is right there. He knows we see him." *Samir, you are so much nicer than I am!*

"You guys do know I can hear you, right?" said Brad. *Oooops!* "Are you ready to unpuddle?"

Miriam watched as Samir rose up, more and more solid – while she remained puddled. *Come on, Miriam – you can do this. I will tense my muscles. NNNNNNGGGNN! Nope. Still water. Now think of hard things. Rocks! Cement! Petrified wood! No! Nothing's working!* Samir appeared next to her. He'd puddled again. "What is happening?"

"I can't unpuddle," she told him. "How is it so easy for you?"

"I have been doing it for years. You have been doing it for weeks. *True. It really hasn't been that long.* Do you <u>want</u> to unpuddle right now?" he asked her. "You could just wait. You will unpuddle at some point. We do not stay puddled forever."

"You're right. I don't really want to unpuddle right now." She slowly drifted around him. "This is very relaxing, but I know they're waiting for us…"

"Oh no! A snake!" shouted Samir.

"AHHHH!" Miriam tensed with fear and immediately unpuddled. Next thing she knew, she was standing on the tarp in the kitchen. Panicked, she looked around on the floor. "Where's the snake?"

Then Samir unpuddled. "There is no snake," he said. "I wanted to scare you to help you unpuddle."

Brad started to laugh. "You actually thought there was a snake?"

"It's not funny. I was really scared," said Miriam.

"And now you're really unpuddled," Brad pointed out.

True. "But I've unpuddled before without being scared," said Miriam.

"But just now you said you did not want to unpuddle," said Samir. *Also true.* "You have to want to unpuddle. Otherwise, you just wait."

"But if I just wait, I could be sucked down a drain or drunk by Bunster," said Miriam.

"But if you were heading towards a drain, or seeing a thirsty Bunster coming towards you, you'd get scared, no? And then you'd naturally unpuddle." *As usual, Brad has a point.*

"But I need to learn to <u>control</u> puddling and unpuddling. Like Samir does. It's the controlling part I want to get good at." *This is frustrating. If I knew I could control it, I'd spend less time being scared.*

Grammy came in from the Wateroomba (she'd spent hours purifying, testing and re-purifying all the water in case ARID had put anything nasty into it) just in time to hear the last bit of the conversation. "Isn't it important to know <u>why</u> you want to puddle?" she asked Samir. He just looked at her. Grammy continued. "It's more than just wanting to puddle for the fun of it – it needs to be bigger than that. *Ooooh, that is so Grammy.* You need to know why. Why do you puddle, Samir?"

"To help my village," he answered. *That's a big why.* "When we lose our water, I can find out where it is going and fix it. So I <u>need</u> to puddle and unpuddle."

"And needing because it's important leads to wanting," said Grammy. *I love when she talks like this.* "If you need to do something just because someone's told you to – like your homework or cleaning your room – then it won't lead to wanting. Really wanting to do something comes when you feel with all your heart that you need to do it. Does that make sense?" Samir and Brad nodded. *I'm not so sure…*

"But how did you puddle in the back of that car when you were being kidnapped?" asked Miriam. "You had to be so scared, and it's hard to puddle when you're scared."

"But I needed to get away from that man," said Samir.

"And you're actually not scared of puddling, are you?" said Grammy. Samir shook his head. *I suppose if he'd been scared of puddling like me, he might've stayed in that car.* "Your challenge, Miriam, is that you're still scared of puddling. The need to puddle has to be bigger than the fear of doing it."

"The more you do it, the more you stop being scared," said Samir. "I promise." *Oh, how I want to stop being scared – the quicker, the better.*

"Think about it," said Brad. "When you needed to get away from Steve, you touched the Globe, even though you were scared. So you've already been in a situation where the need was bigger than the fear." *True… thank you, Brad.*

Grammy put her arm around Miriam. "I know you've only just started to puddle, but it'll help when you get stuck if you know why you do it. You could choose never to puddle on purpose again…"

"But why would I do that?" said Miriam. *That would be insane!*

"Because it's scary," said Brad. "And you are not a fan of scary."

"But it's also amazing," said Miriam. "And I'm a big fan of amazing. If Samir is right, and I'm sure he is, the more I do it, the less scary it'll be. Kind of like learning to swim. Or doing a cartwheel! Right?" She turned to Samir who nodded. *I believe him.*

197

"OK, then why do you <u>need</u> to keep puddling?" asked Grammy. *Grammy is going to get this out of me if it's the last thing she does.* "I get that it's amazing, but what is the reason that grabs you by the heart and makes you need to puddle no matter what, no matter how scared you are?"

It's Mom. It's Mom who grabs my heart, and I don't think Grammy wants to hear that. "Do you really want to know?"

Grammy nodded. "Of course."

"I'm doing it for Mom. *There, I said it.* That's exactly why I will keep doing it even when I'm scared. It's all for Mom! Watch!" *I am doing this for Mom. Mom. Mom would be proud of me for overcoming my fear. Be like water… water isn't scared… let go… breathe… for Mom!* She felt her heart expanding, then her feet turned to water… *It's happening!* …then her legs… *Yes!* …hips… chest… and she'd puddled. *That was the easiest time yet, even easier than when I went into the pond because I needed to find Krakey.*

Two seconds later, Samir puddled right next to her. "Very good!" He flipped over and swirled around. Miriam swirled with him. *Woooo-hoooo! Puddling is the best! I never want to stop doing it!* Suddenly, Samir spread out his arms and legs to steady himself. He floated. Miriam tried to do the same but kept spinning. *I have so much to learn from him!* "Now unpuddle without a snake," he said.

Here goes. Rocks… steel… brick wall… "NNNNNNNNGHHNNG!"

Samir looked at her. "What are you doing?"

"I'm thinking of hard things and imagining I'm tensing my muscles," said Miriam. *Duh.*

"That doesn't work for me. *Come to think of it, it doesn't work for me either.* Think of your bones. First your foot bones, then your leg bones, then your hips, then your ribs and your spine – arm bones, and finally your skull. It's like you are telling them to be bones again."

"That makes sense," said Miriam. *Foot bone, heel, ankle, shin, knee…* Before she got to the thigh bone, she was standing in the kitchen, a solid girl again. *Result!*

Flick, Flack, Fleck

AS Brad's Puddling Workshop progressed, Miriam found that if she just remembered that everything was about finding her mom, she could override any fear. But would that work in every situation? *I'm not sure I could puddle in the back of a car when I was being kidnapped…* To test her skills, Brad designed what he called drills. *Drills? Pa-leeze! That's something Steve would say.* For example, one time when Miriam puddled, Brad suddenly shouted, "You've landed in the sink in the bathroom at your brothers' school!!" Just the thought of that situation made her unpuddle immediately. As she sat there on the floor, Brad and Samir ran around screaming, "Help! A strange girl is sitting in the sink! What's she doing here?" Grammy joined in and imitated Jeff's voice. "Miri? Is that you?? What are you doing here?"

"Quick! Quick! Puddle!" said Samir. But she couldn't. At least, not that time. The more she practiced, though, the better she got at it.

One day, Brad decided to test her "out in the field." *'Out in the field?' Really?* He filled up the kitchen sink, and Miriam put the Asteruba into the water. Bubbles, low-hum, rising on a watery plinth, smell of the sea, whoosh as it settled, blinking lights. It turned into the Globe. Brad leaned in to see if there actually was a Wateruba near where her brothers and father were staying in France. *No, no, no, no. I don't think I'm ready…*

"Well, lookie there," said Brad pointing. *He's having far too much fun with this.* "I believe I see not one, not two, but <u>three</u> lights right near your family."

"Really…?" said Miriam. *I feel sick… What if someone sees me? What do I do?* Brad turned to the aquarium. "Lutine? Do you know which

Waterubas these are?"

"Of course!" said Lutine. "It's Flick, Flack and Fleck."

"Flick Flack Fleck Flick Flack Fleck Flick Flack Fleck!" chanted the Waterubas, swirling around the aquarium.

"Flick!" said Awa.

"Flack!" said Fishman.

"Fleck!" said Pirta. Pirta had an inexplicably deep voice, by the way.

"Flick Flack Fleck Flick Flack Fleck!" As usual, this exuberance led to the Wateruba Tuba. Miriam and Samir put in their earplugs, but Samir stood in front of Miriam with his hand up, as if to say, "Wait." *Samir is waiting to say something. Maybe he'll tell me not to go.* Once Grammy signaled that the Waterubas were finished chanting, Samir pulled out his earplugs.

"I wonder if you can bring back all three Waterubas," he said. *That is not what I wanted to hear!*

"Great idea, Samir!" said Brad. *No it's not!* "Miriam, if you say all three names at the Globe and they all flash and they're together, will that mean you can bring all three back?" *I don't know!*

"That could be hugely helpful when you go to retrieve the Waterubas from ARID," added Grammy.

Um... "Let me get this straight. You want me to try to get three Waterubas on this puddle-jump AND to puddle if I see my brothers so they don't see me, no matter what's going on."

"That's a lot, isn't it," said Brad. He, Samir and Grammy looked at Miriam expectantly.

Yes, it's a lot!! "OK, I'll try..." she said. *I can do this I can do this I can do this.*

"You can do this," said Krakey.

Somehow, coming from Krakey, I believe it. It almost sounds like my mom. Miriam took a deep breath, faced the Globe and said "Flick! Flack! Fleck!" Three lights flashed and a route lit up. Brad quickly photographed it.

"It looks like it's the same route to all three."

"Yes!" said Grammy, fist-pumping. *I've never seen her fist-pump before. She must've learned it from Brad.*

"And from what I can tell," continued Brad, "it'll be plumbing, plumbing, plumbing, with some exciting time in the Atlantic Jet Stream." *Exciting for who??* Brad peered at the photos. "Plumbing, river, lake, sky, way up to the Atlantic Jet Stream, whoosh, down, down to more plumbing. Got it?"

Not really. "Can I try one more thing before I go? *Not asking for permission.* VESI!" she said to the Globe. Nothing. "Well, I guess it's time to go get Flick, Flack and Fleck, right?"

"Flick Flack Fleck Flick Flack Fleck!" came the Wateruba chorus.

Miriam stared at the Globe. *Three at once.* "Think of your mother – and go," whispered Samir. *He knows I'm scared. But I can do this! Mommmmm. Go!*

"Flick! Flack! Fleck!" Miriam said loudly to the Globe. And this time when the three lights flashed, she reached out to touch them, puddled and got pulled in. *Woo-hooo! Into the roller coaster of plumbing! Whoooosh! Thinking about going is so much worse than actually going!* In a matter of moments, Miriam went from plumbing, where it was dark, to being pushed to a place where there was more light. *River!* Then she stopped moving and drifted. *Lake! Vibrating… evaporating!* She went up, up, up. *Into the sky!* Then WHOOSH! *The Atlantic Jet Stream. Oh-oh-oh-oh-ohhh! Bumpy and fast!! Drifting… now falling as rain! I actually love this bit!* Back into plumbing. *Slowing down now. I wonder where Flick, Flack and Fleck are… What if I see my brothers?!?*

When she stopped moving, Miriam unpuddled. She was sitting in a paddling pool with… *ERIK!* Her six year old brother, whom she hadn't seen in weeks and whom she loved very much, was sitting right there, playing with his boats! If she reached out, she could touch him. *It's Erik! Oh, Erik! You've grown! I want to hug you! I miss you!* He hadn't seen her yet. *Miriam, get a grip. You can't let him see you! STOP! Find the Waterubas!*

PUDDLE!! Now! She heard the Wateruba Tuba and saw three Rubas glowing right next to her. Their bodies came out of the ripples, forming around their glows.

Erik looked up. "Miri?!?" Suddenly grateful for all of Brad's drills, Miriam puddled on top of Flick, Flack and Fleck and was on her way home with three Waterubas. *I did it!!*

Manu

THE other Waterubas were thrilled to see Flick, Flack and Fleck. Even though their names were similar, they didn't look anything like each other. *Let's face it. None of the Waterubas look anything like each other. But they're all water – and they all have a Ruba.* It took Brad a while to figure out which was Flick, which was Flack, and which was Fleck. Flick kind of looked like a big tomato with little eyes at the base of limb-like antennae coming out of its head; it had a carrot-colored Ruba. Flack was long and wafty, expanding and contracting as it moved; its Ruba color was what Lutine called 'Hibiscus'. Fleck was a blob with one big eye, one small, with six-fingered 'hands' coming out from its sides. It had a gold Ruba glow. *I don't know how we'd keep track if we didn't have Brad's drawings!*

Miriam watched the ten Waterubas glow and swoosh and ripple. They were obviously chanting the Wateruba Tuba, but she had her earplugs in. *Look at them. Watching them makes me happier than anything. But I can't help it – I miss my brothers and my dad...* Seeing Erik had been discombobulating, but she'd managed not to lose the plot and to puddle when she'd needed to. *The biggest test yet, and I did it!* (When she talked to Erik the next day, he told her he'd had a dream about her. In the dream, she was in the paddling pool. He thought it was incredibly funny. He'd always had vivid dreams so that explanation totally fit in with his world. *Phew.*)

Miriam's thoughts were interrupted by a tap on her arm. It was Samir. *He's solid, so the Waterubas must be done chanting.* She took out her ear plugs. "It is time to puddle-jump together," he said. *What?*

Now?? "We only did it once."

"Are we sure that you can't puddle jump on your own?" asked Miriam. *It would be so much easier if he could!*

"Remember how tired you were yesterday?" asked Brad. Miriam nodded. *All the puddling and unpuddling and drills are exhausting!* "Well Samir and I couldn't sleep and you were snoring... *Probably Bunster, not me* ...so we decided to try to make the Globe without you."

"And it did not work," said Samir.

"The Asteruba just sat in the water like a rock," said Brad. "No bubbling, no rising up, no smell of the sea, no mystery. It was just a rock."

"Which is exactly what it is when you're not around," said Grammy. "So it seems the only way for Samir to puddle-jump is with you. *OK, but do we have to do it now? I'm so tired!* So far, you've only done it together for half a journey – not both there and back," continued Grammy. *True, but couldn't we just wait a few days..?* "We have to find out how it works – or even if it works at all. *I can hear Grammy's sense of urgency. Waiting not an option.* That one time could have been a fluke."

"Fluke?" said Samir.

"An accident," explained Grammy.

"Fluke. I like that word." *Flick, Flack, Fleck, Fluke. Sorry, couldn't help it.*

"Let's think this through," said Brad, making notes in the Book of Experiments. *Thinking things through. My favorite thing to do. Take your time, Brad!* "We're working towards the two of you going into ARID together, right?"

Samir nodded. *Going into ARID. That makes my stomach hurt.*

"So we need to know how long you can both stay unpuddled when you get there, before you have to come back," said Brad. "Also, what happens if Samir gets caught up in spying, and the Globe brings Miriam back without him? *Good question!* No matter what happens, she'll always get there and back because the Globe is her magic, right?"

"Yes, I think it is," said Grammy. "So Samir is the one who has to be careful." *Poor Samir! But I kind of think he's used to it. He puddled out of the back of a kidnapper's car…!* Grammy closed her eyes. *She's thinking.* "Wait a minute. What if I take my campervan into the city and park somewhere near ARID? It's got a sink. So we take the Asteruba, and you could puddle-jump from there! Then either Samir comes back with you…"

"…which is Plan A," Brad jumped in. *He's loving this!!* "Or Plan B – Samir can puddle out of ARID and walk to the van! A getaway car – brilliant!" *Getaway car?? That's so Brad. But also technically it's a van.*

Grammy looked into Samir's face. *She's worried about him understanding. Me, too. I've got it easy compared to him.* "If the Globe brings Miriam back, are you happy to get away by puddling? You'll have to get out of ARID, and onto the street and be able to find the van."

"I can do it," said Samir. *I can't believe how confident he is – and not braggy at all.*

"But we're not there yet. *Brad the drillmaster. But he's right. We need more practice.* How about if you guys do a few practice runs? Start by puddle-jumping together to get a Wateruba and coming back. Simple-pimple."

'Simple pimple' says the guy who's going to sit in the kitchen the whole time. The Asteruba was still sitting in the sink. Miriam turned on the faucet, and the minute the water touched it, the rock-to-Globe process began: bubbles, low hum, watery plinth, settling with a whoosh, cool breeze smelling of the sea, lights appearing. Miriam put on the WTS. Then she faced the Globe and first called "Vesi!", just in case. Nothing. Lutine then spotted the pigeon blue Ruba glow for Manu. "Manu Manu Manu Manu Manu!" chanted the Waterubas, quickly turning the name Manu into the Wateruba Tuba. Before she put in her earplugs, Miriam noticed that having Flick, Flack and Fleck there made the Wateruba Tuba sound different. *They make it sound fuller – it's music from another world! Beautiful!* She quickly plugged up her ears.

Samir did the same.

When the Waterubas stopped chanting, Miriam and Samir removed their earplugs and faced the Globe. "So how do we do this?" asked Miriam.

"I think Samir should be touching you when you reach for Manu's flash," said Grammy. *That makes sense.* "You could either hold hands, or he could put his hand on your shoulder. Whatever works."

"Hand on shoulder, if that's OK with you, Samir," said Miriam. "I need both hands to keep my balance when I get pulled in." *I've never thought about it before, but that's true. That first pull is strong.*

"OK," said Samir, and he put his hand on Miriam's shoulder.

"Ready?" she said.

"Ready."

"Manu!" Miriam shouted at the Globe. Manu's light flashed and the route lit up. Brad quickly took a picture.

"It looks as if Manu is somewhere in South America."

"Really?" *Samir looks excited. Mom, please don't let me wreck this by getting scared.* "Let me try something first," and he reached out and touched the light on the Globe. *Unexpected experiment!* Nothing happened.

"It is definitely Miriam's magic," said Grammy.

"Let's go!" said Miriam. "Manu!!" and this time she touched the flash. And both Miriam and Samir were pulled in. *It worked!*

At first, Samir held onto Miriam's shoulder pretty tightly. *I don't blame him!* But once they were on their way, he found he could let go and still stay with her. *He's really good at steering himself!* "Wooooo-hoooo!" Miriam shouted as they were pulled up into the sky in a speeded-up version of evaporation, and Samir joined in. "Woo-woo-woo-woooohoooo!!" *I love having another Puddler with me!!* They went up to join some clouds, then they rained, then evaporated again, then up again. There was a lot of up-ing and down-ing, then what could've been pipes, then whooshing, then up again and falling again. (Brad told them later that they rained into a city and flowed into its water system before moving on into a river, evaporating again, then being blown as clouds, and finally raining again.) Thanks to Brad, Miriam didn't even try to keep track anymore. There was nothing she could do about it anyway. *I love not having to make decisions! Going with the flow – just like water!* "Slowing down!" Miriam shouted to Samir, who steered himself over to her and put his hand back on her shoulder. Finally, they stopped and unpuddled – to find themselves sitting on a giant water lily. Wherever they looked, huge water lilies covered the surface of the water – big enough to hold the weight of two children!

"Look at where we are…" gasped Samir. *How amazing is this?!*

"Manu?" called Miriam. They heard a soft Wateruba Tuba. Miriam saw what looked like a small lily floating next to the giant lily, glowing blue. *Manu's Ruba!* As she watched, the ripples around the glowing lily formed into what looked like a cloak and rose up out of the water.

"There!" said Miriam, reaching for it. But Samir held her arm.

"Do we have to go back so soon? I want to explore!" *Of course he does.*

"There's no time, Samir. I can already feel the Globe pulling us back, and I do not want to leave you in the middle of wherever we are!"

"Just a little longer," he said, rolling away from her. But before he got too far, Miriam grabbed his leg at the same time as she reached for Manu. "Puddle!!" she shouted.

Samir didn't seem to have a choice. *Did he puddle because I grabbed him or because he wanted to?*

Once she was sure Samir was with her, she concentrated on putting Manu in the WTS. And after some more up-ing and down-ing and whooshing and flowing, they were back in Grammy's kitchen.

Wateruba sidekick

"MANU Manu Manu Manu!" the Waterubas swirled around and chanted when Miriam poured their latest find into the aquarium. Just as they started to chant the Wateruba Tuba – "STOP!" shouted Miriam. They stopped. She turned to Samir.

"Did you puddle on purpose or because I grabbed you?"

"Not on purpose," said Samir. *He's trying to look sorry, but I can see he's smiling.* "When you grabbed me, I puddled." *I thought so!*

"That's another rule for my list for how the Globe works," said Brad. "We can only assume that if Miriam hadn't managed to grab you, Samir, you'd be wandering around in South America somewhere. On your own."

Grammy gave Samir her serious listen-to-me-please-this-is-important look. "Because the Globe is clearly Miriam's magic, you must follow the rules, Samir." He nodded.

"Wait a minute," said Miriam. *I have the most amazing idea ever, if I do say so myself.* "What if we attached a Wateruba to Samir with another WTS, and then if he and I get separated, I'd always be able to puddle-jump back to him?" Everyone looked at Miriam. "Well…?"

"Brilliant…" said Grammy.

"Let's try it!" said Brad.

Miriam asked Krakey if it would be Samir's Wateruba sidekick, and it loved the idea. *Of course it did! Krakey loves everything.* Grammy and Brad made a special WTS for Krakey to attach it to Samir. *All set.*

Emoto

"THE thing about this particular experiment," said Brad, "is that if it goes wrong, Samir will be stuck in another part of the world, unable to get back." *I guess somebody had to say it...*

"How do you feel about that, Samir?" asked Grammy.

"Feel?" Samir just looked at her.

He's got to be as scared as I would be but he doesn't want to say. "I'm not sure we should do this!" said Miriam. "It's too risky."

"We have to do it," said Samir. "We do not know what ARID is doing, but we do know we need to find out and stop it. NOT stopping ARID is risky."

He's right. I keep forgetting how big this is. "You're very brave, Samir," said Miriam.

"I'm just doing what we need to do."

"Just like you do at home in your village," said Grammy. She held up Krakey's special WTS in front of the aquarium. "Krakey?"

Krakey appeared, left ear first. *One minute a reflection, the next a Wateruba! Just when everything feels scary, they show us how wonderful it all is.* "Here I am!" it said, waving. Grammy dipped the WTS into the water and Krakey glided in.

Grammy snapped the top closed, and attached Krakey's sidecar, as she called it, to Samir. "How does that feel?"

"Good," said Samir. He looked down at Krakey who waved. Samir waved back. Krakey waved. Samir waved. *Time to go!*

Miriam dropped the Asteruba in the sink, which Grammy had filled with water. Whooshing, low hum, sea smell, Globe – lights. *Like something from another world…* "I see Emoto!" said Lutine. "Baby Blue Ruba."

"Emoto! Emoto! Emoto!" chanted the Waterubas.

"No Wateruba Tuba, please!" said Miriam. The Waterubas stopped chanting, though Pirta didn't hear Miriam and sang the Wateruba Tuba for a second, but stopped when nobody else joined in. "Emoto!" Miriam said to the Globe. The light flashed; they saw the route; Brad took a picture.

"Looks like it's somewhere in the middle of the ocean!"

Miriam turned to Samir. "You ready?" He nodded enthusiastically. *If he nods any harder, his head will fall off!* He put his hand on her shoulder. "Emoto!" she said again, and this time when the light flashed, she reached for it and she and Samir puddled and were pulled into the Globe – and out into the atmosphere. "Wooooo-eeeeee!" Samir shouted with Miriam. *He looks so happy!*

Miriam noticed that Samir stayed close to her, particularly when they plunged into a thunderstorm. As they were getting tossed around by the wind and rain, Samir steered himself right up next to her so that their two watery bodies merged. *We're still Miriam and Samir, but we're one raindrop!* She tumbled away. *And now we're two raindrops again!* They rained into the ocean and sank down, down, down, through a school of orange clownfish, onto a coral reef. *It's not bleached. It still has its colors. Beautiful! I've seen coral reefs on TV, but never in real life!!* They floated into a hole in the coral where they saw the baby blue glow of Emoto. They stayed puddled. When the Wateruba appeared out of the water, Miriam almost burst out laughing. *It's so cute!* Its head was part of its round body with two little arms that ended in fins coming out of its sides.

"There's Emoto!" said Miriam. Emoto waved. Right next to Emoto was an octopus. Samir had never seen an octopus before. He glided towards it. "Samir! Time to go back! The Globe is pulling me!" As she reached to touch Emoto, she stretched towards Samir, but before she could get to him… he was sucked in through the octopus's beak!

210

Samir's inside an octopus

"SAMIR'S inside an octopus!" Miriam spluttered when she returned to the kitchen with Emoto. "He stayed really close to me when we were jumping, but when we saw an octopus, he had to have a closer look…"

"Of course he did!" said Brad. "I mean, it's an octopus! One of the most truly awesome creatures on the planet!" He started to fill the kitchen sink. "He still has Krakey with him, right?"

"As far as I know." *We need to find him now!!*

"Emoto Emoto Emoto Emoto!" the Waterubas greeted Emoto as Miriam poured it into the aquarium. Brad handed her the headphones as they started to chant the Wateruba Tuba. But she didn't put them on right away. *I want to hear what it sounds like now that there's another voice. Ohh, it's a bigger sound each time… Each Wateruba that gets added makes it sound different… so beautiful… I feel it in my heart…* She started to puddle. *Headphones!*

When the Waterubas had finished chanting, Brad handed Miriam the Asteruba. "So, if he's been sucked into the octopus," said Grammy, "he might either be expelled through the gills, as the octopus breathes, or through the siphon where an octopus ejects water for propulsion."

"Amazeballs!!!" said Brad.

"He can tell us what happened when we find him." *And I will find him!* Miriam put the Asteruba in the water. Whooshing – low hum – watery plinth – sea smell – Globe – lights – "KRAKEY!" Miriam shouted at the Globe. A familiar bumblebee yellow light flashed.

Miriam reached for it. She puddled and was once again soaring through the air. There was no storm this time. She fell into the ocean near the shore and unpuddled as she was thrown up on the beach, landing next to Samir. He was sitting there waiting for her as if he'd just had a picnic and had never seen the outside of an octopus, never mind the inside of one. "Hi, Miriam!"

I'm so so so so glad to see you! "Hello, Samir. Ready to go back?" He nodded and opened the little tub holding Krakey. Krakey waved. Miriam put one hand on Samir and the other on Krakey, and before they knew it, the three of them were back in Grammy's kitchen.

Why be scared?

SAMIR told the others that once he was inside the octopus, he couldn't tell what was going on. Everything looked the same. *That makes sense. What's inside an octopus anyway?* "Something pushed me. Hard. Like the time I was in a hose. *Note to self: Remind Samir to tell me the hose story.* Then I was in the ocean, turning over and over and over. I unpuddled and landed on the beach. Krakey was still with me, so I just waited."

"I hadn't been inside an octopus for ages!" said Krakey. "It's almost as much fun as a water blaster!"

"It's not that much different, actually," laughed Grammy.

"Weren't you scared?" *How can he not have been scared? He was inside an octopus!!*

"I was thinking about what happened. I saw an octopus! *Excited – not scared.* And then you were there. Why be scared?" *I can think of a million reasons…*

Grammy pulled up a video to show Samir – and Brad and Miriam *Who doesn't want to know what happens when you go inside an octopus?* – how he'd been sucked up into the octopus's mouth, into its mantle and then forced out through its siphon as it was probably trying to get away from something. "You felt you were being pushed hard because you were. The octopus was shooting the water out to propel itself forward. Like water coming out of a hose."

"Or a water blaster," added Krakey.

The end of the video showed an octopus shooting through the water. Brad quickly drew an octopus like the one in the film and added a little drawing of a watery Samir flying out the back end. Samir

213

started to laugh. Everyone stared. *We've never seen him laugh before!* "I was octopus poop!"

We go tomorrow night

THE two Puddlers, Grammy and Brad looked at all the information they'd gathered and decided it was time to go into ARID for a recce. *It's easy for Grammy and Brad to say it's time – they don't have to go!*

They were going to jump for… "Splurdge!" said Brad. "I spent so much time getting its story out of it, that I actually kind of miss its horsey face and bizarre leg situation." (Splurdge had what looked like three legs.) So the plan was for Miriam and Samir to puddle-jump for Splurdge. But would there be a water route to it?

"I suspect the room where they're keeping the Waterubas will be sealed," said Grammy. *Hadn't thought about that…*

"And if there's no water route, then I guess our Puddlers won't be able to go," said Brad. "When Miriam first calls a Wateruba's name, its light flashes. Then when she calls it again, the route lights up."

"And that's when you take a picture of it, right?" asked Grammy.

Brad nods. "Then she says the name a third time, and goes. The route stays lit up for about nine seconds after she disappears into the Globe. I timed it. *Of course you did.* If I get the picture, then I can see the route with the app."

"App?" asked Samir. *Ah, yes. He wasn't around when Brad developed his tech.* Brad started to explain how he'd combined a weather app with a map app. As Miriam had heard all this before, she spent the time worrying instead. *Maybe there won't be a water route in. Then what do we do? Give up? I'd really like not to have to go because it's scary, but then what? I need to find out what happened to Mom!*

"Earth to Miriam!" said Grammy.

Ooops! Hello! "Sorry. I was worrying about what happens if there's no water route into ARID."

"How about you don't waste energy worrying until we know if there's a route or not?" said Grammy gently. *That's fair.*

"Think about it," said Brad. *That's what I've been doing!* "We've never seen a flash when there isn't a route, right? *Right.* Maybe that's because there isn't a flash if there isn't a route. That's why we're not seeing Vesi's flash. The Waterubas said that Vesi is on the planet, but just not somewhere where there's a route to it."

Good point. "So if there's no water route, no flash."

"That's our hypothesis." Grammy put her arm around Miriam. "Here's what I suggest. You be all set to go, and if there's no water route, then we'll figure out what to do next. One step at a time, OK?" *Grammy's always so sensible.*

Miriam looked at Samir who hadn't said anything for ages. "What do you think?"

"I think we go tomorrow night," said Samir.

No no no no no! "OK," said Miriam.

Fear

THAT night, Miriam couldn't sleep. She was overwhelmed with fear. It gripped her, clutched at her heart, stirred up her stomach, gave her the shakes. She remembered a conversation she'd had with her mom. The work she did climbing around on glaciers was dangerous. "Do you ever get scared, Mom?" Miriam had asked one time as she watched her pack up for her next trip. *Even her equipment looked complicated and frightening.*

"You have to make friends with fear, Miri," her mom had said. *Friends?? How?? Fear is not friendly! That's like trying to make friends with a tornado!* "Inside every fear is a lesson that will help you grow. An experience that will make you stronger. Do you want to have an adventure that could teach you all sorts of things about yourself, or be too scared to leave the house? *I want an adventure, but I'm so so scared!* Remember what Marie Curie said," her mom had continued as she did a final check on her equipment. "'Nothing in life is to be feared, it is only to be understood. Now is the time to understand more, so that we may fear less.'" *Mom loved that quote.* The memory faded.

Miriam took a deep breath. *Mom… Actually, I kind of get that now… I need to understand more about what's going on at ARID, and maybe then it won't be so scary.* Mom also said, "When you learn about your fear, you learn about yourself." *But I hate feeling afraid! All I'm learning is that I'm SCARED!!*

Miriam turned over, then turned over again, searching for a comfortable position. She tried to relax. She breathed in… and out… and in… and out… *I wonder if I relax and breathe to fall asleep, I'll puddle in bed!* She laughed. *I really don't need to puddle, so probably not. We're going to ARID tomorrow night!! Tomorrow!! Oh no! Here comes the fear! It's like a wave of sick! Breathe, Miriam...*

Then Miriam remembered what Grammy had told her after her mom had disappeared. She'd felt so sad she'd hardly wanted to move. "Don't push the sadness away, Miriam," Grammy had said, holding her tight. "Feel it in your body. Notice the sensations – the heaviness, the dark. Where is it? What color is it?" *That didn't make the sadness go away, but when I watched it, I felt it flow. If I didn't call it sadness and I didn't wish it would go away, it didn't stick. I didn't hold it in. I wonder if that works for fear. I won't call it "fear". I'll call it Felicity. Kidding. I won't call it anything. I'll just feel it ... a wave... a wave of sick... it's around my throat... in my heart... it's moving...*

Then it occurred to her to hum a Wateruba Tuba sound. She hummed; she hummed some more; she relaxed; the fear evaporated; she yawned; she fell asleep.

Operation Arid Recce

MIRIAM was sitting in a tree next to a giant woodpecker. *Whoa! Look at the size of that bird!* It pecked at the tree. Knock knock knock knock! "Miriam! Miriam! Are you awake?" said the woodpecker. *What is that woodpecker talking about?! What? Wait! That knocking is real!* It was Brad knocking on her bedroom door. "Miriam! Get up!"

"I'm up, I'm up!" said Miriam, trying to sound as if she'd been awake forever rather than for just the last two seconds.

"Today's the day! Though we don't actually go until tonight, but you know that," said Brad. "See you downstairs! Ouch!" *Sounds like he ran into the wall.*

When Miriam got to the kitchen, everyone was there. Grammy was putting together the Wateruba Transport Systems, stopping every now and again to take a slug of coffee from her Cloud Lovers mug. Samir sat at the table, calmly eating some toast, watching the Waterubas cavort around the aquarium, one moment ripples, the next watery creatures. *How can he eat? I'm way too nervous to eat. Though if I don't eat, I'll be really hungry by tonight...* Brad was attaching a small camera to a headband. He looked up. "Hello, sleepyhead!" *Annoying.*

"Which Waterubas do you want to take with you?" asked Grammy.

"Definitely Krakey," said Miriam.

Krakey appeared. "Definitely Krakey!" it said, propelling itself in circles with its big ears.

"And Lutine and Flooso. Is that OK with you, Samir?"

Samir nodded. "You know them better than I do."

"Though I'd say that none of us will ever really <u>know</u> a Wateruba."

Grammy tried to hand Miriam a piece of toast with butter and honey, but Miriam wouldn't take it. *Not hungry.*

"You have to eat." Samir stood up and took the toast from Grammy. "What we do takes a lot of energy." He held it out for Miriam. "Go on, eat!"

"Aye-aye, captain!" She saluted and obediently took one bite. *Oh yum! That's so good and now I'm hungry!* She finished the whole piece. "Thank you."

"Thank you," said Samir. "You must not faint during the mission."

"But if you do, we'll all see it," said Brad. He fit the headband with the camera on Samir's head. "How's that feel?"

"Good," said Samir.

"Tap it once to turn it on," said Brad. Samir did, and they all watched on Brad's laptop as Samir took a tour around the kitchen. *That is so cool!* "Another tap, and it's off, but once you're in there, I'd just leave it on."

"OK," Samir agreed.

"What if he has to pee … or something?" asked Miriam. *I'd hate to be wearing a camera in the bathroom!*

"No problem. I'll just take it off," said Samir. And he took the headband off and put it in his pocket, creating a black screen on the computer.

Duh. I should've thought of that. "Good plan," said Miriam.

"I do not want to turn it off, then forget to turn it on again. Like when I forgot the phone on the bookshelf and messed up the plan."

"Dude," said Brad. "You can stop beating yourself up about that… …NOW!" said Miriam and Brad together.

"Aye-aye!" smiled Samir, saluting.

"Speaking of plans," said Brad, opening the Book of Experiments, "here's Operation ARID Recce. OAR. Eight steps." He smiled at Miriam. "Sorry – couldn't get it to ten. *Nice to know that you tried, though!* He started his list.

"1) Drive the Campervan to the city

2) Park near ARID

3) Set up the Globe

4) Miriam and Samir jump for Splurdge

5) Miriam finds Splurdge

6) Miriam returns

7) Samir stays, gathering information

8) Samir puddles and returns to van"

"Excellent," said Grammy, picking up her dog. "I'll obviously take Bunster. So who's going to carry which Waterubas?" She gave Miriam and Samir each a WTS.

"I'll take Krakey," said Miriam. She dipped the container into the aquarium. Krakey slid in, followed by Flooso.

"And Flooso!" said Flooso.

"I'll go with Samir," said Lutine.

Samir scooped Lutine up in the other container. "So if I get stuck, Miriam can jump for you to bring me back."

"Exactly!" said Lutine. "Working with Puddlers is so exciting!"

"I'll say!" said Flooso. "We knew this was coming. We just didn't know when!" *Wait. They knew what was coming?* And they waved and splashed and started to do the Wateruba Tuba. *No time for unnecessary puddling!*

"STOP PLEASE!!" yelled Miriam, before the other Waterubas (and Brad) joined in. "Isn't it time to go?"

221

Tubig

THEY put the nine Waterubas who weren't in a WTS into a nice big glass jug that had a lid and slotted neatly next to the sink in the campervan. Once dog, humans, Puddlers and Waterubas were in, they drove to the city and parked near ARID – steps 1 and 2. Grammy filled the van's little sink with water. Miriam carefully removed the Asteruba from its own backpack – they'd found one that fit it perfectly with room for some towels and sponges and extra containers and even a ladle, just in case. *Not sure why we'd ever need a ladle, but you never know.* Miriam put the Asteruba in the water. Whoosh – low hum – watery plinth – rock turned to Globe – settled with a loud whoosh – ancient sea smell – lights.

"Whoa," whispered Grammy. "I have to say that was even more impressive in this small space."

"Agreed," said Brad.

"OK, here goes," said Miriam, stepping up to the Globe. *My hands are shaking. Hope no one notices…* "Ready?"

Samir positioned himself right behind her. "Ready."

"Splurdge!" No flash.

"Try Jala," said Brad, reading off his list of missing Waterubas.

"Jala!" Again, no flash.

"I was worried this might happen," said Grammy. *What what what? You said it might happen, but you never said you were worried!* "I think they've sealed up the place where they're keeping the Waterubas since we first saw where they were. Even though they don't know what they've got, they wouldn't want to risk anything getting out."

"It also makes sense if they know that someone like Samir is a possibility," said Brad. "They wouldn't want to risk anyone getting in either."

"Slightly horrifying, but you speak the truth," said Grammy. "The thlot pickens."

Now what? Miriam leaned in to look at the Globe. *What's that?* "Is there a light there? And is it still in ARID?"

Brad had a look. "I think it is. Lutine, do you know who it is?"

Samir held his WTS with Lutine up to the Globe. "It's Tubig," said Lutine. "Its Ruba is purple orchid. Beautiful, isn't it…?" *Thank you, Lutine!*

"Tubig! Tubig! Tubig!" chanted all the Waterubas, but stopped before going into the Wateruba Tuba.

"So, Tubig is in ARID, but we don't know exactly where," said Brad, studying the Globe. "It does look as if it's close to where we first saw all the others…"

"Let's hope you don't end up in Eddy's coffee – or in the water cooler in the cafeteria." Grammy tried not to laugh but she couldn't help it.

Not funny. "The quicker we go, the quicker we'll find out," said Miriam. *Am I feeling brave or just impatient? What's the difference?* She stood next to the Globe again and waited for Samir to position himself behind her. *I'm scared I'm scared I'm scared!* "Ready?"

"Ready," he said.

This is for you, Mom! "Tubig!" The light flashed and Miriam leaned in to touch it. She and Samir puddled and whoosh! *When it happens, it's not scary! I need to remember that before I go! I'm so glad I'm not doing this by myself!* Maybe it was because they were only a few blocks away, but it took almost no time before they fell as drops of water and unpuddled. *Where are we?* They'd landed on the floor in a room, just below a vent in the ceiling. As he stood up, Samir tapped the camera on his head. *Well remembered, Samir!* The room had a big desk and a bank of monitors, with images from cameras showing all the angles in another room containing a big pool. The pool had 'rivers' coming off of it, as well as waterfalls, rapids, and a wave machine. The water kept moving, but there were no clouds or anywhere for it to evaporate. *Rather than use the water cycle to keep the Waterubas moving, they're just using gravity. Maybe they think the Waterubas are liquid all the time.* Miriam heard the Wateruba Tuba and saw a purple glow light up a mug of coffee on the desk. *In the coffee? Huh! Grammy was __almost__ right!* She leaned in to have a closer look, and Tubig appeared on the surface.

Whoa. That one looks like it's got wings! Just then, Samir spotted a guard, dressed in a hazmat suit, on one of the monitors. The guard was in the room with the pool.

"I don't know what you are or where you are or even <u>if</u> you are, but I'll make sure you don't go anywhere." *It's a woman. Is she talking to us?? Is it a two-way mirror?* Miriam looked at Samir who had frozen. But the guard carried on walking around the pool. On the monitors, they could see her open a door, then appear on another monitor showing a little alcove, where she removed the hazmat suit. Then she opened a second door – and they could hear the shhhshhh sound from where they were. "It's sealed all right," whispered Miriam.

"And the pool room is right next door," Samir whispered back. "Hide!" *Where??* Too late. The guard stepped into the room. But before she could register that two children were standing by her desk, Krakey started to chant the Wateruba Tuba. Tubig joined in, as did Lutine and Flooso. The Waterubas in the sealed room heard via the intercom and they joined in as well. Miriam and Samir plugged their ears. But the guard slumped over and went into deep relaxation. Miriam gently walked her to her chair and whispered to her: "When you wake up, you won't remember a thing." *I have no idea if that'll work, but it's worth a try! No matter what happens, ARID will be on high alert.*

Miriam noticed she was starting to puddle. She showed Samir that her feet were dissolving, and he signaled for her to go. So she reached for Tubig, glad to discover the coffee wasn't still hot, waved and puddle-jumped back to the van.

Puddle, Samir!

WHEN Miriam unpuddled, she was on the floor, still holding Tubig in a little brown coffee puddle in her hand. She quickly grabbed a sponge and soaked it up. She then squeezed it into the big jug, and poured Krakey and Flooso in with it. "Tubig! Tubig! Tubig!" they chanted once again, overjoyed to see their friend. Tubig swirled the antennae that seemed to come out of its eyes *It is very strange-looking – strange and beautiful!* and swished its wings. They all sang the Wateruba Tuba, but Brad was too busy peering at his computer watching Samir to add his voice. Even with twelve Waterubas chanting (Lutine was still with Samir), without Brad, the sound wasn't loud enough to make Miriam puddle. *Or maybe I'm finally getting better at controlling it...* A completely solid Miriam carried the jug over to join Brad and Grammy at the computer.

Samir was carefully scanning the monitors with his camera while Brad recorded. "He's doing an amazing job," Brad whispered.

This is like a spy movie – but it's real. Wish it didn't feel so dangerous. "Wait, what's that?" said Miriam. They could see an unusual contraption on one of the monitor screens. "I didn't notice that when we were in there." Brad took a screengrab. Samir then scanned the control desk.

"There are all sorts of controls," said Brad. "You can adjust temperature, sound, light..." Then suddenly, the camera swung away as Samir was distracted by the guard.

"She's coming to," said Grammy. Krakey immediately started to chant the Wateruba Tuba, and the others joined in. "They can't hear you in there," said Grammy, "but we can, and it does take the edge off.

226

Miriam, are you OK with it?"

Miriam nodded. *I really do think I'm getting better at it!* And she waved at the Waterubas who kept chanting and glowing. And they all waved back. *They're so amazing and mysterious… Wait! What about Samir!* She turned back to the computer to see the guard shaking her head and looking around. *Puddle, Samir! Puddle! She'll see you!* But she didn't because he did. Before he turned to water, though, Samir hung the camera up where the guard wouldn't notice it (it was small anyway) – but so they could see what was going on. *GENIUS!!!*

"Oh, Samir – you brilliant boy!" said Grammy.

"That guy's a natural," said Brad. "While we wait for him to get back, let's have a look at this weird gizmo." He pulled up the screengrab on his computer. *It looks like a metal box made out of triangles.*

"What is that thing?" Miriam looked more closely.

"It's an octahedron," said Brad. "A platonic solid."

Okay, Mr. Geometry! But what is it for?? One side of the 'box' was transparent, and it looked as if there was water inside. *Is there a glow in there or is it my imagination?* Just then, the door to the campervan opened. "Samir!" everyone called out at once. *I'm so glad he's safe!*

"You did some amazing work back there, dude," said Brad.

"And leaving the camera behind was sheer genius," said Grammy, jiggling with excitement. "Are you hungry? Silly question. Of course you are." She put Bunster down and started to make him a sandwich.

Miriam looked closely at Samir. "Are you OK?" Samir stared at her for a second, then suddenly whooped with joy and started to dance, with an excited Bunster barking along. Miriam grabbed the jug so he didn't knock it over. *Who knew he could move like that??*

"I take it that's a 'yes'," said Grammy, laughing. She picked Bunster up and tried to join in, but there wasn't enough room.

"That was amazing!" said Samir. He unfastened the WTS with Lutine inside it. "Yes, Lutine? Amazing, right?" He poured Lutine into the jug.

"Right!" it said and swirled around. *It's the Wateruba version of dancing!* This time, thirteen Waterubas started to chant the Wateruba Tuba and Brad joined in. Samir, laughing, immediately covered his ears. *Feet liquifying! Help!* Miriam put the jug down next to Brad's computer so she could do the same. She was about to shove in earplugs when Lutine cried, "STOP!!!" It elongated and smooshed itself right up to the glass of the jug so it could see Brad's screen. "Is that... Vesi?"

Operation get Vesi

VESI?! Brad pushed in as far as he could on the screengrab. It was out of focus, but there was definitely a bright red glow. "That's Vesi's Ruba," said Lutine.

"Vesi! Vesi! Vesi! Vesi!" cried the Waterubas, whirling and swirling around the bowl. As they started to chant the Wateruba Tuba, the humans stared at each other, stunned. (Without Brad's voice, the 13-part Wateruba Tuba wasn't quite loud enough to make the Puddlers puddle, in case anyone is wondering.)

"Vesi? We've found Vesi??" said Miriam. *I'm going to cry.*

"Vesi! Vesi! Vesi! Vesi!" The Waterubas continued their chant.

"Do you think ARID has had Vesi all this time?" said Grammy. *I can't believe it. Could that be true? Why??*

"That octahedron looks like some sort of prison," said Brad.

A prison?? "Poor Vesi!" said Miriam.

"Oh, Vesi won't care," said Krakey. "It was once inside a geode for centuries. Wherever a Wateruba is is where a Wateruba is."

"That's true of humans, too, you know," said Miriam. *I'm not sure why I'm arguing with Krakey...* "I mean, we can't be where we're not."

"Yes, but now I know what 'wanting' is, I know that humans often want to be somewhere else," said Lutine, "particularly if they don't like where they are." *I can't disagree with that.*

"So you spend time being somewhere but wanting to be somewhere else," said Krakey.

"Makes no sense to me!" said Flooso.

"Or to me," said Flick.

"Or to me," bubbled Awa.

Or to me when I think about it.

"I'm guessing this 'prison' is made of some kind of hydrophobic material," said Brad.

"Meaning…?" asked Miriam. *How how how how how does Brad know so much?*

"Meaning it repels water, so Vesi can't get near the walls."

"I agree," said Grammy. She carried Samir's sandwich over to look at the screen, forgetting to give it to Samir. As she passed him, he gently took it out of her hand. *Good move. She might have taken a bite before she remembered she had it.* "I'd also be willing to bet that it's in some sort of electro-magnetic field."

Brad moved the picture around and spotted what looked like a red button, only partially in sight. "Maybe you can disable it by pushing that button…?"

"Seems too obvious. But then they wouldn't be expecting someone to be able to walk into their fortress to press it, right?" Grammy looked around. "Where'd I put Samir's sandwich?" *Oh Grammy…* Samir held it up to show her that he was eating it. "Oh, good," said Grammy.

"It's probably there to keep Vesi in rather than to keep anyone else out," said Brad. *Good point.*

Samir finished his sandwich. "We need to go back now."

NOW?!?!?! "But we don't have a plan! We need a plan!" said Miriam. *I don't like this. I'm not ready! Lutine's right – I want to be somewhere else!*

"Then let's make a plan," said Samir. *Yes please!*

"And we'll call it Operation Get Vesi," said Brad. *He's now going to say, "Or OGV for short."*

"Or OGV for short," said Brad.

Shish was with you?

WHILE Grammy, Brad and Samir studied the footage that Samir had shot, Miriam kept an eye on the live feed coming out of the security guard's room. *Thank you, Samir for leaving the camera behind!* The guard didn't seem to suspect anything. *She probably thinks she just nodded off and has no idea for how long. I get that. Like falling asleep reading a book.* There was no extra activity – no panicked phone call. The guard did her 'rounds', going into the room with the pool, looking around, then exiting again. *She has no idea what she's supposed to be guarding.*

Brad was studying an image of the ceiling in the pool room. "Look, there are vents."

"And I bet they have cool or cold air coming out of them to keep the Waterubas from evaporating out of the room," said Grammy. "If they even know that they can evaporate." *I bet they don't.*

"But if they do know, then when a Wateruba gets warm enough to evaporate, it would only get so far before it drifted up to a vent, cooled down, condensed and rained back into the pool. Elegant," said Brad.

"How do we get to the vents?" asked Samir.

"But they can't be a way in, or else the water route would've lit up on the Globe," said Miriam. Samir just nodded. *I'm sure he's as frustrated as I am!*

"We got into the guard's room, so there is a water route into there…" said Samir.

"But now there's no Wateruba there to jump to," said Miriam.

"What about Shish?" said Tubig.

Everyone turned to look at Tubig rippling in the jug. *What??!* "Shish was with you?" asked Miriam. "The last time we saw Shish, it was in a birdbath and got drunk by a bird."

"Shish! Shish! Shish! Shish!" chanted the Waterubas.

"When I saw it, it was in the coffee machine," said Tubig. "There are all sorts of ways Shish could've gone from being inside a bird to being with me inside a coffee machine. I dripped through, but Shish stayed in the coffee grounds."

"But there are only 81 of you, right?" asked Miriam.

"Right!" said Krakey and Lutine.

"The Earth's a big place. What are the chances that you and Shish would be in the same place at the same time?"

"Chances? What do you mean? We're all here, so that's what is," said Krakey.

"It's obviously meant to be or else it wouldn't be," said Lutine. *Yes, but I want to know why!*

"Shish! Shish! Shish! Shish!" chanted the Waterubas. Then they started the Wateruba Tuba.

Instead of joining in, Brad shook his head, amazed. "How can an ancient being that's 99% water even know about a coffee machine?"

"Easy!" said Krakey, stopping the chant. "We're ancient, we're part of everything, and we're aware of it all. You humans will always be amazed by what we know, because you're used to what you know being limited – and you don't even know it!" *HUH??!*

"Too much loo-oo-ooking, not enough see-ee-eeing," added McKibben.

"Too much thinking, not enough knowing," said Lutine.

"The wisdom of the Waterubas," said Grammy. "I feel a book coming on…"

"What we experience is just the never-ending wonder of being on this planet!" continued Krakey. "And get this…" *What??* Miriam, Samir, Brad and Grammy all leaned in to hear what it had to say.

"We're all connected. All of us. No separation. We're the story of inter-being."

"I love that so much, I can't even begin to tell you," whispered Grammy.

Me, too — but what does it mean, exactly? Krakey swished into a backwards somersault and started up the chant again. Because Brad stayed out of it, it wasn't loud enough to make Samir and Miriam puddle. *Good thing, too. We've got to make a plan NOW! We've got to get to Shish before it moves on.*

New guard

MIRIAM didn't need to worry. The reason Brad didn't join in the Wateruba Tuba wasn't because he didn't want her and Samir to puddle, but because he was too busy writing out the plan for Operation Get Vesi, Part 2. "OK, everyone, listen up! Here's the plan for OGV, Part 2! *He's sounding like Steve again… but it's just what we need. Go, Brad!* The goal is to create a water route to Vesi, which probably means turning off the electro- magnetic field or whatever it is that's keeping Vesi in and everything else out, agreed?"

"Agreed," agreed Miriam, Samir and Grammy. *I like when he gets all serious.*

"So here we go." Brad read from the notebook. "One: Miriam and Samir will puddle-jump to Shish, taking Krakey, Lutine and Flooso, as before."

The Waterubas swooshed around the bowl. "Shish! Shish! Shish!" Brad raised his voice in order to continue. "TWO!" The Waterubas rippled down. "Miriam will leave Samir behind – and puddle-jump back to the campervan with Shish. Three: Samir will get the camera he left behind. Four: Samir will turn off the ARID cameras. Five: Samir will turn up the heat. Six: We'll all be watching to see when Samir creates a water route to Vesi. And seven: The second he does, Miriam will be ready to say 'Vesi!' to the Globe and jump."

"Vesi! Vesi! Vesi!" chanted the Waterubas.

"THAT'S THE PLAN!!" hollered Brad. The Waterubas stopped chanting. "What do you think?" *Simple. I like it.*

"It is very good," said Samir.

234

"There's a lot for you to do," said Miriam. "You OK with that?"

"Of course!" said Samir, smiling. *You're smiling a lot more than when we first met you!*

"New guard alert!" announced Grammy. They all gathered around the computer. As they watched, the new guard, whose face they couldn't see, talked to the old guard then walked her to the exit. "Do you think this is just changing of the guard, as it were," said Grammy, "or do you think they wanted the other guard gone? *Why would they want her gone? She didn't see anything... did she...?* It looks like the replacement is a man. It'd be just like ARID to send in a man if they felt the woman had 'failed.'" *You're right, Grammy, but now is not the time for a rant.*

"It doesn't matter," said Samir. "We're going anyway." He dipped his WTS into the jug. "Lutine, please!" he said, and the WTS lit up with Lutine's Egyptian Blue Ruba, and then Flooso's Tiger-colored Ruba as it slipped in with Lutine. *Good old Flooso. I wonder if we have colors that Waterubas can see...* Then Miriam scooped up Krakey. *Bumblebee yellow, my new favorite color.* While Samir filled the sink with water, Miriam got the Asteruba. She gently lowered it into the water, then stepped back. Roiling bubbles – low hum – Asteruba rose out of the sink on a watery plinth – transformed into the Globe – settled – smell of the sea – moving lights.

Awesome. I hope I never get used to seeing that. "Ready?" she said to Samir.

"Ready!"

"SHISH!" Shish's gray light flashed. Brad photographed it. "Yep – it's exactly where Tubig said it would be."

"Shish Shish Shish Shish Shish!" shished the Waterubas.

"SHISH!" When the light flashed again, Miriam reached for it and was pulled into the Globe with Samir holding on. They'd hardly had time to feel they were puddle-jumping when they unpuddled. They were in the kitchen next to the security control room. The guard was only a few feet away, making coffee. *Inconvenient!* But his back was to them.

Miriam and Samir ducked behind a trolley as he took his coffee into the main room. They then moved as close to the door as they could, and watched from the kitchen as Krakey, Flooso and Lutine started up the Wateruba Tuba, joined by the Waterubas in the pool room.

We're all connected. Miriam and Samir covered their ears. The guard raised his head, surprised. Then, as the Wateruba Tuba got louder, he totally relaxed and slumped onto his arms, face down at the control desk.

Miriam and Samir uncovered their ears. The chanting had stopped, but Miriam heard a faint drone. *Where's it coming from?* She opened a little composting bin and saw Shish's feathery head appear out of the water in the coffee grinds. It waved a flipper. She waved her hand, then signaled to Samir that she had to go. He nodded.

Miriam touched Shish, *Yuck! Coffee grounds!* and seconds later, unpuddled on the floor of the van. Brad tipped the coffee grounds she held in her hand into a coffee filter, and held it over the aquarium. Shish eventually dripped into the jug to join the others. "Shish! Shish! Shish! Shish! Shish!" The water looked like it was boiling with their joy.

Miriam noticed Krakey watching from the WTS. "You don't mind if I don't pour you in now, do you?"

"Of course not," said Krakey. "We've got to be ready to go back." Krakey waved and Miriam waved back. *I love Krakey.* "And I love you, too," it said.

"Shhhh!" hissed Grammy. *She's not kidding.* Miriam and Brad joined her at the computer. The guard was still asleep. The image went all over the place for a moment as Samir grabbed the camera, before steadying as he put it back on his head. Then he went to the controls and turned off the cameras in the pool room.

"Now for Step 5, turn up the heat," said Brad. They watched as Samir found the correct control on the panel, then turned the dial as high as it would go.

"We're gonna have a hot time in the old town tonight," Grammy sang softly. She filled the sink with water and positioned the Asteruba right next to it. "Asteruba ready to go," she said.

Samir gently knocked the guard's keys off the desk, waking him. Then he ducked behind a filing cabinet. When the guard lifted his head, he immediately saw that the monitors were all black. The cameras were off. He jumped to his feet and scrambled to find the button to turn them back on.

"Globe!" hissed Brad, and Grammy pushed the Asteruba into the water. Bubbling – low hum – rising on the watery plinth – turning into the Globe –whoosh – settling – sea smell – lights.

The security guard headed for the door to the pool room. *That's exactly what we thought he'd do! OGV is working!* Miriam positioned herself next to the Globe. Her stomach felt like she'd swallowed an octopus. *More excitement than fear, but sometimes hard to tell the difference...*

The guard grabbed a hazmat suit from a hook on the wall and opened the first door to the pool room. Grammy, Brad and Miriam watched, hardly daring to breathe, as Samir followed him in. *Samir really knows how to sneak.* "He's had a lot of practice," said Krakey. *Once again, are you reading my mind?*

The guard was in such a hurry to get into the pool room, he didn't check that the doors had closed behind him. Samir wedged them open, slinked into the pool room, went to Vesi's prison, and hit the red button. "Now!" said Brad. Miriam shouted "Vesi!" at the Globe and a bright red light flashed. *Yes yes yes!!! There's a water route!* "GO!" shouted Brad and Grammy together. Miriam touched the light, and was pulled into the Globe.

We want our Waterubas back

MIRIAM unpuddled next to Samir who was crouching below Vesi's prison. There was nowhere to hide, but thanks to the hood of his suit, the guard hadn't seen them yet. He walked around the pool, looking into the water, *These guards have no idea what they're guarding* then stopped when he saw that the doors into the room had been wedged open. *Uh-oh…* He ran over to Vesi's prison and peered in. "Is it there??" Then he saw Miriam and Samir.

"Miri??!?" The guard took off his hood – it was Uncle Eddy.

Oh no! Oh no! Oh no no no no no! "Samir, run!" said Miriam. *I don't want him to go, but he has to. It's too dangerous for him!* Samir looked at her as if to say, "Are you sure?" Miriam nodded.

Eddy lunged for him. Samir dodged and ran out. Then Eddy grabbed Miriam's arm. "Ow! You're hurting me!" *What do I do? What do I do?*

"I know what he can do, Miri," Eddy hissed into her ear.

"Uncle Eddy, stop!" cried Miriam. *You're scaring me! And this is all because I refuse to admit that Mom died in that accident.*

"He doesn't need to run, does he?" Eddy continued, tightening his grip. "He can flow." *He knows Samir can puddle!* "Did he get in through the plumbing and then let you in? But how? And how did you get past the alarms?"

He doesn't know I can puddle! And it has to stay that way. Miriam pulled her arm away. "We found an open window," she said. *I hope that's possible.* "Shouldn't somebody be fired for leaving it unlocked?"

"Why are you here?" *I guess he believed me.*

238

"We want our Waterubas back."

"But I thought Waterubas weren't real," smirked Eddy. *Oh pa-leeze.*

"Samir was there when your thugs came in and stole them." Eddy started to pace. *This is not what he expected.* "How did you know they were there? By bugging us? You know you accidentally fed a microphone to Bunster." Eddy stared at her. "Uncle Eddy, what is going on?" *I hate this so much.* Eddy grabbed her arm again. "Ow! That hurts!" *Not a flicker of sympathy. Who is this guy?*

"Why is Samir even in Riverside? Doesn't he live in Egypt?"

"He's helping Grammy with her book."

"I knew it!" He pushed Miriam away.

He's being such a jerk. Why did Mom love him so much? And what did it get her? She fell and he didn't! I need to get Vesi and get out of here! But I haven't felt the pull back to the Globe yet. Why not? Maybe because Vesi's out of reach. Idea! Diversion! "I've got to go now. I've got what I want."

"What's that?"

Here goes. "A Wateruba I saw in one of Mom's last photographs." She held up the WTS and jiggled it so that the glow of Krakey's Ruba was visible. "See?" *I'm guessing Eddy doesn't know a Ruba from a tuba. He probably hasn't even noticed that a Wateruba glows, never mind that each one glows a different color.*

"What? How?" Eddy peered into the prison. *Yep. He doesn't know what he's looking for.* "Put it back!"

"No!" said Miriam. *Stand up to him, Miriam! Get him to open the prison so you can get Vesi.*

"Please put it back, Miri. You don't know what you're doing." *Oh yes I do.* He pulled at the collar of the hazmat suit. "Why is it so hot in here?"

"We turned up the heat so the Waterubas you stole will evaporate and escape."

"I always suspected they could evaporate," said Eddy. "What else do you know?" *Nothing I'll ever tell you.*

"Look!" Miriam pointed at the pool. She saw many of the Waterubas she'd found vibrating, spreading out and heading for the vents. "Wooo-hoooo!" "Evaporating!" "Hey, Miriam!" "See you when I see you!"

"Look at them go!" said Miriam, waving. Eddy looked. *He really doesn't see them!* "Bye, Plip! Bye, Plop!"

"Now you're making fun of me. Besides, I don't care about the others. But I do care about that one. And so does my father." *His father?*

"Why? Because it was there when Mom had her accident? And it can tell us what really happened?"

Eddy's face went bright red and he grimaced with fury. "You don't know what you're talking about." *That got a reaction! He's almost growling at me.* Eddy stepped towards Miriam. "Put. It. Back. NOW!!" *Now I'm scared. I've never seen him so angry. Did he talk to Mom like this? Wait... wait... A horrible thought... I can't breathe... Did Eddy push her???* He opened the prison from the top. "I said now."

He opened the prison! I'm feeling the Globe... Stay calm... "All right, all right." Miriam poured Krakey in. But as she did, she scooped Vesi up. *Thank you, Krakey.* "See you when I see you," it bubbled.

Miriam turned to Eddy. "All done."

Eddy looked into the prison and saw Krakey's glow. "Thank you. Now, promise me you'll never talk about what happened here."

As if! "I promise." *Not. Fingers crossed.*

"Wait here and I'll take you home. I've got to turn down this heat!" said Eddy, running out of the room.

But before he reached the desk, Miriam and Vesi were gone.

Your mother is far away

THE minute Miriam unpuddled with Vesi in the campervan, Grammy shouted at her to fasten her seatbelt. *Good to see you, too!* Miriam looked around. Everything was packed away, and Brad and Samir were fastened in, ready to go. Samir had Bunster on his lap. Miriam sat down and buckled up. "Great work, Puddlers," said Brad. "OGV worked!!"

"Yes it did, and we need to get as far away from ARID as possible," said Grammy, starting up the vehicle. "I am not happy that Eddy knows about Samir."

"Don't worry about me," Samir said to Grammy. Then he turned to Miriam. "Thank you for being so brave." *Me? Brave??*

"Thank you for helping me get Vesi," said Miriam. She took the WTS out of its strap and held the container up so she could see the Wateruba she'd been looking for for so long. It glowed a beautiful scarlet. She recognized its two funny long ears and big belly from the shape she'd seen in the photo on her mother's camera. *I thought I'd feel happy, but I just feel so so sad, all over again.* "Vesi! Vesi! Vesi!" chanted the other Waterubas. They started to chant the Wateruba Tuba with Vesi. *I already miss Krakey…*

Miriam held up the WTS to look at Vesi again. It waved. She waved. "Now I can finally find out what happened to my mom. And I can stop believing the impossible." She saw Grammy look at her in the rear view mirror. She turned back to Vesi. "You were there when she had her accident."

"Yes, and so was that man you call Uncle Eddy."

"That's right," said Miriam. "Did he have anything to do with her accident?"

Grammy stopped the van and turned to look at Miriam. "Miriam, what are you saying?"

"You should have seen Uncle Eddy just now, Grammy," sobbed Miriam. "He was horrible. Really scary."

"He is here, and your mother is far away." *What?!*

"Far away? You mean she's dead, right?"

"Dead?"

"Is my mother dead?" asked Miriam.

"No," said Vesi.

I KNEW IT!!! I can't breathe I can't breathe! "Grammy, you know how you always knew that the Waterubas were real, no matter how crazy that seemed…"

"Yes," said Grammy. She was crying.

"Well, I always knew that Mom was alive. And now we both know that we were right all along…"

She's alive!

WORRIED about what Eddy might do, Grammy rang Brad's nan and asked if they could stay with her for the night. "The whole immigration situation is getting out of hand," she said, "and we need somewhere to be that's not my house." Eleanor, being the open and accepting person that she was *Just like her grandson* said, "See you when you get here," and quickly hung up to make beds and find extra towels.

Miriam was given the bedroom where Brad's sister slept when she stayed with her nan. Samir and Brad were sharing Brad's room, and Grammy and Bunster were in the room that Brad's parents used. Miriam kept the bag with the Asteruba in it, plus the jug and Waterubas, with her – Brad's nan didn't seem to need an explanation. *Brad's nan is the best. Just like Brad. And Samir. And Grammy. What a day!* She yawned, took a sip of water from the glass that Brad's nan had given her, and climbed into bed. *Oooh, so comfy…* Miriam was exhausted, but could she sleep? No. This time it wasn't fear that kept her awake, but a mixture of emotions so enormous she could barely identify them. Joy, relief, more joy, a little bit of fear, confusion, and dread. But mostly joy. *She's alive she's alive she's alive! But where is she? Why didn't she let us know? Maybe she couldn't. Maybe she's still in Greenland. Is she being held prisoner like Vesi was? What is going on?*

Then Miriam had an idea, an idea that quickly grew into a plan, a very, very big plan – a plan that she needed to do all on her own. The house was very still. The silence surrounded her like a heavy blanket. She worried that if she got out of bed, it would move the blanket, wake everyone up and ruin everything. She carefully turned over. The silence remained.

OK. The Quest to find Mom. 1) I will quietly get up. 2) I will put the Asteruba in one of the containers I have in my backpack. 3) I will pour my glass of water over the Asteruba. 4) It will turn into the Globe. 5) I will find Greenland on the map. 6) I will put Lutine in the WTS so I can leave it behind when we find Mom. 7) Lutine will tell me if there's a Wateruba in Greenland. 8) I will puddle jump to the Wateruba in Greenland. 9) I will find Mom. 10) I will touch the Wateruba and puddle jump back. 10 steps. Perfect.

Miriam set about quietly, quietly finding a container in her backpack big enough for the Asteruba. *I miss Krakey! I already miss Brad! I already miss Samir! I want Grammy!* She added a step to the plan when she decided to move everything into the closet, just in case the low hum of the Globe appearing might wake someone up. *I do not need anyone telling me not to do this.*

Once in the closet, she put the Asteruba into the container and poured her water over it. There, surrounded by clothes and shoes and boxes of old papers, the Asteruba rose up and transformed into the Globe. *And it didn't even make that much noise!* She used the ladle *I knew I'd need it!* to lift Lutine out of the jug and pour it into the WTS, while the other Waterubas glowed and very quietly swished in and out of sight. She then lifted Lutine up to see the part of the Globe that was Greenland.

"I see two Waterubas there," said Lutine. "Murmur and Squirt. Murmur's Ruba is jungle green, and Squirt's is amber."

"Murmur and Squirt! Murmur and Squirt!" burbled the Waterubas so quietly Miriam could barely hear them. *I love how they just know what's going on! I couldn't do this without them. Puddlers need Waterubas…*

Miriam looked at the two lights. "Which one is with my mom?"

"Think of your mother," said Lutine.

"You mean more than I already am?"

"Think of her with your heart," said Lutine, the tentacles on its head waving in the water.

OK... unexpected... Miriam concentrated very hard on her mom. "With your heart," repeated Lutine. "If you had a Ruba, it would be your heart. *OK... I like that.* How did you know your mother was still alive? With your brain or your heart?" *With my heart, obviously.* Miriam had no problem feeling her mom in her heart. She did it all the time. She thought of her mom in the picture she kept by her bed, smiling like mad. Her heart grew, filling up with both happiness and sadness. *I wonder if this is what Lutine means...*

"Now let's watch the flashes," said Lutine. "Send your heart to your mom and say Squirt."

Miriam faced the Globe. *Mom... Mom... Mom...* "Squirt!" The amber light flashed.

"Now try Murmur," said Lutine.

Mom... Mom... Mom... "Murmur!" The green light flashed so brightly, it almost flew off the Globe. "Whoa!"

"Yes," said Lutine. "Murmur is with your mother. Let's go."

Miriam quickly attached the WTS to her waist, and faced the Globe. "Murmur!" she said. This time, when the light flashed, she touched it, puddled, whooshed into the Globe and was on her way.

Miri? Is that really you?

WHEN Miriam unpuddled, she was in a small room filled with scientific equipment. A woman sat at a desk, looking through a microscope. *Is it?! Is it really?!* "Mom?" said Miriam.

Ruth turned. Miriam would always remember the look on her face when she saw her – complete surprise – and pure joy. She gasped. "Miri?? Is that really you??" She jumped up, ran to Miriam and pulled her into the hug that both of them had been dreaming about for the past eighteen months. *Mom… Mom… Mom… I love you so much! I knew you were alive!* "How are you here?" Ruth asked her daughter, holding her face in her hands. They were both crying.

"Mom. I can turn into water. And that old asteroid in Grammy's kitchen cupboard is some kind of alien technology. It turns into a globe, that shows us where the Waterubas are. Oh, yes, by the way, Waterubas are real."

"That part I know," said Ruth. "What else?"

"I can travel as water travels – from wherever the Globe is to where there's a Wateruba. That's how I got here." She saw a green glow coming from the stage of the microscope. "The Wateruba you were looking at is called…"

"Murmur," said Ruth. "It told me. What happens now?"

Miriam held up the WTS. "This is Lutine. The only way I can get back is by touching Murmur. But I'll leave Lutine here so I can come again. Soon. There's so much to tell you."

"I think I understand." Ruth then covered Miriam's face in kisses. "I can't tell you how much I've missed you…"

Miriam grabbed onto her mom. *I don't ever want to let you go!* "I'm feeling the pull of the Globe to go back. See?" Her feet were turning into water.

Her mother was momentarily distracted by the miracle of puddling, "Look at that!" but quickly regained her composure. And then she was suddenly more serious than Miriam had ever seen her before. "Two things, Miri. Listen carefully. 1) ARID must never know that I'm still alive. If they find out, many people, including you and all of our family, will be in danger. And 2) we must, absolutely must, find all 81 Waterubas."

We must? Why? But there was no time to find out now. Miriam was puddling. She quickly poured Lutine into a glass of water that was on her mom's desk. "Thank you, Lutine!"

"See you when I see you!" said Lutine.

Miriam looked at her mom. *I can't believe it. There's Mom! I found Mom!* "Mom, I love you, and I'll be back!" Her mom blew her kisses with both hands. Miriam then reached out for Murmur. The next thing she knew, she was sitting on the floor of the closet in Brad's nan's house, back in Riverside, Illinois.

TO BE CONTINUED…

Jocelyn Stevenson has worked in children's media for over 40 years as a writer, creator, producer, executive producer. Her credits include: *Sesame Street, Fraggle Rock, Charlie Chalk*, Jim Henson's *Ghost of Faffner Hall*, Jim Henson's *Animal Show with Stinky and Jake*, Jim Henson's *Secret Life of Toys*, Jim Henson's *Tale of the Bunny Picnic. Faeries* (original animated mini-series), *Mopatop's Shop, The Hoobs, Bob the Builder, Thomas & Friends, Barney & Friends, Rubbadubbers, Pingu, What's Your News?, Moshi Monsters: The Movie!, The Magic School Bus.* Most recently, she is a Consulting Producer and Writer for *Fraggle Rock Rock On!* for the Henson Company and Apple TV.

Over the years, she's written books to accompany the series she's worked on, but *The Waterubas Book 1* (soon to be followed by *The Waterubas Book 2*) is her first original book for 9–12 year olds.

Brian Froud has created some of the most respected and highly acknowledged folklore/mythic artwork of our time. In the 1970's, he and Jim Henson collaborated to create *The Dark Crystal* and *Labyrinth*. It was when both Brian and Jocelyn were working with Jim (on very different projects!) that they first met. "I knew that if anyone would understand what I meant when I said that a Wateruba isn't a creature that lives in water, it IS water, it would be Brian," said Jocelyn. "And I was right." With over thirty books in publication and over eight million books sold to date, Brian continues to discover and visually manifest transdimensional worlds today.

I want to thank the following people for their help, insight, inspiration, ideas, encouragement and enthusiasm.

Geoffrey Menin, Tom Livingstone, Marc Seal, John May, Suzanne Bolch, Evan Thaler Hickey, Giles Healy, Natacha Du Pont De Bie, Eileen Sudler, Elizabeth Sobel, Philip Ball, Charles Fishman, Sylvia Earle, Wendy Froud, Brian Froud, Larry Mirkin, Simon Nicholson, Debbie Kovacs, Freddie Stevenson, Ela Carpenter, Rollie Krewson, Daphne Diamant, Deborah Huisken, Charley Feldman, Mira Velimirovic, Rachel Myss, Jeff Carreira, Sally Latham, Charlie Latham, Aflie Latham, Sophie Krzemien, Tim Smedley

Printed in Great Britain
by Amazon